mart of *darkness*
by Phil Granchi

Entry

Trust me, this is the end.

The entire planet will sink back into the Dark Ages.

But it won't seem so bad, as Dark Ages go.

Kurtis McAlsteinetti, CEO of All Mart, the world's largest chain of discount stores. Taken from video recorded during the night of his disappearance.

Everyone gets everything they want. I wanted a 3-day temp job, and for my sins they gave me one.

I was going into the world's largest discount store to witness the end of our civilization and didn't even know it yet. Days away and a few dozen miles along an aisle that snaked through All Mart like an ultra-HD cable and plugged straight into McAlsteinetti. It was no accident that I got to be the caretaker of Kurtis I. McAlsteinetti's memory, any more than being back in Ohio was an accident. There is no way to tell the rest of his story without admitting that, in the end, I slept through most of it. And if his story is really a confession, then I'm pretty sure that no one really wants to hear it.

It would have been nice if I had gotten more information about the mission and my role in the unraveling of all things at the start of the day, but that didn't happen. The scorching hot flight attendant in the apricot flight suit seemed disinclined to provide an orientation session as she rushed through the cabin of the Black Hawk helicopter retrofitted for business travel. Gathering up the remains of our continental breakfast of dark roast coffee and fresh cherry-cheese Danish, she had no time to offer helpful tips to the new guy. Indeed, when she shoved me through the side door over the drop zone, I knew my questions would go unanswered.

To her credit, she appeared conflicted about it, watching me as gravity took hold and started pulling me toward the center of the earth. In the faint wrinkling of her eyes and the wasteland dry smile, I saw in her an element of desire. As if my presence had stirred something in her. An awareness of something she could not possess. Whatever it was, it seemed clouded by a deep black sadness about my predetermined fate, which was in retrospect probably revealed to her as a technical detail in her pre-flight briefing. This paradoxical state was interwoven with an element of surprise that I didn't jump out of the helicopter when asked to do so by the pilot.

Further, there was a streak of professional dissatisfaction in the nature of her duties. Capable of so much, constrained by unknown forces, her only memories of the morning would be of serving breakfast and troubleshooting the helicopter wireless network as my companions were banging out the last-minute details of our world-altering mission. Accelerating toward terminal velocity with the metallic door slicing shut and the helicopter angling back into the cool blue morning sky of autumn in southern Ohio, I saw that she was not a flight attendant at all, but part of something so complex and so expansive that I would never understand.

I landed with a thump onto a mound of thick grass and tried to curl up into a fetal position, already wishing the day would end. Around me, my colleagues had secured a perimeter around an unpaved patch of grass in an immense parking lot. A flurry of hands pulled me to my feet. Without a word or glance to assure my stability, the team sprinted across a barren stretch of asphalt and slipped down a corridor between a long row of RV's.

Choking for breath, running behind these figures from the covers of fitness magazines in the dense, stifling humidity of the parking lot, I saw the fearsome zombie truth approaching me across the green lawn of my quiet artistic life: This was not a simple 3-day automatic temp job that would allow me to pay my rent. And I had not been hired to create a few MetaPoint slides for some presentation they were giving.

Terrified that I might be left alone and forgotten, I sprinted into the cleft of darkness between the parked Class A monster campers. Once inside, the sunlight and rumbling of the eternal paving machines were extinguished. One of my companions flashed a light ahead and whispered something into her wrist pad. Everyone else put on night vision golf visors and kept on running. I stumbled along behind until my eyes adjusted to the darkness.

"VoyEurSat imagery says that the parking lot is expanding at a rate of approximately four hundred spaces per day," barked one of the men. "Without a real-time satellite link giving us coordinates in relation to the arrival and abandonment of vehicles, it's hard to tell how far we have to go before it opens up."

Everyone else nodded that they understood his statement. I nodded as a numb reflex, hoping the one or two neurons of understanding I had would begin to expand. All Mart, our destination that morning, had been promoting the eternal availability of parking spaces at the InfiniPark on buses and trains as far away as Chicago. The ads showed a dour Prime Minister of Liechtenstein comparing aerial photos of his country to those of the InfiniPark. That gave me a vague idea how big the parking lot was, and how difficult it might be to determine our true position as we progressed.

"Is Mister K. still with us?" asked Watson, the team leader, who had introduced herself when we were boarding the helicopter at an abandoned aircraft hangar outside of Fort Wayne at 3 AM. Back then, a few short hours earlier, I had figured that she was the Creative Director in charge of whatever pitch we were going to make to All Mart senior management.

"Sure," I mumbled, noticing how explosive she looked in her flight jacket, black slacks, white blouse, and steel-spiked Mary Janes. Her penetrating dark eyes processed everything around us, reaching decisions about our potential fate at each step. The scent of hot asphalt, the quality of the morning light reaching us through the slits between the rows of parked vehicles were all being evaluated for their potential to either endanger or assist us. Her deep awareness and confidence conspired to take me out of my fear and sent a wake-up call ripping up my spine to the base of my brain. Her combination of beauty and intelligence could induce spontaneous combustion in the walls of any corner office. I needed her as a leader, but I also wanted to provide her with pleasure and satisfaction, in whatever capacity I might be allowed. But, like the meta-flight-attendant, there was so much more. If I touched her sleeve when no one else was looking, and if a second in creation arrived when no one else needed her attention, she would reveal to me the labyrinth of feelings and ideas that sustained her, along with a haiku on the quality of the autumn light, which she had composed in silence, waiting to be spoken.

But I didn't get the chance to dwell in the alternate realm I had created in my mind with her as my spirit guide. Everyone else had followed her down the long dark corridor, leaving me standing there, aching with my entire being. Catching my breath, I moved ahead.

A few dozen yards along, after scrunching myself between a rusted pick-up truck with a rack of moose antlers on the hood and a brand-new minivan maxed out with child car seats in back, I got my first sense of the true magnetism surrounding the new All Mart GigaStore. I had heard the rumors that people were driving in from all over and leaving their cars out in the parking lot while they took up permanent residence inside the store. It seemed a bit exaggerated, as most rumors, and I didn't believe it. But here in the weak light slanting down into the passage, I could make out a mosaic of license plates and bumper stickers on the vehicles that surrounded me. From Maine to Monterey. From the Mystery Spot to Wall Drug—with a host of Crystal Caverns and Prairie Dog Cities in between. There was also the physical evidence of dried sagebrush stuck in the bumpers, southern red clay clumped in the wheel wells and north woods mosquitoes smashed on the windshields. The complete set of geographic points of interest on the continent had been visited by these vehicles and focused on this plain of asphalt in southern Ohio. The owners of these vehicles, however, had long departed.

Ahead, the others moved back out into the sunlight that filled a blacktopped clearing in the automotive forest.

"I think this is a good place for our morning status meeting," said Watson, standing in the middle of the clearing, surveying the space.

"I don't think that's a good idea," said one of the team members. A wiry guy with a military haircut was staring at a running time display on his wrist rocket. "We lost some time flying around that thunderstorm over Wapakoneta."

"I appreciate your input, Major Dalton," Watson said, stiffening. "But we'll make it up on the drive in. We're scheduled to have the newest XR embedded for us."

Dalton edged closer to Watson with no sense of threat, yet confident in his position. "The Surge has already started. We could—"

"Your concerns are noted, Major. Status is going to happen." Watson unzipped the main pocket of her all-terrain wheelie bag and pulled out a desktop holojector.

Dalton had taken a few steps toward the edge of the clearing, as if ready to keep moving. "BizCap will shut us down if there's even—"

"Initiate Status," said Watson, determined.

The team dropped their carry-ons and started whipping out pieces of black-anodized aluminum office equipment and setting up what appeared to be a conference room—table, chairs, projector. I backed myself up against one of the camper vans that served as a wall, not because I didn't have anything to set up but because I realized that I feared being caught in the sudden crossfire. Judging from the way in which some of them were glowering and tossing pieces of equipment at each other, not all of them were happy to be starting their work day. A few hostile flicks of metallic joints later, a few ominous whirs of tiny concealed electric motors, and they were seated around a conference table, most of them reclining in what appeared to be military versions of high-end mesh-back swivel chairs. The fluid ease of their aggressions implied repetition over many years and under a range of climates and conditions.

The woman who sat next to me on the helicopter took a 3-inch aluminum tube from her pack, pulled a tiny lever on it and tossed me my own ultralight mesh chair, which floated toward me like a huge leaf sailing through the autumn breeze. "Helium-graphite composite," she said with a smile.

Summoning what little *prana* that I could muster from the one yoga class I could afford each month, I sat down, adjusted the lumbar support and rolled myself up to the table—hoping I could at least maintain a little emotional distance from their interpersonal battlefields. To give my trembling hands something to do, I opened my laptop and booted up. I took a long deep breath, thinking it would help calm things down a little, but the air tasted like tar and made me feel even more disoriented. Then there was the distant rumbling of the paving machines that was now echoing inside our little enclave in the vehicular wilderness.

"You guys aren't really working for an advertising agency, are you?" I said, attempting to be heard above the tumultuous startup tones of laptops, tablets, spheres, orbs, external drives, routers and satellite video conference monitors that covered the table.

Watson, like the apricot jump-suited flight entity, seemed surprised at my question, as if I should be certain of their identity—as well as mine. I could see her mind trying to figure out why I would even ask that, and then considering it an ill-timed joke of poor taste.

Several of the others fidgeted with pieces of equipment to indicate that they were eager to get the meeting started. One guy, who looked like he might have had an earlier career modeling boxer briefs, cranked some knobs on a titanium alloy espresso maker that was spewing steaming, foamed milk into some paper cups, which he then distributed around the table. Dalton rattled the base of a wire-framed satellite dish, testing its integrity—and thereby also confirming that all necessary information flowed from this table to distant points of contact.

After Watson somehow reconciled my confusion in her mind, she turned to me and spoke. "Couldn't compromise the mission. We don't tell until you need to know. Standard orders for disclosure."

"That's fine," I said, gripping the sides of the chair, "But now that I know you're not an agency pitching some new letterhead to All Mart—which you didn't tell me, by the way, but which I figured out from the stealth lounge office suite—who are you?"

"Department of Commerce, Special Forces, Shopping 233rd Airborne. We're a Discount Outlet Unit and our mission is to keep peace in the marketplace," said Watson. "I'm Senior Director of Untraceable Operations and I think we're ready for our morning status meeting. If it's alright with you, I'll introduce the team as we go along. Trusting they'll keep their personal feelings to themselves for purposes of serving the greater good."

She turned toward an early middle-aged guy with a perfect all-natural non-spray copper glow. He might have been in his late thirties, mid-forties, or even protofifties, depending on how you weighted the faint leathery quality of his skin in your calculations. "This is Stanton. Senior Manager for Consumer Reconnaissance."

Stanton looked up and gave me a smile capable of etching glass, fixing my gaze for an extra few seconds to ensure the caustic effect. He then swallowed his obvious disdain for the entire endeavor, only because his immediate supervisor had specified he do so. After taking a sip of his latte, which seemed to provide him with a scant ray of joy, he made his report:

"Demographics for this area of the parking lot are what we expected. There's good correlation between high school dropouts and early acceptance of Convert status. High school graduates who haven't converted are camping close to the store and hanging on to the few service jobs left over in Springdale. The commute is becoming more of a hassle each day with the Truck Wall blocking the roads, so we'll likely see those people converting within the next quarter.

"For the benefit of our special guest here with the blank stare, the Truck Wall is the line of trucks created by the constant arrival of deliveries from all over the world, that are inching their way to the loading docks at the back of the store. Most of the main roads have been permanently gridlocked so that shoppers and employees are using back roads or going overland to get to the store. Hence the people arriving through the corn fields we saw this morning. Obviously, this makes converting to being a full-time resident an advantage, for both shopping and working.

"What's really surprising is the number of college graduates and former professionals working at All Mart. Current students are converting remotely while still on campus and leaving their cars in the next county to the east, which is, ahh," he glanced at a map that flashed onto his 23-inch PhantazmaPad. "Lancaster County. McAlsteinetti is probably recruiting heavily in the local J-C's and universities. I've got a mole working inside the Wright State University Job Fair as we speak.

Ignoring Watson's request for restraint, he continued. "This mission's a cesspool. And our enigmatic freelancer here with the clueless look on his face that is suspiciously real better not slow us down because I have brunch reservations at Frizzo in Manhattan Beach on Friday."

"Great." Watson smiled to acknowledge his minor diversion from the agenda and swiveled her chair toward the other woman. "This is Hardin. Associate Director of Promotional Tactics. Heavy hitter skill set. Serving double duty as both communications and medical officer. Quickly, please."

The rumbling of the paving machines was being replaced by the chattering of thousands of voices, amassing nearby.

Hardin—with perfect complexion, green eyes and dark hair pulled back—was still pulling even more equipment from her carry-on. After retrieving a headset and fixing it to her ear, she looked over, smiled and commenced. Her strong voice rose above the gathering crowd. "We've secured press, radio, television and major internet traffic for the local area. All Mart is currently running its Pilgrims' Pride 85% off on selected ticketed items, with a free plastic turkey stuffed with candy corn for the first five thousand shoppers each day. I just want to add that I'm excited about being part of this team. I'm happy to be back in the field with some of you and looking forward to working with the rest of you for the first time. As some of you may know, I have some personal interests in this mission, but I assure you that I'll keep those well separated from our work."

She nodded to indicate she was finished, which brought the tiny headset microphone down in place at the edge of her lips. She then commenced a clipped yet quiet conversation with someone speaking to her from a remote location.

"Great!" snapped Watson. Pointing toward the sole African-American who was still working on some equipment next to Hardin, she added. "That's Klean, whom we affectionately call Morpheus, Executive Director of Media Ordinance and pilot."

Wearing hipsterish business casual slacks and a leather jacket, Klean had produced a 256-inch flat-panel display from a black metallic case the size of a Himalaya After Dinner Mint. After verifying that the screen was working, he took off his jacket to reveal his rippling arms and torso and hung the jacket on the back of his chair. Sitting, he acknowledged me, shot a territorial glance toward Stanton across the table from him, and then bent over a gleaming 27-inch OmManiPad. "We're now feeding live video and sound of the mission to Naperville, White Plains, Irvine and the Airborne Retail Market Surveillance plane over Tyson's Corner. At 0400 this morning, while we were in transit from Fort Wayne, the plane scanned the current floor plan from high altitude and sent me a 3D rendering of the entire store for us to run on our VisorVids. The store is growing at a rate of about five hundred meters each day. But we won't be going to those new areas. We're headed to the older, core regions of the store that are no longer under construction, so today's floor plan should be accurate throughout the duration of our mission. I'll register that floor plan with the original GPS data so we have a real time display of every possible aisle, shelf and end cap if we have to run without lights once we get in there. Actually, I can e-mail you the 3D file right now. Special Skills Temp Guy, you'll get one, too."

Klean tapped a few times on his keyboard, which was followed by the simultaneous chimes on multiple devices as his message arrived—scarcely audible above the rumbling that had become a constant roar. Exchanging a fist bump with Hardin and a final glare toward Stanton, he signaled that his official report was complete. "Happy to be here. Hardin and I go all the way back to start-up days at CytoKron. And several of you I know through your—poorly documented...successes...on missions such as this."

"Excellent," said Watson. She pointed toward the buff guy with dark brown hair who had delivered the coffee drinks. "That's Lawson, Associate Managing Special Counsel for Psychological Finance. If you ever wondered what caused the Russian bank meltdown two years ago, Lawson might know. But I'm sure we'll never know too much more about that."

A continuous stream of people in golf carts and scooters were now flowing past us in between the rows of parked vehicles.

Lawson, the male underwear model, pulled some collated and stapled copies off a thimble-sized color printer that sat in the center of the table and handed them out—taking an extra second to heave one in my direction like it was some sort of rotating kung fu knife thing. Following this up with a sneer in Klean's direction, he began. "We're currently operating at 41°28'14"N 86°54'33"W. We're in the southeast quadrant of the InfiniPark. We're on pace to meet our numbers for the mission. So far within our budget for the flight, drop and set-up. The hand-outs have the relevant spreadsheet and bar charts. And the weather report for tomorrow morning inside the store looks good. Shouldn't be anything standing in the way of our freelance line item here doing what he needs to do. As for my weekend plans, I'll be para-gliding in Maui no matter what El Blanko here does or doesn't do."

He directed a cold fusion stare in my direction—reassuring me that I was in fact El Blanko and no doubt referring to the fact that I was gazing into space with a blank expression, hoping that some indication of my purpose there would arise from the void.

"Nice work," said Watson over the roar of a purple school bus loaded with people wearing purple ponchos that rumbled through the clearing, though shaking her head at Lawson's rudeness.

She then nodded toward Dalton, who had unpacked a single netsphere and was sitting with his pack positioned by his side—ready to heave it onto his back again in the next instant. As a squadron of passenger airships bearing the All Mart logo buzzed over our heads at low altitude, he looked up and winced.

"And that's Major Dalton," Watson continued, "Acting VP of Market Guidance Systems. On loan from the E-Berets."

"We're all on the same team," said Dalton, watching the airships fly off before glancing at me in a non-nuclear-reaction-inducing sort of way. Unlike Stanton and Lawson, his awkward half smile communicated that he was not aligned with any of the competing factions and that my presence was appreciated, though poorly understood.

Turning toward Watson, he toggled a joy stick at the side of the streaming sphere that moved the antenna he had set up. "I've tracked internet and wireless usage in the entire county via HackSat. The printable coupon page on the All Mart site has had twelve million downloads since 0500. The full-time shoppers from the surrounding towns who saw today's All Mart commercials on *Good Morning Now Buy Something!* will be showing up here in any second. We're in for a rough ride. I'd recommend we clear out—*now*. As you can tell from the aerial activity, the Surge is underway."

With that final comment, he unplugged the joystick and sphere and stuffed them into the front pocket of his pack.

"That's impressive, Major Dalton. Thank you." Watson appeared tormented. On the one hand, she seemed satisfied at the magnificent display of group multitasking that we had all witnessed. But she was also concerned about the androgen slinging aspect of the meeting and the impending issue of the Surge.

Dalton had returned his wrist rocket to countdown display, watching as thousandths of a second flashed past. "I think that's about everything and we should ab-"

"We're not quite done. We haven't heard from K," Watson said, looking over at me with desperate haste. "The mystery man."

"I'm a production artist," I said, sensing we needed to be in a hurry, while attempting to pump a little baritone into my voice. My ego was derailed by then and I was still a little shaky from the helicopter drop, so I didn't even mention that I considered myself a screenwriter more than a production temp, who like so many artists before me, had subjected themselves to less satisfying jobs in order to support their craft.

My sense of identity in the moment was further clouded by the as-yet unexplained spray of toxicity that Stanton and Lawson continued spewing in my direction. Even on the flight down they had been blasting stink eyes at me from across the aisle and had left foamy dabs of testosterone on the leather seats.

"With some special skills, as we understand it," said Watson. She took a moment to plumb my thousand-yard stare for some non-verbal indication that these special skills might also make me a candidate for some witty and challenging repartee. But then, sensing a potential complete absence of wit, she turned back to her screen.

Then, after what felt like hours, I noticed that everyone else was packing up stuff so we could get the hell out of there—but at the same waiting for me to make some introductory remarks about the high degree of training that had gotten *me* selected for the operation. That is, contribute something to the meeting. Which was not an easy thing. For the last ten years I hadn't created anything you could touch, or even use in any practical way. Instead, all I did was manipulate pixels that were on-screen representations of printed or online materials that promoted goods and services to people who existed as stored records inside another server that I never even saw. As a production artist with limited design skills of my own, all I ever did was take other people's designs and move them around a little. Sometimes I was asked to build some slides for management presentations—which is what I thought I was doing on this job. But more often, when I wasn't cranking out rewrites of my screenplay about a mafia boss who decides to join the Peace Corps, the Agency mostly placed me at direct marketing agencies—usually working on credit card offers.

Over the past few years, I had established myself as proficient in laying out letters that told recipients they were pre-approved to receive an insane low-introductory APR if they signed up for whatever AbsurdlyMassiveBank card we were pushing that week. The people who succeeded in the direct mail industry were as creative, hardworking and intelligent as those in any other field, so I don't judge them for my discomfit, nor the direct mail industry itself. The problem was, my own credit score was approaching single digits and the employment prospects for production artists continued to decline as even children could now perform many of my daily tasks using mobile apps on their entry-level smart phones and tablets—probably with more skill and enthusiasm. To make matters even worse, my technical portfolio consisted of a fake line of cereal boxes I had created with pictures of clocks draped over bowls of corn flakes— *Breakfàste Surréal!*, I called it. The Agency, preferring a more serious approach to the portfolios they shared with their potential clients, tolerated me because I showed up on time and got the job done. Which was not a given in the world of freelancers.

The whole special skills thing was also troublesome. And a bit of a surprise. When the guy from the freelance agency called the previous night, he made reference to my online resume, which I hadn't updated in years.

He seemed very interested in being quite sure that I was proficient in all the software l had listed there. When I told him that I was, he sounded relieved and offered me the job in the next breath. Fast forward about 12 hours and the clock was ticking. With everyone waiting for me to say something very important. Recognizing my inability to do so, I pulled out some stock stuff I carried around for these situations. In retrospect, the lines sounded like they were pilfered from an on-field post-game interview with an offensive lineman who had for a few seconds gathered the attention of the entire country by recovering a fumble on the 1-yard line to preserve a victory for his college football team.

"I'm just here to make this j-, uh, mission, as successful as I know we all want it to be. And I'll do whatever I can. To be a team player. That's what I do,"

I could see both Stanton and Lawson looking at me as if trying to figure out some hidden meaning in my blundered introduction. A second layer of their meaning was implied in the way in which they each crumpled whatever piece of paper or cup was in their hands at the moment. That is, they loathed every last carbon atom that constituted my physical presence on their turf. Hardin laughed nervously. Klean and Dalton were both studying me—waiting for a tell that would allow them to fully know whether or not I had anything worth betting on. I studied their faces for some possible clues, something to grip onto that would allow me to improvise a little, maybe get some hints as to what special skills I was supposed to have. But they were all avoiding eye contact at the moment. In a last-ditch effort to look and feel useful, I started typing. Nothing like the clicking of a laptop to add some relevance to our existence.

After a few seconds of this, I noticed that Watson was *still* waiting for me to make my contribution to the status meeting, even though everyone else was packed up and ready to move on. I guess a floundering explanation of my presumed role in the mission wasn't enough. She needed some next steps.

"Uhh," I tapped a few keys to appear as though I was flipping through some notes, "I've been leaning toward, a, uh—comprehensive approach to hit all the buttons on all the key holiday themes. Family. Value. Buying power. Deferred payments." I furrowed my brow in the general direction of Watson. "I'm also looking at some woodsy themes. Families like trees. We are the forest.

The tag line I'm working with is *'All Mart helps you save your own rainforest.'*"

As soon as I finished speaking, a 50,000 megaton F-bomb exploded inside me. There was little in my life that I knew with certainty, but the fact that I had uttered the lamest possible creative offering to a staff meeting anywhere in the world at any time in history became one of them. But I couldn't take it back. Wishing to the core of my non-specially-skilled being could not make it so. I should have just shut my pie hole and admitted that my presence on the mission was some obvious mistake. That one short second of courage might have spared me the burden of becoming the sole bearer of this message of our doom.

"That's, great, Mister K." Watson's facial muscles twitched as she bent forward and collapsed her high resolution holopad. The panic flicker in her eyes, reflected in her screen, spoke the clear truth of what she was thinking. Although she had an idea of what my special skills were supposed to be, she was faced with the suspicion that I might have no skills whatsoever that were pertinent to her mission. Let alone special ones. Stirred into the sadness that smoldered inside her, I could see her eyes waking to the recognition that I wasn't attempting to be either witty or humble at the status meeting that morning. She had awakened to the fact that it might be much worse than she had even suspected. That I might, in fact, belong to a new class of clueless. This path of reasoning was balanced against her hope that I did possess innate, hidden special skills, far from obvious in my demeanor and presentation, the nature of which had not yet been revealed to her. "Any other issues?" she asked, with attempted fake serenity.

"Well," muttered Lawson, studying a piece of equipment he was stuffing into a sack. "The thermocouple in the BivouCaff seems a little off. I won't be able to get the Americanos in the next phase over about 175."

Watson tensed her lips. "We're in the field," she reassured us. "We have to expect such hardship."

Multiple simultaneous alarm buzzers then came alive inside the surrounding RV's—with the simultaneous automatic flickering of fluorescent lights coming on. The inhabitants were waking up.

"Great proactivity on finding the problem before it got out of hand. As for me," she said, standing up from the table so that Lawson could collapse it again. "I've finished my portion of the diversionary MetaPoint presentation for All Mart Senior Management. I'll incorporate your slides—which look great, by the way, thanks for getting them to me—in time for our meeting in 26 hours and 18 minutes. They look great. Now, in regard to our goal. Hardin and I met yesterday afternoon to review McAlsteinetti's medical records on the Patriot Portal and found that he's had a recent EKG, which showed something called a right bundle branch block. Sounds encouraging, right? Well, Hardin said it wasn't a big deal, and unfortunately, the extirpative cardiologists at the Department confirmed her assessment. It's probably just an anatomical variant in his case and won't help us much. Otherwise, his lipids look good. His blood pressure hovers around 127/70. There's been some intel suggesting he plays on an intramural basketball team a few days a week, but nothing we can track with certainty. His PSA was low. And he had a colonoscopy at the store's main clinic last week that revealed a single polyp, which was benign, and some diverticuli. The photos are in your packets. Bottom line, we're unable to synchronize our efforts with any supposed natural causes. Which presents a challenge, but one which I'm sure we're all up for."

Throngs of pale, sleep-addled people were stumbling out of the RV's and heading toward the store—seeming to be unaware of us. Dalton and Klean herded us toward the edge of the clearing, careful not to touch any of the RV shoppers, fearing, as we all did, that they might waken and enquire about our presence.

Watson's voice strained as her team huddled around her, revealing a hairline crack in her confidence. "The chatter in the grid is that McAlsteinetti is planning something so horrendous that it'll change the face of business in this country for the next thousand years. Obviously, we can't let that happen. So –" Determined, she scanned the faces of all those assembled. "Let's get this covert human resource intervention on the road."

Lawson was feeding the handouts into a shoulder-mounted shredding device with Department of Commerce logos and other sponsors all over it. The others had already packed up the computers, tablets, monitors, scanners, antennas, routers and storage devices and collapsed all their chairs and stuffed everything into tiny pouches, leaving them a few sacred seconds to guzzle the last of their coffees and lob the cups into Lawson's shredder.

As I prepared myself to leave, I heard my phone buzz inside the pocket of my computer bag, announcing the arrival of a text message, which I instinctively read. *"woodsy? u bring me woodsy after all these years?"*

The area code was 614, which I knew was Columbus, OH because my brother had gone to school here, but I didn't recognize the number. My first thought was that the message was sent to me in error—but my cell phone was 312. So that didn't make any sense.

'who is this?' I texted back.

The immediate response to my question provided no usable information. *"WE ARE—THE FOREST????"* I looked around to see if any of my companions were pranking me, but they were all digging into their packs at that moment.

"I feel it evokes the human spirit in union with ecoconsciousness," I typed back.

Then, it seemed like a tenth of a second after I hit send before another reply reached my phone: *"I feel it evokes an inflammatory bowel response."*

Whoever it was that I was dealing with didn't know anything about marketing. Employing an ancient human trait of dismissing information that conflicts with our internal view of ourselves and the world, however, I stuffed my phone back into my bag with a few extra foot-pounds of force.

By then everything was packed and all the trash and documentation were obliterated to the point of making our meeting non-existent—although it didn't seem to matter to the shoppers around us. Unshaven, sleep-hair tangled, coupons clutched in their limp hands, they wobbled through the clearing.

"On my mark," said Watson, bent down in the center of our few remaining square feet in the clearing. "Three-two-one. Initiate shopping camouflage attire sequence."

In unison, the team transformed.

A minute later, no more, and I was standing with my computer bag, ready to make the run toward the store entrance. But where Watson once stood, there waited a housewife in a lime green jogging suit with silver reflective fluting running up the arms and legs. Her hair frizzed out to impossible angles, becoming more visible as her head reappeared from beneath a dispersing cloud of adhesive spray.

In place of Stanton, I saw a repairman—or an installer—of what I had to presume was mechanical or electrical equipment of some obscured nature. It was impossible to tell exactly what the company did from the generic *AAAAAAA-1 Systems* company name embroidered onto the right breast of a bright blue cotton-polyester shirt blend, with polyester by far the majority fiber. The company name, chosen no doubt to optimize placement in the yellow pages of old, was countersigned on the left breast by the gold embroidered and equally generic: *Del*. His hair was a series of oily tracks that conformed to the exact shape of his head. Scuffed boots protruded from beneath the rumpled cuffs of matching bright blue work pants.

In the space occupied by Dalton stood a craftsman, with paint-splattered and sawdust-encrusted denim pants and shirt that hung loose on his wiry frame. Upon the smooth, bony chin rested a wispy goatee. From beneath a University of Akron baseball cap trailed the matted locks of a bleached blond mullet. His hands, fitted with prosthetic blackened fingernails, fidgeted with a leather tool belt slung with hardened steel tools of cryptic trade.

Klean seemed the least changed, though the gravity of his person was diminished. He had simply pulled a V-neck cotton sweater over his t-shirt, and his leather jacket had been supplanted by a tweed blazer. His spiked-sole boots had been swapped out for soft brown Mirkenshlöcks. Square, trendy, wire-frame spectacles replaced the brushed-metal sunglasses.

Hardin's slight, muscular torso was encased in a pink hooded sweatshirt emblazoned across the front with red-glittered hearts. Her thin, powerful legs were lost beneath multiple folds of fleecy, elastic-waist slacks and a new abdominal bulge. Round and overhanging, it was a swelling of sufficient size yet odd enough shape to require the closest possible clinical scrutiny in order to determine if it represented the joyous beginnings of new life or the ravages of languid and mostly-recumbent years that had followed her presumed days as a pom-pom girl, or member of the flag corps, or any of the numerous sports-related pep or drill squads that displayed the blooming teen physique. Maybe the Dance Team. It was unknowable by then. The quiet surrender of her face testified that membership on such a squad twirled lost in the past. I honestly could not tell if she was acting, getting into the role, as it were, or actually experiencing the pained history of her costume. With cheeks and eyes like that, she had to have been popular and competitive in those early days. Penultimate to this look of quiet suffering, she wore a flesh-colored plastic neck brace. Through my recent memory of Hardin the professional I discerned that the cervical spine restraining device was in fact a telecommunications system, with earpiece and mouthpiece fitted into tiny grooves at the apex of the shiny plastic collar.

Lawson was gone, and in his place stood a figure of uncertain occupation. His pleated taupe slacks shimmered in the sunlight. His teal work shirt had a swooshing logo at the breast that might represent a water purification enterprise, or an insurer of agricultural machinery. Like so many corporate names and logos, and like Stanton's costume, it was impossible to guess at what the company in question did. *Aventra*, the logo read. And nothing more. On his head, he wore a baseball cap that bore a different logo—a blue frog—which further confused the matter of his vocation. His relationship to Hardin was also ambiguous. A liaison between them was hinted at by the identical bright orange Bengals jackets that they placed over their retina-piercing unmatched apparel.

The whole 'sequence' puzzled me. "Why are you dressing up if you guys have a meeting scheduled with All Mart senior management?"

"Focus groups say it's better if we blend in. Less chance for retribution," said Watson, hurling me a Canton McKinley High School marching band jacket at the maximum possible velocity recorded for a marching band jacket of any affiliation. But she wasn't smiling. None of them were. Frowning in unison with them, and to avoid any more projectiles—either textile-based or verbal—I put on the jacket while the others stowed their business-jump gear. But even with such a decisive, market-driven answer from Watson, some unseen facet of their true intent was revealed in their costuming. It wasn't that they were trying to lampoon the fashion sense of those who shopped at All Mart, in which case the costumes were cartoonish representations of shallow archetypes. Rather, they were acting out some truth of their individual realities which could not be spoken.

In my mind's eye, I saw that each of them resembled their original embodiments with an additional twenty years tacked onto the bill, and with a few zeros slashed from the bottom line. For an instant I imagined that I had witnessed some unspoken penitential rite, and the figures assembled had become sacrificial avatars of their former or future selves, or perhaps shadows of their ancestors who had arrived in this country and passed through these forms. Further, by shape-shifting into this assortment of non-executive track workers, they had also assumed the emotional burden of these lives on the opposite rim of the socioeconomic divide. Their impressive job titles and physical forms guaranteed that they had gone to the best schools and had the best opportunities. There were multiple athletic and academic scholarships among them. With all their skills, there was nothing they could not master. But after the change sequence, they seemed not even two-dimensional, more like one. As if everything that they once were had been stretched to a thin film that conformed to the exterior contours of their physical bodies. But I didn't have the time to wonder what might lie inside.

Watson disappeared into the flow of RV shoppers—lost among the many other women wearing equivalent attire. Lawson's hand whacked the back part of my shoulder, urging me to move along—a little harder than I thought necessary since I had just met him.

"You'll be fine," Lawson said, his toxic smile sprinkled with loathing..

Eager to demonstrate my worth, I rolled my shoulder blade a few times until the dull stinging pain was gone, and then jogged ahead.

Migration

"We cannot support the conclusion with any appreciable level of guaranteed certainty in regard to the position that Miss Hardin was employed by the Department of Commerce at the time of her so-called Conversion to residency status inside All Mart. Furthermore, I might add, the Department of Commerce has not now, that we know of, nor ever, as of which I'm aware, employed a special forces unit per se for the purpose of conducting clandestine business transactions or compulsory changes in employee physiological status."

Rex Troglett, Undersecretary, Department of Commerce, Office of Antitrust Operations, in a press conference to answer allegations of a failed takeover of All Mart.

A few hundred meters north of our base camp, my heart started pounding and I couldn't catch my breath. I found myself mashed into the river of humans heading toward the store.

"Who are you really working for?" asked Lawson, looming at my shoulder. "Existential Reassignment Associates? BlakOpTemps?"

"What?"

"Come on, K. Don't waste my time. Stanton and I have been around this track a bunch of times and your name and face have never crossed our radar." Lawson was smirking, figuring that I was being coy. "Where did you get trained?"

"I have no idea what you're talking about."

"I heard those guys from Department of Transportation special forces are some steely mo-fos."

"What?"

"Are you EPA? National Park Service Marmot Team 9?"

"I lay out documents on a computer before they get sent off to printers," I said. "It's a shrinking industry. People can do it on their freaking cell phones."

"Please, we're on the same team here. No one comes into our unit from the electronic side unless they've been doing ultradeep stuff. Text hits. Server-side regime changes. That kind of thing."

"I move pixels around on a screen. That's it."

Lawson edged away from me still smirking. "And it looks like someone invested in getting you a zero-threat personality implant. Nice work. Who did it?"

"I've always had this personality."

"No one in this business is that dull," Lawson growled. "Come on! Throw me a bone here. Who was it? Iliescu? In Bucharest? I heard he's good but I didn't think he was that good."

"I've never even been to Romania."

Lawson smiled. "Sure," he said, shaking his head and trotting ahead into the crowd.

I tried to catch up but then let it go. I mean, I had no idea what I would do or say if I had caught up with him. It wasn't in me to try to explain to him the obvious misunderstanding in regard to my hiring. And I had already revealed my undeniable unsuitability for the mission at the status meeting. A few more F-bombs vented off under my breath as I closed my eyes—figuring there was no way I could get out of the flow of shoppers moving toward the store and deciding to move along with it.

After a few more steps, I felt another body jostling in close and moved over to guard myself.

"Don't worry about him." A warm hand rested on my shoulder.

Looking over, I saw that it was Dalton and felt a little relief. I didn't think I could stand any more shrapnel blasts to my ego at the moment.

I think he sensed that I was getting close to being overwhelmed and was trying to get me through. "We'll head off to the left just after we clear the Babel Babes."

I nodded that I understood and that I wouldn't be bailing out quite so soon.

"Klean has located the shop ship and texted me the coordinates," said Dalton. "Just follow me and keep your cool. It can get pretty hot in the cart acquisition phase."

I had no intention of attempting any heroics. I had shopped at smaller All Mart stores in La Grange years ago before they even had Babel Babes, but I knew those visits could not prepare me for this encounter. Rumors about the All Mart Store Number 1 experience confounded any meaningful understanding of what went on inside. Still more legend grew around the unknown fate of the thousands who Converted and were never heard from again. The media got its sharpened pens into the most ridiculous of these myths—free cell phone service for life in exchange for your soul, kidneys being swapped for 8 terabyte MP7 players, a new contagious disease sweeping through the store. Plus, tales of untold riches—free dental care and daily tanning breaks for Converts.

As we approached the store that morning, any prejudices I might have brought with me were shattered. I figured everyone in North America had heard of the Babel Babes by then, but no magazine quote or even first-hand account could convey the power of the *a cappella* chorus that greeted the herd as we neared the cavernous entrance to the store. The chatter of the crowd was overpowered by the multiharmonic, multigenerational and multilingual voices of several hundred Babel Babes welcoming us to All Mart. In between the people in front of me, I caught my first glimpse of one of the fabled Purple Ponchos and I knew we were close. In between the arias, I caught single words from the handful of languages I had studied in high school but still couldn't speak, plus bits and pieces of languages that I recognized from my foreign classmates in college. French, Italian, German. Greek—but also Arabic, Farsi, Urdu, Tagalog, Thai, Cantonese—spoken in multiple dialects and in multiple ranges of pitch. Then, as the crowd started to fan out inside the store and we passed beneath the shadow of the 1,500-foot ceiling, I saw them in their full array. An entire century's worth of female *National Geographic* cover girls, spanning the entire visible spectrum of color, the complete statistical distribution of fitness levels compatible with life, and several geologic ages of time—all wearing identical Purple Ponchos with name tags reading *Welcome to All Mart* in their native languages. One of these women in particular caught my gaze. Ivory skin and moist ringlet hair, brown eyes that met mine and narrowed as she smiled.

"*Incoming!*" hissed Dalton, dragging me out of the path of a purple plastic shopping cart that was hurtling toward me with 50-mm wheels wobbling. Grabbing my arm, he cleared me of the inscrutable paths of multiple carts and shoppers that were all changing directions and maneuvered me toward an open space between the long rows of carts. As we approached, the other members of the team stepped out from different regions of the cart-human melee and moved in our direction.

Klean got there first and grabbed a canvas tarp covering what I thought to be some piece of derelict machinery. With cavalier disregard for the *Employees Only* signs decorating the tarp, Klean had the thing uncovered in seconds. To me, it looked like a brand-new family-sized electric shopping cart. A unified gasp rose from the team.

"Here's my baby," said Klean, untying some cables from around the huge motor near the back of the hulking frame.

"I've heard the rumors about these," said Lawson. "But I–"

"Never thought it was real? Guess again," said Klean. "A buddy of mine in logistics told me they were going to plant one of these in here for us."

Klean had climbed into the cockpit and started powering up. The others climbed into side cars attached to the main frame of the shopping cart. When they each started punching buttons and I saw heads-up display systems flickering to life on the inside of the small wind-screens, I knew this was no mere electric shopping cart from the All Mart fleet.

"Wha-a-t is it?" I stuttered.

"It's an extended range Fully Automated Tactical Assault-Shopping System, or the FATÁSS XR," said Watson, using what sounded like a French pronunciation for the acronym. "Hummbris wanted to market a consumer version but the autobionics of it were way too advanced. More than a few good test pilots lost it with this thing at the Twentynine Palms Proving Mall."

Klean cranked over a circuit breaker and the sound of what might have been a turbine rose to a scream from beneath the dull gray frame of the beast. Through the louvered cowling on the hood, I could see the power source glowing as Klean continued running up the engine. I stood there and watched, waiting for the flimsy looking covering to start melting. When the engine blazed up to white hot and reached banshee howl decibel, Klean must have seen what I was thinking.

"Beryllium-fiber composite," he yelled, tapping the engine housing, "this stuff can handle any temperature and all the shear of rapid-sequence discount shopping."

"We ready?" asked Watson, scrolling through what looked like a Sunday newspaper insert that was projected onto the screen in front of her.

"Just need to make it look the part," said Klean, turning to me. "Hey K, do us a favor and grab one of those signs off one of those other carts."

I was still standing at the edge of one of the long rows of the store's real carts. I looked over and saw that a purple plastic placard was attached to the front of each cart by tiny plastic clips. Each of the placards displayed in a different shade of purple lettering some variation on a feel-good message for shoppers. The one I grabbed read: *Questions? Look for a Purple Poncho!*

The cheap plastic clip that held on the placard snapped with minimal resistance. Shaking my head at how chintzy the thing was, I handed it up to Klean—who slapped it onto the front of the ship and motioned for me to climb aboard.

The remaining workspace on the huge shopping cart was an elevated turret that sat in the center toward the back. Attempting with little success to increase my speed, I monkeyed myself up into the turret and settled into a contoured, cushioned seat. At the edge of my field of view, I saw both Lawson and Stanton snarl as I sat down in front of a contoured black glass control panel, avoiding touching it for fear that it would light up and I would have to do something.

Watson, who hadn't noticed that I was sitting there, looked at her watch and pointed straight ahead. Klean gunned the turbine and we shot out from between the more primitive human carts—entering the flow of shoppers heading down the main aisle of the store. I wasn't surprised to see plenty of other electric carts. All Mart had made notable efforts to provide shopping support for people of all ages and with all manner of disabilities. There were also droves of the purple push carts, with many other shoppers carrying purple hand baskets. Klean navigated us through all these without anyone even noticing our passage. The disguises were working. We looked like an extended family of shoppers who were picking up some items during the early morning hours of a regular working day.

Dalton was fixated on a holographic display that was projected in the dashboard space in front of him. It seemed as though this represented the region of the store that surrounded the XR. In it, each successive end-cap display and aisle was rendered in dots of green light. On his screen I could see the translucent individual ruffles on a baby onesy hanging on a nearby rack. Each item around the onesy, including the display on which it hung, was annotated with what appeared to be real-time pricing and inventory information. He touched the screen and it zoomed out to reveal an overhead view of a few hundred square miles near the store entrance. The upper right of the screen looked like a mountain range. "Make for the Wholesale Highlands," he said without looking up. "I think we'd all like to get up there before the Black Light Blowouts kick in."

The sound of those words silenced the background chatter of the crew. For myself, I pushed down the crawling eel in my gullet with the reassurance that I was with professionals and that their numbers provided me some measure of protection from the unknown hazards that awaited us ahead. They all looked busy and it was easy to imagine that our safety was their top priority.

Then I noticed it wasn't their instruments and control screens that they were focused on. It was the constant input of text into multiple hand-held devices that held them. And their on-board monitors were not displaying live mission information as I imagined it, but MeToob mashups of everything we had done so far that morning. It was hard not to re-live the embarrassment of earlier that morning when I saw Stanton snickering with cruel ecstasy as he watched a video of me dropping out of the helicopter.

Opening up my own laptop, as much to hide as to figure out my role in the mission, I was not surprised to find that the FATASS had its own wireless network. Nor was I shocked to find a link on the Department of Commerce website to their online store where you could buy a consumer edition tactical assault shopping system—including a junior-sized version for the kiddies. Along the side bar of the website were links to the multiple Blither and Fritter feeds surrounding the mission. @TanStan was my new buddy Stanton, who was at that moment in the middle of skewering the Department of Commerce for outsourcing 'immoblztns.' Everyone else was chipping in comments about the cushy seats on the FATASS, or posting photos of themselves on FaceHook. And it didn't take much in the way of arithmetic to figure out that Lawson had started his Where's Kurtis? blog during our morning status report. I hadn't even gotten through the first paragraph when Stanton fritted 'all mart chain demise imminent #corpdust.' Then there was a selection of fan sites, photo galleries and video commentaries in multiple languages that continued to multiply as we traveled. On a normal work day, I might have glanced at some of these to try and get a better handle on the team and the mission. But I didn't. It might sound insane, but I felt something drawing me to sit and watch everything that was going by as we moved.

Sitting in the observation turret of the FATASS, I had the first eerie twitches in gut that everything was going to unravel. Not only for us, but for most people on the planet.

Kurtis McAlsteinetti's plans to blow up the world economy and his freak-show rant on the night of his departure were not the stuff of tabloids, nor would they get much traction on the talk show circuit. But they also weren't the kind of thing that Wall Street carnivores would have pounced on during his 20-year reign over the All Mart chain of discount stores. This was insider information *nobody* wanted.

At the end of the day, I suppose most newspapers, magazines, networks, blogs, portals and vortals were unwilling to relay his prophetic message detailing the implosion of Western Civilization, as well as his role in it, given that they were owned by the very corporations that were hoping he would go away. And even though he sold it pretty hard, the whole trippy-dippy Einstein vs. quantum physics angle didn't do much to spice up his prediction that our great technological nation and many others like it would soon be toast.

But, as an old friend, and someone who's trying to redeem his own squandered life before it's all over, I figure I owe it to him to tell this story. Plus, there's the small matter of me being one of the few of people left who can.

Problem was, from the minute the helicopter took off from an abandoned hangar outside Fort Wayne, I was in way over my head. But it wasn't only me who was determined to fail in what I had been hired to do. Disaster was built into the organizational chart on both sides of the conference table. Even now, searching for more clues in the memory that gets grainier with each consecutive playback, nothing about the job made much sense.

"Mister K, have you ever heard of Kurtis McAlsteinetti?" It was Watson, speaking through a headset from the front of the shopper, trying to get me up to speed on the mission.

"Of course," I answered, sitting up in my seat. Even though I wasn't aware of our connection at the time, I was aware of his existence. Who hadn't heard of McAlsteinetti? Books about All Mart's formula for success had dominated bestseller lists for years. And no one could escape the company's popular talking amoeba commercials that were shown every few minutes on every major network, cable channel and radio station. Then there were the Babel Babe swimsuit pop-up ads on the internet that compelled viewers to click through again and again despite solemn vows they wouldn't. And because 24/7 wasn't enough, All Mart bought huge chunks of air time during halftime of the Colossal Bowl every year. Last year's spots featured Jerry Jensen, owner of the Dayton Defendants, building a new stadium with the money he saved at All Mart. McAlsteinetti's own rambling voiceover as the mysterious inner source telling Jensen to shop at All Mart was recognizable from the million other commercials that the store ran worldwide. I, like billions of other average citizens, was very clear on the existence of Kurtis McAlsteinetti. By the way, when you become one of the top 3 richest people in the world, people stop asking you questions about your odd and awkward-to-pronounce multi-ethnic amalgamated surname. But I'll get back to that later.

"This was monitored out of Cambridge, Ohio, east of Columbus. This has been verified as McAlsteinetti's voice." Watson was flipping through a series of play lists on her OmegaPod. Finding the one she wanted, she tapped the screen to play the clip over the FATASS sound system.

"I'm here with Sammy Snail, the in-store mascot for this week's HALLOWEEEN RAZOR SALE—where we slash our prices so far you'll scream! We have latex masks of the world's scariest politicians! This week we're featuring the entire US Senate! Plus fake teeth, vampire coffins and haunted patio castles! And costumes to transform your kids into the stars of All Mart's hit series Aquatic Adolescent Guerilla Fighters! Get Sammy Snail, Che Crabera and Mao Tse-Tuna all for HALF-OFF! Help make my dream come true that you'll never need to shop anywhere else! That's my dream! Happy Halloween!"

Watson clicked off the radio ad and fast-forwarded to another. "That was on September 28th, two days before the new store opened a few years back. This next spot followed on the evening before the Grand Opening Sale."

"We must sell them, then you must grill them! Pig after pig, cow after cow, chicken after chicken! And they call me crazy for offering you our selected cuts of USDA meats for a fraction of what you'll pay at Corky Porky! What do you call it when people refuse to shop at All Mart? They lie! They lie about my plans to give you great bargains for our Grand Opening in Circleville! And don't forget the kabobs! I love them! How I love them!"

"This was just before he lowered the prices on his entire meat stock by over 75% at all his stores around the world. And the prices have stayed there since." Watson shut down her OmegaPod and slipped it back into the pocket of her jogging suit. "Kurtis McAlsteinetti was one of the most imitated businessmen this country has ever produced. He was brilliant and bankable in every way, and he was a heckuva venture capitalist. Humanitarian man. Bit of a player in his early days. Not much fun at parties, lately. Prone to rants. Kinda' boring, I've been told. And definitely not much of an athlete. But CEO's all over the world have tolerated his maverick ways because he moved their goods. Then he started expanding Store Number One. After that his promotions, his marketing, have become unsound...Unsound."

That last fact was not something Watson needed to tell me. With ads like those, the whole world knew the guy had moved on from reality as we knew it. It didn't take a psychiatrist, or even a first year MBA student, to know the guy had left the building in every possible way. Whatever fingernail grasp of sanity he once possessed had now slipped away and the robust viability of his core business was in a glorious swan dive over an ocean of red ink. But that didn't stop us from shopping at his stores. All Mart stores worldwide carried everything—from brake pads to mattress pads, from Margie° dolls to drywall, from smoothies to Uzis—at below rock-bottom, Center of the Earth PricesSM that couldn't get any lower. But they did, and I had a feeling Watson and her team weren't happy about it.

Going up that aisle was like traveling back to the earliest beginnings of commerce in the New World—when vegetation rioted on the earth, when the big trees were king and when the single mercantile in the village contained every good known to both colonists and citizens of the Motherland alike. A turbulent stream of shoppers moved along; an ambient selection of classic 60's Revolution Rock rendered in pan flute and marimba played from speakers hidden high above. The air warm, thick, heavy, sluggish. There was little joy in the constant overhead fluorescent brightness that saturated the enclosing merchandise in an otherworldy palette of false color. But it didn't matter. Choked with product, the long miles of discount floor space ran on into a glaring, ever-expanding distance. On the narrow side aisles, which fed shoppers into and out of the main flow of traffic, Purple Poncho'd workers restocked each purchased item in flowing choreography of perfected global inventory—the ethereal purple summit team culminating the long voyages of trucks and ships that arrived from around the globe. The broad main aisle splayed through promotional dioramas, with single files of shoppers first channeled through a full-scale mock-up of an Ohio campground, complete with tents, fold-up chairs and tables, serious lantern power, plastic cookware, hatchets, ATV's and fleece-clad mannequin campers huddled around mannequin campfires with flapping paper flames and red and black faux-burnt plastic weenies. A little further on, the traffic was diverted into a high school gymnasium scene where mannequins wearing budget-conscious formal wear were suspended in revolving painful slow dance beneath programmable home laser light displays. The mannequins were even set to Awkward Smile Mode to display their sparkling Allthodontic hardware.

The flow of traffic slowed to stop-and-go as it passed by rows of tables with myriad punch delivery systems and ultrafructose cookie trays that were brought over from the unseen grocery provinces of the store. You lost your way on that aisle, as you would in a desert without the sun or stars for reference, and with increasing frequency you ended up bumping into the mannequin trees and roll-away basketball backboards adorned with crepe paper, trying to find the main aisle again till you thought yourself overtaken by an unseen power that had rendered all persons, trees and rocks in lightweight yet durable molded plastic. A power also capable of suppressing the Indian Summer sky, experienced as a round yellow icon on the main control panel in front of Klean that monitored the outside weather, obscured by tinting of the skylights overhead. And once you were captured by this force, your connection to the domain of actual humans dissolved, making all non-mannequins seem cosmically distant from where you now were, driving your cart among the still, glass-eyed pre-game revelers in a promotional tail-gate mock-up of The Ohio State University stadium parking lot, complete with red- and white-clad The Buckeye mannequins huddled around mannequin kegs and billboard-sized propane-powered mobile theaters, losing yourself so that your shopping became in fact another existence. There were moments when your deep time past came back to you—as it will sometimes when your mind is somehow cleared by a fleeting disruption of your own thoughts, without your knowledge or will, in a way that you can neither stop nor start. Arriving in this sudden fashion, this past of yours comes not as a welcome reminiscence of amber-lit childhood, but in the sound of an unrestful, teeth-grinding dream, remembered with a shudder amongst the overwhelming unreality of this strange terrain of actual merchandise placed upon these both undead and unliving approximations of plants and animals, resonating with the perpetual hum of an electric motor, the voices of shoppers and the tinkle of the overhead AllMuze. The Doors' "Light My Fire" being played down tempo on a glockenspiel barely audible, at the farthest edge of perception. To be clear, this perpetual dream sound beneath the music in no way resembled the clear voice that might speak to you in the absolute silence of a meditative state. Instead, it was the gray noise of an implacable force in dominion over the part of you that was captive to the store and its endless opportunities. It crooned over you with a patriarchal aspect, though without any perceivable instruction for your future.

After a while, though, I found I could tune the whole thing out if I went deep into my head. At that point, with my special skills still unknown to my colleagues and myself, and not yet reconnected with Kurtis, I was still committed to finding some way to be useful—rambling through the catalogue of what skills I did have and examining their suitability for the needs of meeting the CEO of a massive business consortium. I have to say, it wasn't looking good. But my blue collar eastern European immigrant lineage had wired into me the notion that I needed to do my best at whatever task was before me. Even if it was cleaning toilets or riding along in an electric shopping cart with an executive level special forces unit. After all, this was one of the traits that had kept me alive in the freelance pool for so long.

After some unknown time interval, during which I had managed to filter out the wide-scale butchering of the great classics of 60's rock, my mind was jerked back to the actual presence of being in the shopping cart. I couldn't explain how this collar-grasp back into reality worked, but it had something to do with the part of your brain that wakes you up in the middle of the night at the exact moment that your closet door creaks open the slightest fraction of an inch—even though your bedroom window sits four feet away from an elevated train platform. It's as if the brain can be comfortable with a raucous pattern of noise while sleeping, but even tiny perturbations of the pattern signal an alarm to wake up. I've never been a parent, but I was sure that all my friends with children could recognize minuscule variations in the coughs, sniffs and breathing of their children. In my case, there were plenty of strange sounds along the main aisle of the store that evening, but something had changed in the quality of one of those sounds and a part of me that I didn't understand had noticed this change and alerted my conscious mind.

Without even thinking about it, I turned my attention to Klean—who was bent over his instrument panel, tapping on a row of lights on the engine performance readout.

The persistent hum of the FATASS was fading out.

Seconds later, the high-tech assault shopping system jolted to a halt as the engine stopped. A few nearby shoppers beeped the horns on their carts, mumbled some all-inclusive expletives and raced around us. The few with push carts and on foot flowed past us as their attention remained focused on the surrounding goods. They didn't even see us.

"Morpheus?" Watson's voice conveyed an expectation of full accountability.

"Workin' on it," said Klean.

Lawson looked up from his latest blog entry and pointed in my direction. "It's probably K trying to run another operation through the control panel."

His words were spiked with the insinuation that my ultradeep state special forces training had given me the ability to cause the machine to malfunction through some futuristic technology that only myself and two other people in the world knew about and could be activated by the simple action of my mind. Watson's face told me she thought this might be a reasonable hypothesis. All eyes fell upon me for confirmation.

"I didn't touch anything," I said with the first breath of certainty I felt since starting the mission. "I was just sitting here."

Doubting my every word, Lawson nodded and climbed out of his seat to survey our position in the aisle. The rest of us piled out and stood there, staring down at the dead machine. Klean leaned over to release a breaking device with a deep metallic thunk and we all started pushing the 2-ton heavily armed shopper out of the main aisle. No other shoppers stopped to help. Which was good I thought, because by then it would have been hard to explain the fact that we hadn't put anything into the cart that might allow others to believe that we were really shopping. Especially since we were smack in the middle of Hardware Heaven, All Mart's extensive in-store building supply department, with three members of our party dressed as possible contractors. Here, more than anywhere, the empty bins and cargo netting on the shopper were sure to arouse suspicion. Indeed, it would only be a matter of seconds before we attracted the attention of a Purple Poncho'd sales associate who was trained to shout 'May I help you?' at anything that emitted heat in the infrared spectrum.

Once the XR was rolled into a deserted side aisle, everyone shut down their social media apps and looked real busy. Dalton was shaking his head, restraining himself from reminding Watson that he had advised against the prolonged status meeting.

"Our schedule is meaningful," Watson said, climbing back into her command turret near the front of the vehicle. She opened a scheduling app on her wrist pad and started moving icons around on a screen that appeared to correspond to individual minutes along the timeline of our mission. "With a specific event requiring our presence in a place that isn't here at a time in the near future."

That sounded veiled and threatening, and everyone else took it as an indication they had better freaking figure out what the hell happened to the power systems or she was going supernova.

Klean had his head under the hood but his voice sounded unfazed. "Looks like the primary and secondary power take-off systems failed." A sound similar to that emitted by a pipe wrench striking an automotive transmission came out from under the hood. "The static electricity harvesting module seems to be working. It's taking power directly from the surrounding air as it should. We just can't get any of it."

Watson's face looked like we were driving past a sausage factory in mid-July. The fact that the problem had been identified in the first minute since we stopped wasn't what she had in mind when she suggested without saying so that she wanted an actual *solution* to the problem of the non-functioning of the shopper. An immediate solution was preferred—as a few of the icons on her wrist pad had started flashing red and others were cycling through a little animation of a mushroom cloud. I suspect these indicated her task checklist had fallen behind the mission clock as Dalton had warned against hours earlier. Dark hair swirling in violent glory, she leaned over and attempted to bang some numbers into her onboard control screen. When that failed, she pulled her cell phone from the pocket of her jogging suit and started scanning through her contacts for someone accountable. "Dalton, get S.T. on my private com channel—*now*."

Dalton jerked the portable satellite dish out of his carry-on and had it up in a few seconds. The others, giving up on getting their own panels to work, had restarted their hand-, wrist- or shoulder-held devices and looked very busy.

"Can you patch it through to my headset?" said Watson.

Dalton punched about a hundred numbers into the keyboard feeding into the dish. "Not with her dead in the aisle like this."

"So put it on the speaker." Watson's eyes were white-hot pinpoint lasers.

Dalton rapid-fire key-punched down through the nine layers of the automated customer service call center at Dominational Dynamics, Inc., the company that made the FATASS, pausing to slam the "O" button a bunch of times in hopes of getting an actual person. After a series of hopeful clicks, a genderless recorded voice came on the speaker and announced that Dalton had reached the division of the company that specialized in suburban defense systems, that he was calling outside of normal business hours, but that didn't matter anyway because this particular division had been sold off from the parent company five years earlier. The message continued by adding that if he needed actual parts and service for his tactical lawn mowing system, he would have to call his local authorized dealership. And last, they appreciated his business anyway.

After another Byzantine excursion through the catacombs of the call center, Dalton lucked into an irreproducible combination of menu selections that promised to lead us to an Assault *Shopping* Specialist. Knowing that the odds of ever getting to this place in the menu again were nonexistent, we all waited with our breath held as he punched in the final zero that should lead us to a call center specialist. After another thirty seconds of *"Let It Be"* performed on a hammer dulcimer, a single electronic ring sounded and a voice clicked onto the speaker.

"Shopping Technology, this is Trevor, how may I assist you today?"

"Hello, Trevor," Watson was all dripping business honey, "This is Roberta Watson from Special Forces, how are you today?"

"I'm fine, thank you," said Trevor with perk! You could hear him smiling. "And you?"

"Good. Good," said Watson. "Listen, we're here in Ohio working on the McAlsteinetti job for All Mart, and we're having some trouble with the new XR shopper they sent out to us."

"Is that the XR version 3.02.6.1.4, or XR 3.02.6.1.3?" chirped our man Trev. "Both are currently operational in Department of Commerce squadrons."

"Morpheus?"

"Excuse me?" peeped Trevor.

"I'm sorry, Trevor. I was just talking to our local guru here."

Klean moved his head to examine what looked like a VIN plate beneath the front main windscreen. "Uhh..."

"It should be on the cover of the manual that you will likely find in the in-dash accessory storage area," said Trevor.

"You mean the glove compartment?" said Watson, leaning over.

"As you wish," said Trevor. He sounded like a therapist I once had in Chicago.

Watson leaned over, popped open a compartment and pulled out a tri-fold brochure that had 'FATASS XR 3.02.6.1.4' printed in bold black lettering on the front. The brochure contained a few words of text on each page, in 8 different languages, warning us that we shouldn't attempt to eat any of the plastic or metal components, that there was a slight risk of electrical shock if we tried to drive the thing underwater, followed by a 5-panel cartoon which consisted of stick figures in various positions in and around the shopper, demonstrating how to control its many functions. Watson opened the brochure and turned it over in her hands. "It's the point four."

"Ahh, excellent choice," gushed Trevor. "Although I must report that there has been some problems with the aft frozen-food storage hydraulic system."

"The aft—?" said Klean, who had started surfing what looked like a FATASS user message board on his laptop.

"And could that cause the whole unit to shut down?" asked Watson.

"Well, madam, it's hard to say." Trevor hesitated. "What sort of application have you been, mm, applying, with your XR?"

"We're in the field on a job in Ohio."

"And can you please describe for me your level of usage of the product in question? Would you characterize your activity as somewhat light, light, somewhat medium, medium, excessively medium, or excessive?" Trevor had begun this question with the engineered warmth that he displayed with his earlier interchanges with Watson. As he continued, however, I had the impression that a new arm of the FATASS Assault Shopping Specialist Training Flow Chart had been entered.

"So far, just cruising to the job site."

"And how would you characterize this activity, as an approximate *level*?" Trevor exuded the patience of a thousand years at the end of a call center line, gentle in his reminder to use the required terminology for the characterization of their usage of the company's products.

"Light." Watson snapped.

"Somewhat light, moderately light, intermittently light, or severely light?" Trevor wanted total clarity on the issue.

"Light. Just light," Watson had reharnessed her impatience—though her gaze had shot up to the ceiling, which suggested her internal reactor was heating up.

""So you're saying," gulped Trevor, wavering from the clean lines of the flow chart. "You're cruising to the job site—I'm essentially using your own words here—which seem to imply at some basic level that you're operating the XR."

"Yes, that's right," said Watson.

The faintest crackle of the satellite phone system marked the 15 second pause that followed. In that time, I envisioned Trevor's mind cycling through the various strengths and weaknesses of the three options given to Assault Shopping Specialist trainees in how to deliver the worst possible news to users of his company's products. The first option, the warmest approach, might allow Watson to believe—wrongly, Trevor would have to admit—that things were going quite well under the circumstances. The last option, in which he gave her the worst possible news in the most detached possible way, would without question result in a thermonuclear chain reaction capable of blasting a hole from Watson's location in Ohio, through the entire thickness off the earth's crust, skirting the mantle in a direct path to toward the call center where Trevor worked. He couldn't see the flashing icons on Watson' scheduling app, but he had to believe at some level that no matter what he said, the chain reaction might still occur.

"Well," he hemmed, way off the flow chart dialogue for an instant, then choosing a path that was skewed toward cutting his losses in terms of generating a positive 3-question survey at the end of the call and focusing instead on getting Watson off the call faster. "*That's* your problem. You seem to be actually *using* the shopper."

"Say that again, please," said Watson, replacing a strand of hair that had fallen across her face.

"Do you have the warranty handy?" You could hear the squeak of Trevor's pants as he squirmed in his chair. There was an air of lightness to the squeak, as if one of the call center supervisors had logged onto the call and was, silent to our ears, reassuring Trevor that he was on firm ground and he need not worry about admitting any actual weakness in the company's products. The microscopic print of the warranty was the final word.

Watson attempted to toss the manual to Klean, but the damn thing was so thin that it floated on a passing current so that he had to reach out and snatch it from the air. "Component parts made in Ningxia Province, Guatemala, Surtsey Island...blah, blah...assembled in Mexico...hmm, blah...," he read after securing it. "Ah, here: '*Warranty includes defective materials or parts subjected to reasonable entropy over the period of one month from date of purchase.*'"

"Sounds promising," said Watson.

A few more seconds of crackling silence passed as Trevor's throat clearing crossed from his unseen location in a call center to a commercial satellite somewhere far above earth in market-synchronous orbit and then back again to our location inside All Mart. "Actually, I'm afraid it's quite explicit."

"Yes?" prompted Watson.

"The warranty says nothing about actually using the shopper. It simply covers the premature physical decay of the parts and materials that might occur in excess of what is expected from the gradual dissipation of matter as a consequence of the continually expanding cosmos."

"And what does that mean, exactly? For my purposes. As a consumer. At this moment. Here in Ohio with this product of yours that is no longer functional?"

"Yes," said Trevor. "The warranty will cover replacement of parts and materials only if the shopper is maintained in a vacuum, without exposure to electromagnetic radiation of any type, not limited to visible light, also to include ultraviolet or infrared light, and at a temperature that does not vary from that of the assembly plant by more than one thousandth of one percent of a single Kelvin. And I'm sure you're aware that a change of one Kelvin is equivalent to a change of one degree Celsius. So there's not a great deal of tolerance in this regard. I don't know what they keep the factory temperature at, but it is reasonable to state that you have varied from it considerably. It is not my intention to question your ability and desire to operate within the parameters of the warranty, nor do I mean this as a criticism of your business practices, of course, it's a likely scenario that you have varied the temperature by more than the stated percentage of one degree Kelvin. Especially considering the fact that you're in Ohio. This is something that does occasionally happen with our products."

"In what way?" asked Watson. Her question sounded innocent, but the downturn of her mouth showed that she had been there before and knew what was coming next. Perhaps she had operated missions with previous versions of the FATASS.

"It greatly displeases me to report that you have voided the warranty on your shopper by, your, uh, use of it."

Watson pulled off her headset and picked at some unseen specks on her jogging suit. Then she reached over and wrenched the controls to the satellite dish in front of Dalton and pressed the "PARK" key. Holding her cell phone with both hands close to her mouth, she then unleashed a raging Class V hurricane of words, insinuations and anatomical commands which one could imagine were compiled from the highlights of an entire century of commercial fishing operations off the Aleutians, sprinkled with outtakes from the collected early works of Martin Scorsese, with bonus material provided as condensed excerpts of onstage rants of unemployed, gin-guzzling British punk rockers of the mid to late 70's. Then, with each of us still reeling from attempting to visualize some of the proposed body part insertions, she took the phone and placed it onto the tiled floor next to the shopper, hefted a short-handled sledge hammer from a toolbox in the center console, got onto her knees and exploded the phone with a single crushing direct blow. After repeated blows she pounded the remaining specks of smart phone into smart phone dust, took a backup phone from her pocket, turned it on, and tapped the flashing parked call button on Dalton's keyboard.

"Well," she said, returned to absolute calm. "This is most unfortunate. But I understand your policy."

Trevor sounded relieved that Watson had taken his explanation of the warranty so well. "Have I answered all your questions today?"

Watson's jaw tightened, but she still managed to salvage some warmth. "Yes, you've been a great help, Trevor. Thanks."

"Would you like to receive some additional information from our special forces travel partners?"

"We'll pass for now."

"I understand, thank you for calling Dominational Dynamics Retail Technologies."

"Goodbye, Trevor."

"Goodbye, Ms. Watson. And have—"

The speaker phone clicked off. A light jazz version of *Purple Haze* swelled from the overhead speakers.

Klean, who had been studying the flimsy owners' manual throughout all but the most colorful of Watson's riff, raised his index finger, as if to signify the identification of a key point. "Says here that a complete schematic can be found in the on-board help module. Which, of course requires the power and control systems to be operating." Tossing the manual over his shoulder he turned back to his laptop.

After a few quick scans of the FATASS XR message-board postings on his OmManiPad, however, he was back in business. "But I can re-route the auxiliary battery that supplies the soda fountain and get us back on the trail."

Dalton watched as a few other shoppers passed. The traffic had slowed to a trickle, which seemed to correspond with the faint shifting of the artificial lighting to a violet blush that felt like twilight. "How long you figure, Morph?"

"Hard to say. Couple hours at least. I'll have to splice into the main power line from the static harvester. Then re-route the thirty-two individual circuits that lead into the flavor fountains."

He snapped the cover plate off the ice-crushing unit and was already working.

Watson didn't take her eyes off her wrist screen. Some of the mushroom cloud icons had become tiny cartoons of swirling black holes. "Will that give us enough power?"

"The carbonated beverage distribution system is the one piece of hardware on the ship that can never fail," said Morpheus. "The hex-lithium battery can keep it going for weeks."

"Is that your final answer?" Watson said icily, knowing that long battery life was different than electromotive force.

"The soda fountain, or CBDS as the manual refers to it, was adapted from a San Francisco Fire Department fireboat."

Watson fired a nervous, questioning glance at Klean. "It's a frickin' water cannon?"

"Yup," Klean allowed himself a fractional smile.

Though Watson looked satisfied at this answer, she took no noticeable pleasure in the magnitude of the wattage available to us. All the mushroom cloud icons on her screen had vanished, except one, which had morphed into a swirling animation of a black hole. Everyone else also looked a little worried. Klean continued working and the rest of us set up some folding chairs in the aisle and each pulled the clicking laptop ruse again in our own little ways.

As the light inside the store continued to fade with each passing minute, I noticed that the core team members were abandoning the updates of their social media apps. But it wasn't the limited light that was bothering them. There was something dangerous hanging in the air that I didn't understand. How could I? I had no idea where we were going and what we were supposed to be doing. Hardin initiated a hushed, edgy conversation with someone on her neck communicator, probably at a central monitoring office for the agency.

Dalton and Watson were re-arranging icons on the scheduling app. Lawson and Stanton had gotten out of their pods and were helping Klean run a series of wires across the deck from CBDS batteries to the main engine housing—participating at a new level of cooperation that had me worried.

I had found an addictive game on the AllMart website where you get to kill groundhogs by throwing kittens at them but had to stop playing. There were too many unknowns and I couldn't focus. With the onset of darkness came the seeds of terror.

"Let's get the hell out of here—this place is starting to creep me out a little." Watson didn't even look up from the scheduling app. The single animated black hole was now sucking in all the other icons on her desktop. I wasn't sure what that meant in terms of wrist pad's operating system and licensing agreements between the various manufacturers of the software she was using, but it couldn't be good.

Before I could even shut down my own laptop, the XR was whining again and everyone else was in position. The store was dark by then and the giant shopping cart was silhouetted in the soft green light of all the display panels. Hardin and I jumped into our pods as the vehicle started moving. Klean saw that we were seated and hit the throttle. In the high-beams of the forward ShopLights, I couldn't see any other shoppers around us, so Klean punched it and had us going about 45 knots down the aisle.

"What's the big hurry?" I mumbled over to Hardin.

"The Black Light Blowout," she whispered, looking over at me with a curious mixture of both horror and pity—as if I, as an adult male, had asked her where babies come from.

The Black Light Blowout was the legendary territory of Converts. Between 10:00 PM and 4:00 AM of each night in All Mart, the entire store was darkened. Without prior advertising or marketing to inform customers what products would be featured, ultraviolet lights—that is, so-called black lights— would click on to highlight individual items for a period of time that was also not advertised. If found and brought to a black-lit register before the light illuminating the product went out again, these featured items were sold at 99% off the everyday low price, or even the special Center of the Earth Prices. Any item in the store could be chosen for a Black Light Blowout—no matter how big or pricey—and multiple items might be featured at any given time, with the time of illumination by the black light ranging from under a minute to several hours. During one of the early sessions of the Blowout, entire pallets of motor oil were featured for the entire duration of the night. There were no rules or patterns that could be distinguished among those who attempted to study the Black Light Blowout. The reasons for this remained obvious to those on the outside who attempted to interpret the meaning of this promotion. Few casual visitors to All Mart had attempted to negotiate the treacherous depths of these markdowns, and many who had dared enter these aisles in darkness ended up converting to resident status and were never heard from again. It was assumed so that they could continue to attend the nightly Blowout. As a result, none of them could be interviewed—leaving any factual information about the Blowout to be sparse indeed. Myths of shoppers emerging in the daylight with next-generation All Mart branded KPhones for which they had paid pennies persisted. At the other extreme of shock and horror were the tales of those who sprinted miles through the darkness, arriving at the nearest black-lit Purple Poncho'd sales associate as the light shining on their chosen item flickered out. Even as we raced into the vinyl-tiled void before us, we could see spheres of luminous indigo surrounding the chosen items throughout the store, followed by the screams of the distraught Converts echoing at first far off, and then, emerging from the shadows beyond the glare of our headlights.

I'm not proud of what happened next, but for completeness of this story I must reveal the facts as I saw them.

We weren't more than a few hundred yards down the dark aisle when a black light flicked on in an adjacent aisle off to my left, which I was able to see because of my position on the turret.

"I need that!" I yelled above the silence around us.

Klean slowed the vehicle down—all eyes turned on me. It was the first thing I'd said with any confidence all day and they noticed.

"Come again?" Watson replied.

"In the next aisle—the thing with the black light on it. I need it. Stop this hog and turn around." I stood up in the turret and was pointing over the next aisle. "I need to get over there."

"We're kind of in a hurry," said Watson.

"For the mission. I need it for the mission." I had no idea where that came from. It came out of me. There was not a single quark of truth to what I had spoken. But the fools didn't get it so it didn't matter that I was lying to them. The purchase of this device would enhance my existence after their trivial non-humanitarian mission. With the vehicle starting to accelerate, I jumped down off the turret and started sprinting up the aisle. At first my legs wobbled from sitting most of the day but I found that my desire to reach the black light was like a high-octane injection. Coca leaves, light roast coffee and sugar cane dumped into a juicer and then blasted into my veins for immediate superhuman speed.

Cutting down a side aisle I left the path of the headlights of the shopper and entered into the purple radiant aura of the next aisle. My focus was perfect. I had shaped shifted into a lion—no, not fast enough. I was a German-engineered intercontinental ballistic cheetah converging on prey in the moonlight. I covered the final 20 yards toward the object of my intention in what must have been thousandths of a second—noticing in mid-stride that a thin, pale figure was also approaching the black-lighted center of the aisle from the opposite direction. An interloper—whom I judged far weaker than me. The paleness of his skin created the impression of a fragile immune system without access to sunlight and pigmented root vegetables. Poor bastard had somehow fallen off the steep, slippery sides of the food pyramid without knowing the joy of a single serving of whole grains—and now his life as he knew it was going to end. Arriving on the ground, my speed-of-light reflexes stopped me at the precise spot of the aisle where the black light was focused on the device of my longest dreams. A hole opened in the center of my chest when I saw that the top and middle shelves were empty—cleared by figures I hadn't even seen in the dark seconds before my arrival there, each of them already closing toward a register where they could complete the transaction that would define their own place in the cosmos. In the trillionth of a second available to me, I saw them, arriving there inside my mind, weeping with the exhilaration and exhaustion of an entire life. Seeing in that same non-measurable unit of time the corner edge of a single remaining unit on the bottom shelf, pushed toward the back by the hasty fury of another hand reaching to grasp the device in a single movement as they ran past toward the register. The corner of the box was marked by a single greasy fingerprint, decorated with the unmistakable crumbles of Kaptain Kurt's HyperKrisp Fried Chicken. I gasped—my heart filled with radiant hope. My hand reached out and I found that I was bending toward the lower shelf. The motion slowed by the coca leaf turbine that had become my waking mind.

As my fingers closed upon the corner of the box, I felt that intervening between my perception of a glossy printed cardboard package was the feeling of the thin, bony fingers of another creature. The pale, slug-eating forager. By then, I had become a suborbital drone, my mind and strength could cross entire hemispheres in seconds, driven by something outside my ability to comprehend. I gripped harder and tried to pull the box toward me. Feeling immediate resistance, my Mach 9 mind saw in slow motion the device moving away from me and toward the bare pale chest of a wire frame male figure, flaming eyes locked on me from behind a full face scraggly beard littered with small bits of chicken breading and biscuit crumbs. I felt the muscles in my arms start to tear at the opposing force of the man's movement to bring the device closer to his chest. In the same space of recognition of the pain as my arm was pulled against the full resistance of my shoulder, straining the socket so that I feared that it had become dislocated, I knew that I had underestimated the strength of this man. Knowing my erroneous assessment of his power as the bones of my arm socket held fast, screaming pain toward the center of my brain. Pain and simultaneous knowledge that this man had bested me. In some dim corner of the media storage department where we now battled, in the seconds prior to our meeting at the edge of the box containing the single remaining unit available for consumption, he had injected into his veins a superior cocktail of gingko biloba, sucrose and 100% Organic Orbital Escape Velocity Nicaraguan light roast con plutonio.

I felt my lungs and throat emitting a growl from deep inside my anger, slashing my free hand to grab onto the other edge of the box that he had squeezed close to his chest—finding then that his bony hand had fused to the edge of the packaging. My entire weight levered against his hand, I stumbled backward as he broke free of my grip and headed off down the aisle toward the register. Catching my balance, I sprinted after him, forgetting all things about myself. Knowing that what he held was mine and I would have it back.

Waking, I found myself lying on the ground next to the register, my shoulder raging in pain—remembering as I came to the wrenching movement of my opponent. He was gone. I imagined him in his lair licking the grease from his fingers and beard as a victory celebration of his purchase.

"He's dead." It was Stanton, leaning over my face. I felt a nudge in my side with a boot. "Let's go."

"He'll live," said Hardin as she checked my pulse and gave me a quick sternal rub. I had forgotten that she was also a physician.

I sat up and shook the cobwebs out of my head.

"He's slipping away, let's let him go in peace." Stanton stood up and climbed back into the XR.

I started to cry, not from the pain or from Stanton's obvious dissatisfaction at my ongoing life, but because I couldn't remember what the device was that had so consumed me. It had units associated with it that represented very large numbers was all that I could remember. "What was it? That he bought?" My voice cracked and blubbered.

"We were hoping you'd tell us," said Hardin. Her soft but powerful hand rubbed my aching shoulder.

"Get him up and loaded." Watson's voice came from the direction of the front of the shopper. "Then find us an alternate route."

Hardin and Klean helped me to my feet, which felt spent of whatever imaginary force had been propelling me in my pursuit. More or less deposited in my seat, I slumped back and assessed my partially dislocated shoulder and a sore aching in my belly from the impact of my interloper's head. Surrounding the area of physical pain was a debris field of fried chicken breading stuck to my band jacket that provided added insult to my loss.

"We need more than an alternate route. We're not just a few miles off course, we're now a few *light years* off course." Lawson was seated on the edge of his side pod with his arms folded. "*And*, K here almost blew our cover."

"If it wasn't for K's diversion, we wouldn't have seen her." Hardin was half-turned in the communication pod.

"You're not even sure it was her, you said that yourself." Lawson raised the pitch of his voice to perfect condescension and attempted to reach out for Hardin—causing her to recoil to the farthest edge of her pod away from him.

"It doesn't really matter how we got here—we need to get ourselves moving again toward the Mezzanine," said Watson, still staring down at her wrist pad. The Mezzanine was the home of All Mart's corporate offices and professional services. A complex of offices, conference rooms, suites and apartments elevated above the sales floor in the geometric center of the store. This was the last recorded location of McAlsteinetti and the source of all communications to the outside world from All Mart senior management.

It might have been my delirium, but it seemed as though the swirling black hole on her screen, which had consumed all the desktop icons, was starting to pull inward on the aluminum frame of the device itself. As I watched, she banged on the I/O button in an obvious attempt to turn the damn thing off before it no longer existed. When the screen went black, she looked toward Dalton in the navigation pod. "You're sure?"

"I'm afraid—" Dalton said. His voice cracked, "it's the only way we can get back on schedule."

"You're *sure?*" asked Watson, almost childlike, relinquishing her commanding presence.

Lawson had become his usual offensive self again. "You don't want to stop at an Insulin Island and ask someone who knows their way around inside this dump?"

"Either that," said Stanton. "Or we call in a gunship and torch the Mezzanine. The mission is screwed anyway, thanks to K Force here." It was hard to imagine what could cause an intelligent man, accomplished in so many ways, to be so angry all the time

Whatever was the only way to reach wherever it was we were trying to go, none of them wanted any part of it.

"You're absolutely sure it's the only way?" asked Klean of Dalton. He didn't want to go there either, but at least he sounded a little more confident in our chances of getting through whatever it was.

"I've run the topographic scheduling algorithm four times now," Dalton confirmed. "The only sure way to get us to our meeting, even close to on time—accounting for the time we lost with the engines down, and then adding the time spent chasing down K—is to head through Gherkin Gorge."

The words alone stirred in me a sense of wonderment and terror. It wasn't that the Gorge was advertised very much, or that it was all that mysterious. Rather, Gherkin Gorge was more than an unprecedented feat of creative floor space management, it was also the single most-photographed bulk food display of all time.

Watson was back to full command. "Let's get moving."

Dalton hesitated. "It's not really that simple."

"What isn't simple? We drive through the giant stacks of pickle drums and we get to the other side. It sounds very simple." Watson was already adjusting her shoulder harness.

"There may be technical challenges." Dalton didn't sound convincing.

Watson turned toward our driver. "Klean, please weigh in on this."

"I can get us there and I can keep us moving," Klean said, revving the engine. "But I'll need to use the real-time topo data to get us through."

"Fine. We have the data you sent us this morning. Very nice proactivity. I like that. We're good. Let's go."

Dalton looked nervous and didn't seem prepared to reveal some other fact that disturbed him. "I'm a little concerned about the—"

"The what, Dalton? The French and Italian tourists on chartered day trips from Vegas? Worried we might spill their espressos? Worried that we'll offend their cultural sensibilities as we drive past at high speed while they're walking along with their guide books? Worried you'll be asked to take their picture with them standing in front of a jar of garlic-stuffed olives the size of a refrigerator? Klean?"

Klean leaned over the engine readout panel. "This thing's built to withstand high speed maneuvers in tight shopping situations."

"It's not—" Dalton trailed off.

Watson was already scanning the pickle specification section of her on-board catalog of goods and services. "I agree with Klean. It's not a great choice, but it's our only choice and, as mission director, I'm going to authorize a deviation of our course to make it happen."

Dalton shook his head as he tried to expand the range of his local radar display to show the Gorge—or at least the part of it that was closest to us. "I just -" he murmured, wiping a wave of sweat off his forehead.

"You *what*, Dalton?" asked Watson.

"I don't think it's a good idea. Period."

Watson cocked her head, perplexed. "And what experience could lead you to this conclusion?"

Watson sounded concerned. But the few extra drops of high fructose corn syrup in her question made it clear that there was some dark fun that she was weaving underneath that sultry, dispassionate professionalism. Maybe Dalton had become the foil she sought.

Dalton sighed and looked up from his monitor. There was a sadness in his face, having to explain a few things. First, that he wasn't interested in Watson, which I couldn't even imagine how that could possibly be at the moment. Secondly, that he had no factual information to support his conclusion. "It's a hunch. That's it. *I just don't think it's a good idea.*"

By then, Watson had taken off her wrist pad and slipped it into a sleeve at the side of her briefcase. It was clear she didn't have time for hunches. Strapping herself in, she pointed off to the left, indicating to Klean to drive on without further discussion of the route. Klean swiveled the XR around a sharp 90 degrees and took us into a narrow aisle filled with orthotic shoe inserts that was paved with ancient cobblestone pattern high-impact vinyl flooring. The top edges of the displays were capped with foam blocks that had been carved and spray-painted to look like ancient building stones—which confirmed that we were somewhere in Pharmadelphia, even if we couldn't see the temple skyline that marked the center of the medication metropolis inside the store. Another of McAlsteinetti's great gifts to consumers was *99 days for 99¢!* on thousands of common generic drugs.

Dalton, jaw clenched, looked over at Klean and the two reaffirmed that their displays were reading the correct information. Klean was watching the real-time topography on his VisorVid, which was the very information that he had generated earlier from the spy plane data. Dalton studied the holographic image that the shopper itself generated with its own local side-scanning radar.

Both seemed to breathe a little easier with the knowledge that the two data sets agreed with each other in terms of our location: in the Shoe Insert Department, toward the north end of Pharmadelphia, with the configuration of the aisles in both data sets matching. More to the point, a few short kilometers from the towering Wholesale Highlands and the mouth of Gherkin Gorge.

But the Black Light Blowout had also caught up to us.

A few yards ahead a black light flicked on to illuminate a display of Doktor AlleFuß store brand silicone-gel arch supports. A long, wailing, feral cry—seeming to come from the next aisle over—split the night and was followed by the racing patter of bare feet on the tile floor. Klean jammed the throttle forward and kept the XR well past the red-line until the cries faded behind us in the dark. In case any of us had felt some momentary comfort by the high quality of the technology we had on board, we were reminded that the evolutionary path toward lower prices was the domain of flesh—with little regard for the lines and figures of mathematical space that allowed us to navigate in the dark. I may still have been a little delirious, but in that same moment of acceleration I saw what looked like one of the swirling black hole icons appear *on the control screen of the shopper itself.* This icon, however, was different in that the tiny animations of entire galaxies that covered the desktop, plus folders named for each of the team members, including a black folder with my name on it, were being sucked toward a singularity at the center of the screen.

Dwindle

Pretty birds
Pretty flowers
Pretty sky above me as I lie here by the
window
Aisles that ramble on through the
tattered corners of my wide-awake
dreams
Forever...
Why are all the people screaming?

From Willows and Rivulets, the collected poems of Major Anthony Dalton,
United States Army, 101st Digital Division (Medical Retirement)

At high speed it wasn't more than a few minutes before we arrived at the mouth of the Gorge. Whatever gasping reaction I had at hearing the mention of the Gorge was superseded by the jaw-plummeting, eye-bulging, breath-extracting site of the Great Gates of Giardiniera—a 1000-foot high portal of stacked 55-gallon glass jars of Italian vegetable mix, each with the familiar purple label of the Kurt's Klub brand of bulk foods. Even Dalton, who had shown such apprehension at coming there, stared straight up at the clear glass edifice as a young boy might marvel at meeting a professional basketball player. Or upon arrival at the foot of El Capitan in Yosemite Valley. It reminded me of the immense fortified entrance to a lost Mesopotamian city that I had seen in an online virtual tour of the Louvre. Decorated with carved sandstone bulls with human heads, winged lions and other bestial guardians, which were brought to life by the flickering of oil lamps, the gates would have towered over the heads of travelers who arrived at the ancient city in the middle of the night. As a known tourist attraction, the Gates of Giardiniera were also lit from both above and below. The light passing through the brine caused the jarred veggies to cast tortured and irregular shadows on the floor and nearby displays, and on ourselves. Across Hardin's face I saw the distinctive shadow of a chunk of cauliflower, magnified from a beam of light high above. On Klean, I saw the crenulated edge of a crinkle-cut carrot, but sharper, suggesting a closer source of light, perhaps from an unseen fixture ensconced in a nearby wall. These and many other shadow forms played upon us as we sat gaping skyward.

Despite the fact that an electric tour van was emerging from the Gorge filled with tourists who appeared to be elated at their experience, even at that late hour, no one, including myself, seemed to be enjoying the scenery. Awe for a few seconds was one thing, but after that, my companions again seemed edgy about something ahead that I didn't understand yet. The Gorge seemed so benign. Tourists wearing sandals wandered around inside there every day without incident. But no one in our vehicle looked like they wanted to go in there. After rewinding the entire ordeal so many times in my head, at some point I decided that our diversion to the Gorge may have been a subconscious distraction. An unspoken pact the team members made with each other to delay our meeting with McAlsteinetti—and what they might have to accomplish once we got to him.

Dalton and Klean each allowed themselves a cool, minimalist nod to indicate that their displays still matched. Then they drove us between the towering pillars.

Immediately I understood why Dalton seemed so spooked about this place. In the absence of tourists, there was a brooding, serpentine quality to the layout. The spires of low-priced megajars of pickles were not stacked in neat rows, but in a sinuous fashion like the carving of rock by a meltwater river. A river, like the presumed ones that flowed on Mars, that was now gone. Regardless of the actual or suggested presence of such a river, the effect of the rapid changing of direction required to traverse it was quite real. The familiar nausea, which in my adult life had steered me clear of the once-beloved TiltAHurl and most other carnival rides, was filling my body with a cold-sweating uneasiness. Simultaneously, my mind became aware that my late-night snack of All Mart's patented instant self-frying mozzarella sticks was threatening to return to the outside world. As long I kept my eyes straight ahead, I was fine. But that was a non-trivial undertaking. The high-beams of the XR fell upon a shifting pastiche of garish color and design. At one turn, the smooth glass walls contained kosher dills. Around another sharp bend bright yellow sweet pepper rings constituted the vegologic strata. Still further along, my insides were yanked around another turn to see that we were enclosed by a pale green, red-accented cliff of pimento-stuffed cocktail olives.

"We should have walked," I gurgled.

"I suggested letting you do that after your half marathon with Sasquatch." Lawson reached up from his side car and chucked a small plastic bottle of spring water in my direction. Slamming it into my soft midsection with a faint *glug* sound, the instantaneous dull pain served to take my mind off my nauseated state for a second—long enough to consider that maybe Lawson had a few molecules of kindness floating around in that hulked out body of his.

But our course had become more erratic and my head was jerked away from offering him a few words of gratitude.

Klean seemed rattled and I sensed that our guidance had shifted from something controlled and regular to an improvised, moment-to-moment reckoning of our direction. Indeed, Klean stared down at his instrument panel as if viewing the unfolding horror of yet another stock market massacre, wide-eye staring at the actual path in front of him, with additional tiny rapid eye movements to view the image being projected inside his VisorVid.

"They moved 'em," Klean choked.

"What?" Watson appeared to spin around in her seat. Or maybe I only perceived that she was spinning since everything else was.

"They moved the jars. The floor plan is different from the VisorVid. They moved the jars since this morning when we scanned the store."

Klean was using his whole body to muscle the shopper around the vaulting displays of pickles. The engine of the FATASS groaned. The tires squealed with each turn and cut-back. "Dalton, can you tell me what's coming up?"

Dalton's face was inches from his holographic display, attempting to figure out what manner of malfeasance had befallen these innocent towers of hamburger relish. The tiny rendering of the XR with all of us aboard on his display showed our movements in real time. But it was pointless, and we could all see that he knew it, too. The radar was good, the best that deficit spending could buy, but with the XR moving at high speed to within millimeters of the glass walls, it could not distinguish our own ever-changing position from the walls themselves. And the sweet female voice on the talking GPS on Watson's phone, which she had flicked on seconds earlier in an attempt to help out, had become a repeating mantra of 're-routing,' As we moved to within a few hairs of the smooth glass of the enclosing pickle jars, the tiny holographic representations of the walls and the shopper merged with our own tiny holographic representations. With each turn, the changing green depiction of the back end of the shopper, the front end, or the entire port side including our own limbs, became continuous with the shimmering green obelisks of pickles.

"Hard right!" The GPS wailed. Watson had upgraded to the Special Forces Voice Package. "Hard left *now, motherfu-re-routing.* Soft right *Get out! Get outta' there, now!"*

Klean dripped with sweat from the monumental effort of guiding us through the maze. By then, it seemed as though we were fishtailing out of control. The years of education and whatever tours of duty Klean and the others had spent at top-secret special-forces shopping simulators had not prepared them for this.

Lawson grunted as the impact of the XR against a jar of baby dills caused his side car to snap off and rocket toward the other side of the aisle where the ragged metal edge of the car punctured a drum of Hamburger dill chips. The side of the mammoth jar buckled. A torrential slurry of pickle slices slammed the car on its side and swept Lawson onto the floor. The jars stacked higher up tumbled out into the aisle and shattered in succession as they hit the floor. The air around us filled with splashing green foam and one-inch cross-sections of deadly cucumbers. Our lungs filled with salty waves of garlic, dill and other natural flavors and spices. At the first breath, this evoked a European deli, but became overpowering as we found ourselves lost in a briny fog. A stray Polish dill projectile exploded on impact with the side of my head, causing me to wobble in my turret. Then, as I neared falling into the brine myself, the sudden yaw of the entire shopper pushed me my back down into my seat. The tide expanded as nearby stacks of jars started to collapse and the shopper itself was being floated further up the aisle while Lawson tried to swim in the Class Five green-water that engulfed him.

"Haarrr-din," Lawson was screaming as he tumbled further from us in the rapids.

Hardin, her face gnarled in fear, leapt out of her seat, leaned over and reached out toward him, wincing as she strained against the telecommunications device around her neck.

"Somebody, please!" is all she managed to yell.

Dalton climbed out of his seat and prepared to dive, but a raft of pickles slices knocked him sideways.

Stanton fashioned a paddle from one of the side bulk-food scoopers and attempted to keep the XR oriented in the stream, lest we should be capsized and all thrown into the froth. Klean wrestled with the steering. Watson pounded a keypad on her control panel, perhaps initiating a rescue sequence that would not come since the panel was dark, short-circuited by the pickle juice surf that was battering the shopper.

Then Lawson was gone.

His screams became muffled. Glimpses of his flailing limbs and the orange tiger on the back of his Bengals jacket became less frequent in the receding swell. Powerless, we watched as he was carried out along one of the narrow side canyons that cut back into the deepest part of the gorge. Back out toward the main floor, or deeper in the heart of the highlands. I couldn't tell for sure which direction he was headed.

Even if we could tell where he was going, we couldn't save him anyway. It was impossible to turn back. Huge mounds of pickles, intermingled with tusk-like shards of glass, blocked the aisle behind us. And the overhead lights remained off, so we remained a tiny island of light in the dark and cavernous maze. All we could do was follow the stream that flowed in front of us—with the one behind impassable.

"H—h—e was taking me to Tuscany for my birthday," Hardin sobbed. But her face was conflicted. Was there a semblance of relief in her words?

"Keep moving," Watson ordered. Dalton gave up attempting to call out directions, leaving Klean to drive us through the roaring current alone— which seemed fortuitous. We could all see that he was watching the waves and riffles in the flowing brine to discern the way through the walls ahead, so that our passage again became steady. It might have been hours. It's hard to know how long we rode in silence. There was no way to turn back—on all possible levels. We were committed to moving ahead. Over time, we passed through pale green cliffs of pickled tomatoes, followed by the blazing fall colors of the red and yellow roasted pepper mix, which gave way to the spring-like hues of olives stuffed with garlic, almonds and jalapenos. All this time, minutes that passed into hours, the rushing pickle river carried us along. When the flow ceased and all that remained of the current was little more than a puddle, the walls around us opened and we were free of the briny grip of the Gorge.

Klean pulled over and we stopped. Hardin's sobs were intermittent by then and the low whine of the engine replaced the roar of the current. The Black Light Blowout must have ended during our run out of the Gorge, and a silvery luster informed the entire store, becoming brighter by the minute.

We all sat there and observed the changing quality of the light. Despite the horror of Lawson's passing, a gentle peace settled down around us as we waited at the edge of the Gorge. The particulate matter suspended high up near the ceiling -which amounted to real smog in the artificial light—progressed from the morning tones of swollen purple and into long hopeful shades of orange. Hardin's sobs had become sniffles, followed by a brief rustling as she composed herself, in respect for the gravity of the moment.

"The Buyer's Dawn," whispered Stanton—sounding almost moved. Perhaps my premature labeling him as a token testostobot was inaccurate. "Another one of the rumors from the depths of the Mart."

"But why?" whispered someone else, with what sounded like reverence.

I'm not sure who it was who had spoken this question, which I was also asking inside. The air and merchandise continued to evolve through the soft, delicate spectrum of a pearl. The oranges shifted into yellow, with ever bolder white arriving as the overhead lights became still brighter. Looking up, I noticed for the first time that there were skylights recessed into the ceiling, well above the hanging light globes, though they appeared as squares of darkness against the artificial morn. The real dawn outside had not yet even begun. It was not surprising that the stylized dawn of the Mart should precede the actual dawn of the natural world.

"Why would they take the time to turn on the lights so slowly? And make a fake morning?" asked Dalton.

"No one knows for sure," said Klean. "The psychiatric literature on McAlsteinetti's motivation remains pretty thin. Why he does anything is anybody's guess."

Hardin's eyes were damp with tears as the lights grew stronger. Her shoulders seemed weighted and she was bent forward in her pod by an intense gravitation field that was fixated on her alone. I didn't know what she saw in Lawson in the short time that I knew him, but there had to be something in him that was lovable. Then, as I looked on, I saw the weight on her shoulders lessen, as if she was unburdened of one task and gearing up for another. She had another mission to accomplish that was hers alone. Finding that inside herself, some surviving part in her moved her right hand to tap the touch screen of her communications console. She began speaking a few soft, unheard words into her telecom collar, making an official alert to the mission controller that we were short one employee. But more so, signaling to us that she was willing to continue on with the business of our journey. Tapping the screen again to close the communication, she turned to me with a tired look of focused clinical concern. "K, how's your head?"

In the fury of the storm, I had forgotten that I had taken a pickle to the head. I felt a little sore, but nothing I couldn't live with. I rubbed the side of my face and dislodged a few mushy cucumber seeds smeared into my sideburns. "I'm fine."

Klean had returned to the cockpit and was running a systems check. "Might have to send you off to see Doctor Beanwater!" he said laughing.

The reference to the urban mythical Dr. Beanwater was well timed. The healthcare equivalent of Johnny Appleseed, Beanwater had arisen in pop culture as a doctor that you could see who would make your symptoms disappear but then you wouldn't remember seeing him. This fantasy sounded like something we could all use at the moment.

With everyone else preparing to get us moving again, I took a few seconds to dry my hair with some paper towels from a dispenser on the control panel of my turret. As I was getting re-oriented, I had the notion that we were being watched. The half turn of Hardin's head against the restriction of her neck brace showed that she also felt it. Klean reached for the glove box but stopped as three figures leapt from behind a crevice in the canyon and onto a ledge of olive jars that stood beside us.

"I'm sorry about your friend," said a lean figure wearing a peasant skirt and hiking boots, with long flowing curls partitioned into alternating segments of brilliant orange and green. As she leapt down off the ledge, her unshaven legs became visible as the skirt flowed behind her.

The two other figures followed, both male, wearing mid-80's vintage wool slacks and rumpled cotton flannel shirts that looked as though they were acquired at a thrift shop.

"I'm Ren." The young woman's wide smile compelled Klean's hand to move away from the glove box. "And these are my friends, Quinoa and Pesto. You guys should get out of here as fast as you can."

Watson stood up to meet the young woman at eye level. "That's our intention. What do you know about our friend? Actually, he was more like an employee. But it doesn't matter. W-R-E-N? What can you tell us?"

"R-E-N," said the young woman, correcting Watson. "Short for another name by which I was once known, who no longer exists. We were tracking you across the Gorge. We saw him get dumped into the river but were too high up in the pass to do anything. We saw some Converts fish his body out back toward the Gates."

"Was he –?" Hardin interjected.

"Hard to know. He was covered in little bits of shredded carrot and pimento."

A fleeting glimmer of hope crossed Hardin's face.

"Tracking us?" Klean had moved out of the driver's pod and stood beside Watson.

Ren held up a tattered spiral-bound notebook that she was holding by her side—scribbled on every visible page with florid multicolored hand-written notes, embellished in the margins with swirling water, earth and moon motifs. "We're monitoring non-shoppers moving through the Gorge and up toward the Mezzanine. It's part of our class project."

Watson was leaning over trying to read the notes. "Project?"

"Field Studies in Compassionate Insurrection. CI543. I'm a senior at Humboldt State. In northern California. Quinoa and Pesto here are Junior Suggestive at Antioch."

"Why here, all the way from California?" asked Watson. Ren handed the notes over and Watson was flipping through the pages, looking for clues.

"I grew up around Cleveland. My pop came down for a football game a few years ago—just before Christmas. Big mistake. Never saw 'em again. I'm sure he's in here somewhere."

Hardin had lifted herself up against the weight of her sadness. "Did you see any women, about my size, similar build, pass through here last summer?"

"Maybe. You do look kinda' familiar. In a quasi-non-previous lifetime sort of way. Not to suggest that I haven't known you in a broader sense of our shared participation in a universal consciousness. Just that I might have really actually seen you in an optical sense in this plane. Possibly on the cover of a cereal box. Or its equivalent."

Hardin didn't answer. She was staring down at a photo on her phone—a young woman who looked like her, smiling between two Babel Babes.

Ren turned and said something to one of the others, who stepped forward and presented us with a bundle of wax-paper-wrapped clusters that looked like something you'd find on a forest floor, possibly left by bears. On closer inspection, they were globs of oats and sunflower seeds held together by thick honey, with suspicious dark green leafy bits mixed in.

Quinoa—his name was embroidered along the rim of the beaded man-purse that had produced the bars—chuckled. Noticing our hesitation, he presented the bars further. "It's cool," he said. "The green stuff is kale."

Klean and Dalton both reached forward and extracted the sticky globs from the wax paper and half-yoga-bowed in thanks.

Watson took a step to follow Ren, who was already scampering back up onto a display of small-car-sized jars of sauerkraut. "We need to know the fastest route to the Mezzanine."

Ren half-turned, propelling her gypsy print skirt into a swirl that was lifted from the poems that either Quinoa or Pesto, or both, had written about her. Her every living moment was likely the subject of verses that were sequestered in small leather pouches hanging around their necks, in the humid enclosures of their flannel shirts. "No brainer," she said. "It's a straight shot if you can make a crossing."

"We have amphibious capability," said Watson.

"Then you better get moving. If we know you're here, then others do, too." She took a sacred few seconds to *namaste* us and then she was gone. Quinoa and Pesto flipped back their man-purses and scrambled up the slope behind her.

"That's not what I wanted to hear," said Watson, jumping back into the command pod.

Dalton and Klean were both looking at the larger scale maps of the store, pointing out specific paths that would lead to the central Mezzanine where McAlsteinetti was known to reside. Dalton watched as Klean drew a line across what appeared to be a broad central clearing.

"We made up some time going through the Gorge, which was what we hoped." Klean said, giving the shopper a once-around before getting back aboard. The immeasurable force released by the collapse of the canyon wall had pulverized millions of pickle chips into green slime that covered the vehicle. In addition to inspecting for damage, he was removing the largest patches of green pickle matter that had collected on the axles and the engine housing. "And then, we actually got out of the Gorge even quicker once the, uh–" He stopped wiping for a second before continuing in silence.

Hardin seemed to be listening to some other transmission on her neck phone, so she may not have even heard Klean's unintentional tiptoe along the edge of grief.

"Lawson was the best field barista this outfit ever had. And sweet Jesus, could that man build bar charts," Watson said, straightening, putting what her team already knew onto the pyre. After that, it was clear that whatever moment of silence we were going to get for Lawson was over. Once Klean had got back into the cockpit, she continued. "Let's head for the Food Farm, we could all use a hot meal."

Stanton snorted. "That's an unusually stupid idea from someone as smart as you."

"Stanton—" Watson grimaced, causing what appeared to be two additional crevices to form in the soft skin at edge of her eyes. "You know this is a safe, professional environment where we all support each other. Why don't you just tell me that you're really thinking? No need to soft pedal."

"Okay, then –"

"We have to eat," Watson interrupted him. In her face, along with the wrinkles, was the meaning behind them. It might have been the light, but she appeared even more fierce and more delicate than before.

"The food there is crap and we'll all be smelling like fried egg rolls for the rest of the mission," said Stanton. He held up a unit of plastic wrapped sandwich concentrate he had pulled from one of his packs. "Plus, we have food on board."

"I'm in command of this mission," said Watson. "I agree that the quality of the food may not be what you're accustomed to, but it's also a primary gathering place of Converts. It's possible that we might gain some useful information by stopping there."

I didn't know it at the time, but I was witnessing the expressed good intentions of her publishing heiress mother and the full body armor toughness of her Marine Colonel father. Suddenly she was no longer someone I needed to fear. She may have hated me for screwing up her mission, but she didn't want me to die because of it.

"The Uniform Code of Military Justice–" Stanton was sniffing an unwrapped food packet.

"We're going," said Watson. "That's it."

"– demands that I resist any order that I feel to be immoral and likely to produce potentially harmful emissions –"

"Discussion over."

Then I saw it—the binding force that was driving Watson to continue, fighting pushback from Stanton but also seeking to answer the questions that had arisen about what we were going to do if we ever even got to the Mezzanine. The force had become recognizable as sadness, lining the thin furrows in her cheeks. Not a defeated sadness. It was thousands of miles from that. It was more like an unexpected connection to old wounds that were hidden beneath her professional edge.

Stanton didn't quit speaking as he struggled to chew the hyperviscous food product he had pulled from the storage locker. "Not to mention the long-term effects of partially hydrogenated –"

"Shut it, Stanton," said Watson. "Sharing session is over. Klean, let's move."

With the sadness engaged, she had become paradoxically radiant. Competing forces within her had resolved into a pure and commanding state. I knew there was no way for me or anyone else to ever possess or govern this emergent property of her. And Stanton saw it, too. Shaking his head, he half-slunk down in his pod and pretended to study a financial readout gauge close up as he spit his mouthful of food back into the package from whence it had come.

Klean had us moving again, faster than I would have preferred under the circumstances, but no one else seemed to mind. By then, we had settled into the pattern that full-speed work resumed after delays of any sort. The departure of one of our team was no exception. Displays and devices buzzed and chimed with incoming messages and outgoing data, with everyone keeping their hands and faces supremely occupied. For me, I wanted to watch the light change a little more and continue to study the lines in Watson's face. But driven by the desire to stay employed, I flipped open my own laptop and tried to look busy. Still hoping that my own mother wasn't lying when she told me I was here for a reason. Trying to awaken a lost belief that somewhere inside me, underneath the recent wreckage of my ego, there were a few short bits of DNA that might, if the environment turned right, still be expressed as a usable, perhaps even special, skill that might help someone else in the world.

We hadn't gone more than a few kilometers when I felt the XR accelerating. Which brought back the fear and nausea from the Gorge.

"Can you outrun 'em?" Watson yelled to Klean.

"Maybe," came the short, leave-me-the-heck-alone-while-I do-my-job reply from Klean.

Everyone else had dropped whatever it was they were doing and focused on hiding every piece of equipment that was within their reach. In a seamless display of cool thinking under intense pressure, they had stowed every computer, tablet, reader, writer, calculator, hard drive, monitor, keyboard, mouse, copier and banner printer that had seconds before littered the deck of the shopper. Smart phones and GenieUs phones were stashed deep into the zippered and VelGrabbed pockets of their cary-on luggage.

"*K!*" Stanton shouted. "Lose the laptop."

"*Why?*"

"*Now!*" Stanton yelled.

But before I could even get the screen closed a voice amplified through a speaker commanded me to stop. "You there, with the laptop. Steady now. Close it and we close you!"

As he pulled the XR off to the side aisle, Klean looked ready to explode. Whoever these guys were, it was the wrong time for their arrival. His narrowed eyes went on to explain that there was no possible time throughout the history of the universe that would be an acceptable time for them. As we slowed to a stop, five figures clad in black jeans and polo shirts with black pocket protectors rode down a scaffold suspended from ropes that were hanging from a silent gyro-copter hovering over our heads. After hitting the ground with a thud that echoed back from the Gorge behind us, they attempted to disentangle themselves from the ropes that supported the scaffolding—which only served to increase their entanglement. Their movements were accented by high frequency bursts of 4-letter words in multiple languages, recognizable as such not through the actual translation of the word, but more from the context of adult men in locked combat with inanimate objects, pieces of hardware or any combination of materials that contained cables, wires, lines or even simple strings that might become formed into a knot by the slightest pull in the wrong direction. The knot tightening with each new utterance of the chosen word. A cataclysmic birthing of arms and legs began. Which resolved itself into a few of the five or so men becoming free of the ropes and scaffolding with surprised looks on their faces. These happy few, after ensuring their freedom with one or two cautious steps, began running toward us where we waited in the shopper, parked at the side of a broad aisle. The spring-loaded KrustyKreem Law Enforcement Pastry Deployment Packs strapped to their backs made me think that we might be able to defend ourselves against them.

"Don't even think about it," whispered Dalton, who must have figured out what I was thinking as I watched them encircle the XR. "These guys might look like they're out of shape, but they're incredibly athletic and powerful. Like sumo wrestlers, but for software updates."

"Who are they?" I whispered back.

"Upraiders," Dalton hissed.

"Upgraders?" I asked again.

"Well..." Dalton said, wincing. "Let's just say they're IT personnel, working somewhere in the borderlands between mildly annoying and completely meaningless, in a realm far adrift from necessary and helpful."

But I didn't have a chance to ferret out who they were and why they were stopping us while in the middle of a mission. The muzzle of a Ninjita 1000-Watt battery-powered screwdriver was pointed straight at me. Similar tools of varying computer-devastating potential were aimed at everyone else.

The guy who seemed to be the leader wobbled toward Watson. I believed him to be the leader because he had the biggest jumble of pens and miniature screwdrivers stuffed into his black pocket protector that bore a Department of Commerce logo with a lightning bolt crashing through it. "Are you the McAlsteinetti Project Mobile Field Office?"

"Yes," Watson said without even looking at the guy.

"Assigned to continually relocate the office until the time of your meeting with McAlsteinetti at ten AM?"

"Yes." Watson had engaged her polar ice pack mode of professional demeanor.

The guy didn't seem to mind. He seemed accustomed to being ignored. "That's good," he said. "We were hoping to intercept you before your gear got too outdated."

"Well, here we are," Watson said, from the icy darkness of deep winter at the south pole.

The leader guy lowered his screwdriver and used the end of it to poke at Watson's carry-on bag lying on the deck next to her. "Any electronic equipment, today, ma'am?"

"Nope, just what you see installed on the vehicle itself. It's brand new and doesn't need any updates."

"Seems kind of strange, all you higher-ups out here without any personal computers or assisted consciousness devices."

"Our mission is classified," said Watson. "No room for clutter."

"I see," the leader said and moved to the back of the shopper where he kicked the lever for the rear cargo hold. "And back here?"

"Empty."

I heard the cargo door clang open but didn't dare turn around, what with the power tool pointed right at me.

Everyone else followed Watson's lead and looked straight ahead with their faces frozen. Hardin seemed unnerved. I could see that her forehead was sweating. But that could have been the fact that the collar around her neck wasn't ventilating very well. Or more worrisome, her fear that the Upraiders had been tipped off that our operation had been issued one of the new generation of medically-themed surreptitious communications systems—the thing she was wearing around her throat.

But since I had never encountered actual upgraders in the work setting, I had no idea what to expect.

"Mind if we have a look around?" The leader asked with false deference, reassuring me that there was plenty of reason to fear these guys.

"Help yourself," Watson responded with 9-foot-long icicle courtesy. "Mind you, we're on a tight schedule."

"Oh, we know all about that swirling icon on your mission control panel. We've seen that thing before in this outfit," the leader said while strolling over to me and allowing the Phillips head of his power screwdriver to hang inches above my laptop.

With two of the other guys keeping their power tools aimed at us, the remaining two searched everything on the shopper, poking the various pieces of luggage with their screwdrivers. I thought Klean and Dalton might scream as the Upraiders punched, nudged, banged open and slammed shut each one of the several hundred cargo and personal storage areas that were placed around the perimeter of the shopping cart. With their power tools raised, they patted each of us down—causing Klean, Stanton, Hardin, Dalton and Watson to snarl in their own idiosyncratic ways as the donut-fed hands moved along our arms and legs.

When they got to me they stopped and stared at my laptop like a pack of corpulent coyotes.

"And what do we have here?" asked the leader.

"He's a freelancer," said Watson, her words containing the approximate amount of warmth one might experience on the surface of Pluto.

"Freelancer, huh? Contracted to whom?"

"To us," said Watson. "Leave him alone."

Like a demonic bad actor in a B-grade horror movie, the leader was lifting the screen on my computer with the very tip of his screwdriver. "So, I gather that you're not familiar with article 16, section 7. Department of Commerce

Specifications for the Timely Upgrade of Electronic Equipment *Under Contract.*"

"Article 16—" Watson glared at the leader but it was too late.

Before I could reach out to stop them, not that I *would* with all torque pointed at me, the leader hefted my laptop onto a black portable workbench that one of the others had set up in the aisle. Before any of us could even scream, another of the black-clad figures was removing the screws that would allow them to remove the motherboard from its case.

"No, please," Watson pleaded. "It's him that's contracted, not the computer."

"Article 16, section 7, *paragraph 1,*" laughed the leader.

"Here, take this!" Hardin tossed them one of the many AromaPhones that I had seen her conceal moments before. I felt a wave of gratitude that she above everyone else—so in danger herself—was trying to distract them from my computer.

But the leader picked up the omnidirectional olfactory conferencing device and laughed even harder as he turned it over in his hands.

"Superseded by metabolic conferencing. Hit the market last month," he cackled and tossed the worthless piece of equipment back onto the deck, where it clattered to rest a few feet from Hardin. "We don't even *service* those anymore, let alone upgrade 'em."

Meanwhile, another of the Upraiders had whipped out my hard drive and shoved it into a black minitower that he had set up on yet another black workbench. In an instant, he was clicking and dragging a hideous collection of icons representing utilities and patches for the most diabolical, obscure and useless improvements to my operating system.

And then, the screws were tightened so that no human could ever again get inside the case to repair their havoc, the work benches were folded up, and my computer was clunked down onto the deck in front of my turret.

We all remained motionless, powerless, as the five figures fumbled to get back onto their scaffold elevator, and then waved up to the gyrocopter crew.

When the last of the figures was up and away out of our sight and the gyrocopter had flown away, Watson relaxed and turned to me. "I can't tell you how sorry I am."

"Maybe it won't be so bad," Klean said.

"Thanks for trying, Hardin," is all I could think of to say.

Hardin smiled with sympathy. Everyone else followed with a respectful nod in my direction and then set about the task of unpacking the equipment they had buried deep inside secret compartments in their luggage.

I reached down to pick up my computer from the deck, but before I could even cradle it into my arms, Klean had the XR moving along the aisle. Thrust back into my seat, I lifted the screen and pushed the power button.

The machine booted fine.

But when I noticed that my chosen wallpaper had transmogrified into a freakish scene from an undiscovered Hieronymus Bosch painting that depicted the torments of those who hadn't made the cut on Judgment Day, I knew that the worst was yet to come.

Indeed, I spent the next two hours trying to get the file for my screenplay to open. I was distraught because this was the new version I was working on in some of my spare minutes on the trip. When it did open, the number of wise Kenyan villagers who befriended the mafia boss had doubled. Pozzo and Lucky from *Waiting for Godot* were written into most of the scenes, and the locations had been moved from Mombasa to Buenos Aires. *What? The? Hell?* I had no idea software existed that could so deeply alter the structure and content of existing files.

As for other applications, attempting to launch MetaPoint seemed to control the dimmer switches for nearby lighting displays. And though I could not be certain of the connection, double clicking on the Compost icon appeared to cause a tick in Dalton's shoulder. I thought at first he was shrugging off some insect, or maybe a speck of dandruff, but then I noticed that the movement coincided with my attempts to place some older files into the compost bin on my desktop. But he also twitched a time or two when I wasn't cleaning up the hard drive, so the real nature of his movement remained a mystery.

And so it would be. Our arrival at the Food Farm forced me to abandon my investigations of both my computer and Dalton's unconscious movements.

Klean didn't slow down as we rolled past the 400-foot statue of a soft pretzel that marked the main gate. About a dozen other motorized shopping carts were parked around the statue and Klean maneuvered the XR around families that were climbing out of their vehicles and heading toward the main feeding areas. Many of the other parked vehicles were family models with seating capacity and hopper space equivalent to that of the XR. A quick glance at Watson revealed that she was certain that we weren't standing out against the crowd. Consistent with the recommendations of her focus groups, we blended. Even with one of the side cars busted off. Possibly *because* one of the side cars was busted off. Most of the other shopping vehicles looked as though they were veterans of many long and gory Black Friday Door Buster skirmishes. A few watchful adult Converts smiled and waved from the long rows of tables as we sped past, further suggesting that our presence and haste were nothing unusual. Without waiting for orders from Watson, Klean followed the signs that directed us toward the drive-through lanes.

The Food Farm was a landscaped faux-farm, complete with acres of plastic corn stalks, sponge-rubber pumpkins and inflatable hay bales that reflected the harvest theme. A few scarecrows—which seemed to be mannequins that were displaying AllHart brand industrial-grade canvas work clothing—stood along the fence lines. There appeared to be a *real* petting zoo in one little fake pasture, which made me a little suspicious of some of the clods of organic matter that some of the smallest and grimier kids were tramping around on the floors of the serving and dining areas. But everything else was fabricated and focused on providing visitors with fast, affordable food and drink. To that end, all the farm buildings—the sheds, multiple barns and rows of artificially-aged farmhouses with wrap-around porches and wrought-iron lightning rods—were individual food vendor stalls.

The effect of these installations was disorienting and felt more than a little contrived. It was ridiculous to see the words 'Turbo Panda' in a font suggestive of Kanji characters over the front porch of what looked like my grandfather's farmhouse. But the forcing of the farm motif was protean. Nearby, there was also a farmhouse, woodshed and windmill Ricky Renaissance Pizza, Peach Caesar Fruit Drinks and Uncle Twisty's Pretzels, respectively. And beyond that, the vastness of the Food Farm comprised pretend-ramshackle buildings that housed Burger Prince, Burger Duke, Burger Duchess, Burger Earl, Burger Lord, Burger Viscount, Burger Empress, Burger Mayor, Burger City Council Member, Burger Emir, Burger Sultan, Burger Sheik and Fries, Burger Khan, Burger Shaman, El Presidente del Burger, General Burger, Burger Revolutionary, Burger Grass Roots Civic Leader and Burger Burghermeister. There was also Steak Breakout, Steak Inside Job, Steak Heist, Steak Blitz, Steak Invasion, Steak Conquest, Steak Occupation, Steak Crusade, Steak and Awe, Steak Jihad, Le Coup d'Steak, Pretzel Steak, Pizza Steak and LiquiSteak. The Middle East and the Mediterranean were well-represented with ShwarmaShack, QuickKaBob's, ZoomKaBobs and SoniKabobs. In one long section, there was the aforementioned Turbo Panda followed by Golden Dragon, Imperial Dragon, Golden Panda, Imperial Panda, Panda Dragon and Golden Imperial Panda Panda. Plus Taco Mondo, Tengo Taco, Tiene Taco, Tenemos Taco, Taco Tu Madre, Taco Tio, San Taco, Sangre de Taco, Nuestra Señora del Taco, Taco Por Favor, Taco Me Gusto, Donde Esta El Taco, Taco Me Llamo and Taco de Leche. And a host of pizza joints boasting the traditional crusts and regional topping styles of Chicago, New York, California, Schaumburg, Berwyn, Des Plaines, Elk Grove Village, Arlington Heights, Nutley, Bloomfield, Hackensack, Floral Park, Manhasset and Great Neck.

No one seemed to mind that the names of these places didn't fit with the farm theme. Quite to the contrary, casual shoppers and Converts were lined up 10-deep at every one of these establishments in order to await their breakfast. The fact that every possible stall and counter was open for *breakfast* further compounded the oddness of the place. I paled to imagine what form of eggs and hash browns might be available at LiquiSteak.

The foot traffic thronging through the central portion of the Farm slowed us to a crawl.

Stanton's resistance to our visit to the Farm seemed all but faded. "I do need coffee. Right about *now*," he said.

In the absence of Lawson, no one had taken on the task of staffing the BivouCaff, which placed us in the dangerous predicament of having to outsource our caffeine supply. For our benefit, and most humans on planet earth, there was always a Queequeg's Dregs close at hand. The closest kiosk that I could see from our parking spot was set up in a corn picker painted with AllMart purple. About twenty others were scattered around that section of the Farm serving coffee, scones and quiche pops from a variety of silos, troughs, tractors, combines, hay wagons and grain elevators. Beyond that, I could see the familiar sight of Mokie the White Chocolate Whale—Queequeg's corporate mascot—spouting puffs of steam into the morning haze at other convenient locations, well off into the distance.

Watson turned to address the crew. Her face showed more than 30 hours without sleep. She was worried. "We only have time for the drive-through. Stay frosty. I want decisive orders. Standard menu items only. No substitutions that could slow us down or arouse suspicion."

Everyone, including me, nodded that we understood. Watson didn't point it out to us, but the images of entire galaxies swirling into a giant black hole on her main console had further evolved. Whatever point of no return we were headed toward had been passed. All possible permutations of a successful mission according to the scheduling algorithms had failed and we had entered into a new phase of impossibility. In place of the massive spiraling black hole at the center of the main control screen of the XR was a depiction of a superheated exploding source of all new mission possibilities. At that point in the animation, formless energy blasting out from the center stripped away all recognizable software icons from the desktop. As I watched, three faint new logos started to appear, pixel by pixel, in the top left corner of the screen. Watson glanced down and also saw them. She had probably anticipated their arrival from her in-depth pre-mission training, and knowing their significance, edged her body over the screen to obscure them from our view. But not before I could make out the words that were visible above the recognizable symbols of a sledge hammer, a spear tip, and crossed sticks of dynamite: Liquidate, Terminate and Detonate. These were the three core applications of the AmeriSoft NationBuilder Invasion Suite.

The arrival of these icons on Watson's desktop suggested that control of our mission had been notched up by more than a couple of pay grades. Watson was no longer in charge. A new clock was ticking and we hadn't gotten the memo.

Watson muttered a few words under her breath as she sat back down in her pod. Klean, ever watchful, darted the XR through the traffic and got us into the BlastThrough lane. A robotic arm holding 2 adult-sized and 2.1 child-sized touch screens descended on us from above and matched our speed so we didn't need to stop.

"K, I'm getting Taco Madre. Who's in? Klean?" Hardin had gripped the 23-inch monitor and pulled it toward her. Klean was reprogramming our route into the navigation system as were accelerating along the straight, wide-open lane that lead out of the Farm beneath a series of overpasses for pedestrian traffic. He was in no mood to be messing with a touch screen.

"37-Layer burrito. Grilled chicken. With QuesoMaximo," I yelled above the howl of the surrounding traffic. Hardin flipped through the menus on the screen and selected my choices as she found them.

"Same thing," said Klean as he maneuvered the XR through a gauntlet of carts arriving and departing the BlastThrough lanes. "And here's our trajectory once we leave the Farm. Heading 283. Their radar should register our speed."

"Got it," said Hardin. "Either of you interested in trying Kurt's Klub Cola Nothing? Free with purchase of 37 Layer Burrito? It's giving me the option."

"I'm good." Klean had a plastic 64-oz Guzzlr mug bracketed to the side of the driver pod. He must have grabbed one while they were picking me up off the floor after my Black Light Blowout encounter.

"Sure," I said. I didn't want to delay us, but it did sound like something I wanted to try.

Stanton punched in the orders for Watson, Dalton and himself while Hardin finished the orders for Taco Madre. As they pushed aside the screens, a green light flashed in the lane ahead. Seeing the signal, Klean touched a lighted button in the center column which depicted a cartoon image of shooting orange flames.

I still wasn't sure what sort of propulsion system the shopper had, but it seemed to me that we hadn't even begun to exploit its full potential. In a few tenths of a second, I was slammed back into my seat and we were veering out from the perimeter of the farm and into a broad, straight aisle. As I glanced at the digital compass reading on my own control screen to see that we were indeed on a 283 degree heading, I heard the hiss of our incoming MunchieMissile. The ballistic food container deployed a parachute a few seconds before impact and then made a dead-on soft landing in the center console between Klean and Watson.

It didn't take long to discover that the orders were all screwed up. Stanton was fuming when he discovered that the soy latte he ordered from the Queequeg's Grand Banks Central Sail Through contained a mere 5 shots of espresso. Apparently, he could tell by how much his ears rang as soon as he took the first sip. Dalton had received a 9 Piece Goat Grab instead of the Oasis Salad with side of baba ganoush from QuickKaBob's. Hardin had been given a Cinco Carne Enchiladas plate rather than the Tostada de Vegetariano, and Watson had received a Yellow Belt Kid Meal from SushiNow! that contained a microscopic California roll, French fries, a fortune cookie, and two 3-inch tall karate action figures that would bow to each other before and after matches. Klean and I got the correct burritos and sides, but I was stuck trying to figure out how to consume my single serving of Kurt's Klub Kola Nothing. The free sample came as a tiny foil pouch with the list of ingredients detailing what the product didn't contain: no natural or artificial sweeteners, no coloring, no caffeine, no gluten, no soy and no water. The tag line on the pouch read: *'The Experience of Cola. With nothing else!'*

As I studied the edges of the packet, looking for some clue as to how I might get it to work, out of the corner of my eye I saw a face pop up in a webcam screen on my laptop. A dim, thin face came onto the screen, whom I didn't recognize. When the voice said, "Dude, just pull the tiny tab to begin your cola experience," I recognized it as McAlsteinetti himself. Then the video clip stopped and I saw that a little set of controls were beneath the face on the video screen if I wanted to play the clip again. In the bottom right corner of the screen were the fine print words: 'Copyright to PERPETUITY, AllMart Enterprises.' This had to be something that the Upgraders had installed, but why would they be planting All Mart applications on my machine?

Unwilling and unable to process any of this, starving as I was and with my burrito getting colder with each passing second, I pulled the tiny paper tab on the bottom of the packet. A small cloud of brown dust formed in front of my face, like when you tap on a puff-ball mushroom as a kid. I felt that a few particles of the dust had entered my nose on the next breath. It's hard to explain what happened next. In my mind I perceived a cool, fizzy feeling in my stomach, with the memory of a huge gulp of cola that I might have taken on a humid August afternoon after riding my bike for 50 miles with my two best friends—whose names I couldn't remembered. Nor could I be sure that they even existed. Rather, I felt the laughter and sense of fun that would arise as part of a mythical, idealized bike ride on a summer day with two best friends I never had. I was experiencing how the presence of these two young men—who knew every detail of my catastrophic 9th grade dance with Marcie Wiggins and my loathing of algebra—would impact the perfect quality of the cola experience. Which was then followed by the complete, deep sensation of satisfied thirst.

I took a bite of the burrito, and then tapped the Cola Nothing puff packet to release another cloud of fine brown dust. That whiff took me to the shores of Lake Michigan, again in August, though ahead in time by more than 10 years, reclined in a beach chair with an icy tumbler filled with bubbly cola at my side. In the chair next to me was the complete image of Daniela Piazzaloni, the Italian political science student in the US for a semester who had attended my Com 114 class. The curves of her smooth, tanned skin radiated the full heat of the late afternoon sun. Her modest one-piece bathing suit conformed to the time frame of the vision, but I found it no less appealing, since the experience of the cola had heightened my senses to all that was present in that moment.

'There,' said McAlsteinetti's voice on the tiny video screen on my laptop, 'that's the idea.' Followed by the abrupt disappearance of the video screen from my desktop.

With no knowledge of how much time had passed, my consciousness arrived back in the rear turret of the XR. My burrito had been consumed and continued taps on the Cola Nothing packet allowed no more brown dust clouds. Everyone else had also finished their meals and were preparing for the next phase of our journey—passage through Electropia, the electronics province of the store.

Electropia was one of the most product-rich environments ever created in the history of consumer economies. With players, recorders, speakers, processors, monitors, printers, scanners, copiers, 4-in-ones, all-in-ones, drives, tablets, pads, rads, scads, routers, outers, phones, home controllers, drones and clones—plus the requisite software and accessories that defined the entire spectrum of human-binary interface. Aisles wider than anywhere else in the world accommodated the extra-large boxes that held self-expanding Great Wall Ion Jet televisions, which had become the standard by which all other televisions were compared. Few other retailers or discounters had foreseen the future in the way that McAlsteinetti had by building a high degree of flexibility into layout of the new store. In particular, Electropia was built from Day 1 to accommodate ever-increasing sizes and numbers of consumer electronic goods. The enormous volume of merchandise that was sold also required that the shelves be overstuffed at the start of the day to keep up with demand. The net effect was one of confinement. The merchandise was way too dense for even my comfort, and at some points overhung the path so that the lights were blocked out. As we glided into the video game region, I saw a clearing ahead, which came as a welcome surprise: just our luck, we had ended up in the SIMergency aisle which featured all the various editions of the popular large metropolitan area county hospital emergency room simulation game—on the very day of the new release of *Code Blue Resuscitation Room: Unrated.* The aisle was packed like a Third World fruit market. The clearing ahead wrested my attention from the brawling shoppers, game boxes and life-size holographic patient characters in a way that I had never experienced.

Ren—the wandering waif we had met earlier at the outflow of the Gorge—had told us to attempt a crossing, so I knew we were coming here, but I had no idea what to expect. I was surprised at how moved I was by the massive scale of what was ahead. It reminded me of seeing sunlight through a thick grove of pine trees and knowing that the ocean was ahead. I had seen radiant light splintering through redwoods while driving in Northern California, rounding the crazy bends in the roads that cut through the coastal ranges. In a similar way, I could see that the store opened up, but without the definitive sunlight of that encounter in the redwoods. The artificial light wasn't the same, and the sounds were those of another place—laughter, screams of delight, and an odd, continuous fluttering sound.

A few seconds later we broke out of the aisle and for the first time I saw the expanse of the Videocean—the shallow in-store sea of close-out DVD's, AllRays and molecular-encoded video streams that had galvanized the growing international reputation of McAlsteinetti as a merchandising and programming genius. This was the feature that had made Electropia the true sapphire in McAlsteinetti's reigning scepter. It was impossible to argue that any of his competitors had conceived anything that even approached the majesty of this ocean. The fact that he had started producing his own content which one could stream from anywhere was unmatched among brick and mortar stores. Offering that same content as heavily-discounted as molecular-memory modules that were available in-store upped the ante even further. Still, other stores had attempted to rip-off the video pond concept—with pitiable results. The most famous failed imitator was 'Loch Fliks' at BullZye, a much smaller body of videos that harbored an animatronic monster. The machine was built with such haste and so little regard for safety that it never really worked. When it did spew video boxes from its mouth as intended, the aim was bad and they never got the velocity quite right so the thing tended to topple toddlers and really older shoppers who were trying to catch the boxes. No one got really hurt, but it was scary too for parents and care-takers. Within days, and not mentioned in the press, 'Fliksie' disappeared into the murky depths of bad marketing ideas. As a whole, these efforts amounted to a temporary distraction among serious viewable content consumers. All comparisons were humbled by the unmatched size of the Videocean, and the streaming and retail-box video market remained in the firm grasp of All Mart.

Photos of the ocean were in numerous print and online ads and on television commercials, but I'm sure I was still looking dazzled as the others jumped out of their pods and deployed the outboard skis that would allow us to glide out across the sea.

Close to shore, day shoppers and kids waded in the shallowest reaches, grabbing quick bargains and running back to the plastic-sand beach. Others went further out in pedal-powered paddle boats. It was the wide plastic paddles of these boats that produced the repetitive fluttering sound as they whacked against the plastic of the ancient DVD boxes, the smaller cases of the intermediate age AllRays, and the miniature rectangular boxes that contained MEV streaming codes with their patented anti-piracy explosive smiley face TV's on the spine. I could see children grabbing boxed sets from beneath the gunwales of the tiny boats and holding them up for their parents on shore to see. Passengers waved from a house boat still further out on the sea. Near the horizon, beneath low, white cumulus puff balls created by the cloud generators, video stock freighters moved through the mist dumping new titles out into the middle of the sea to replace the hundreds of thousands that were taken out each hour by the shoppers along every inch of shoreline.

A continuous network of aisles that encircled the entire periphery of the sea was intended as a scenic byway that would keep traffic moving. But that didn't seem to be working. Shoppers who slowed down to grab armfuls of boxes from the sea had choked traffic to a crawl. Thus, the quickest path to the other side was to cross it, which now made Watson's earlier comment to the young vixenish Ren about 'amphibious capability' clear in my mind.

"Whatever you do," Watson warned as the XR skimmed off the beach with the wheels lifted into the underbelly, "don't look down."

That was easy for her to say. As a screenwriter, my interest in film was academic and I was immune to impulse video diving. Plus, it wasn't like I even owned one of the new AllRay infinite-resolution, ultraviolet frequency players. I had no interest in those little boxes. Moreover, I figured I would forego buying one of the new molecular encoding picodrive streaming receivers and go straight for an Everything On Demand Permeative Media System that would be available before the end of the year. Thus, I was confident I could peek at a few boxes without adverse consequences as we headed out to sea.

The bright orange discount labels captured my gaze. *$1.99 for movies that were still in theaters. How could this be?* My mind leapt to the possibilities for updating my video library that had become available to me—and there I could remain for years.

Hardin reached up from her side car and jerked on one of my pant legs. "This is serious."

"But, they're so cheap," I said, as if falling toward sleep. As though taken to the edge of a dream world and left standing, unsure in which direction I might fall.

"Yes, I know," said Hardin. "But you don't know how deep it goes."

"I, uh—" I didn't have a good response for her.

She was facing me straight on—which made sense, because she couldn't turn her head very well with her neck brace phone and had to sit right in front of me to meet my eyes. But even though she didn't have a choice in her position, it seemed no less effective.

She was right of course. I had no idea when or even how a buying spree might stop. My credit cards had exceeded their maximum limits and had entered into a parallel world where the familiar concepts of balance and minimum payments had lost their meaning. The rate of expansion of my debt had at last tunneled beneath the supposed endpoint speed of light and proceeded at a velocity that smote the quantitative certainty of physicists and credit appraisers, alike. How could my balance at the beginning of each month get to its value at the end of the month without violating our preconceived notions of compounded interest?

Indeed, who knew? But the truth was, the whole thing had become unreal by that point.

Artificial clouds puffed out from the vapor generators placed away from where the shoppers most congregated. In between the clouds, high above us and circling something far ahead, I could see what looked like swarms of metallic gnats.

"Got it," said Dalton, tapping the center of his radar console, which showed a jagged wave of green color moving over the ocean and converging on the Mezzanine. The audio signal from the radar was the dull sound of something heavy moving over crushed glass. I knew no one had the time to explain to me what the hell the green wave was, and I was too afraid to ask.

"Commerce? Is Shardley shutting us down?" Hardin was straining to look against her neck collar to look up. "Or did Labor Special Forces launch this stuff? Or someone else?"

Dalton tapped one of the individual points of light on his screen with his finger. "Not Commerce radar signature. Looks like private ownership. License issued under the Corporate Protection Amendment."

Watson was ignoring the Liquidate Main Menu Screen that had appeared on her console, leaving untouched the *"Yes"* and *"Not Now"* toggle buttons that were asking if she wanted a Tip of the Day before beginning the day's financial dismemberment project. "The impatient bastards could have at least waited until we gave our presentation."

I felt a wave of sadness as I waited for someone to acknowledge Watson's comment. Even if the mission had been taken out of her hands, she was still our commander and had kept us alive this long. Sitting there in the turret, with our purpose even more obscured and our leader rendered powerless, I hit a wall. I wanted the damn thing to end. I was a near washed-up production artist, convincing myself that somewhere inside me was a screenplay that someone else would bring to light. More than anything, I wanted my quiet, insignificant life back.

At least the breeze seemed real. It made sense to me that the store would have its own atmospheric circulation patterns. With the air conditioners going on in different regions of the store at different times, and with features like the Farm and the Videocean allowing air masses to pick up speed, a stiff head wind across a flat place like this was a certainty.

What I could not explain, however, was the peculiar quality of the circulating air. Stale came to mind, but this seemed much older. There was also the suggestion of things that had died generations earlier. If anything, the scent conjured the vision of a natural history museum. Perhaps a dusty one in Egypt that contained the desiccated remains of Pharaohs, with the untidiness of their excavation already completed, and all that's left for the visitor is to observe the contents of the gilded wooden boxes.

Any further reverie on the quality of the air was interrupted by sudden evasive movements of the XR. Klean was making sharp, alternating turns to avoid what looked like clumps of seaweed that covered the surface of the sea.

The repeated passage of vessels such as ours had shaped the billions of video cases into hummocks that appeared to be huge ocean swells. Moving over these mounds was like pitching and rolling in an actual boat in rough seas. The orange discount stickers on the plastic boxes appeared as orange caps on the tips of the waves, so that the illusion of heavy weather was even more pronounced than if the sea were gray. The overhead lights reflecting off the plastic cases added an oily sheen to this suggestion of roughness in the sea. Amidst this plasticene squall, I caught sight of a navigational buoy several hundred yards off the port bow. When Klean steered the XR toward it, I knew that he had seen it, and I knew that it was significant.

"What's it say, K?" Watson yelled back to me. "Can you read it?"

I pulled myself up to look through a ShopScope that was mounted on the edge of my turret. Cranking up the zoom, I focused in close on the buoy. It was not floating, of course, but appeared to be attached to the top of a pole that extended to about where the surface of the sea of videos would be. The perceived floating part of the buoy was painted with purple reflective paint so that it could be seen from orbit. "It says Sargas-," I said. "But I can't read the whole—"

"Sargasso Savings," said Watson, interrupting me, then uttering a rapid fire string of monosyllabic words from the loosening confines of her once tightly-wrapped seams.

"I thought they were outlawed a few years ago," said Stanton.

Hardin looked up from the com pod. "Seems to me that California and Vermont outlawed 'em. Think that had more to do with emissions from the boats than anything else."

With that, some long strips of green plastic webbing wound up into the starboard ski, banged around on the metallic frame of the underbelly of the shopper, spooled themselves around the propulsion hub and caused the entire mechanism to freeze up with a resonant *clunk*.

"And they're designed to do just that," said Watson, ripping off her headset and slamming into onto her console.

Meanwhile, with the arrest of the starboard ski, our momentum had taken us into a spin. After a few 360's we shuddered to a stop in the middle of the sea.

With my head somewhat recovered from the spinning, I dared to have a look around. The starboard ski was bound up with the plastic webbing, which I could see had multiple boxed sets of MEV's stuffed in pockets along its length.

"The idea," Klean was saying for my benefit, since I had not identified the whole name of the promotion from the fragment of text I had seen on the buoy, "is that everything that gets stuffed into the Sargasso Savings web is sold as a single unit, with the lowest price in the set determining the price for the *entire* unit. Most customers love them. People sail out here with the intention of getting caught like we just did."

There wasn't much joy in the telling. We couldn't move and we were being approached by a squadron of what looked like the All Mart coast guard: three bright purple raging fast cigarette boats that were converging on us from opposite directions.

"They're gonna' want a freakin' Salty Dog Discount Code!" Watson seethed as she unbuckled herself, jumped off the shopper and started yanking on the webbing that was wrapped around the ski.

"And if we don't have one?" I asked. For once, I was out of my turret and had leapt down to help Watson free up the ski, with Stanton right behind me.

"They impound the vehicle." Hardin was typing on her communications console.

"Can they do that?" Klean asked, trying to restart the engine.

Watson was straining against the resistance of a long strip of webbing, "You have to register at the customer service village in Electropia in order to be eligible to receive Sargasso Savings. Without the Salty Dog code, we'd technically be shoplifting."

Hardin was shaking as she struggled to remove the stupid neck brace communicator. "They're blocking all satellite and wireless so we can't download one. We gotta' get the hell out of here."

"We were briefed on this," said Watson straining in unison with Stanton and me against a 4-foot wide strip of webbing that was weighted with multiple boxed DVD and MEV compilations. "You saw the pictures of the New Zealand Team after their encounter. And those guys were all experienced ShopBlacks."

Meanwhile, the cigarette boats were bearing down on us from three sides. On the decks of the boats, I could see their crews wearing festive purple maritime-themed uniforms and costume purple lifejackets.

Then I noticed that Stanton was closing his eyes every few seconds—as if refusing to look upon the fiery pillar of a heavenly messenger. I figured out that he was avoiding looking at the titles of the boxed sets that were entangled in the webbing as he worked.

Watson had also noticed Stanton's wavering spirit. *"Hang on, Stanton. Just a few more seconds."*

A screeching sound blasted across the ocean, as if some sleeping giant with black metallic spikes for scales had been awakened from slumber.

In the next fraction of a second I entertained the possibility that a divine enforcer had arrived and was about to announce the reckoning of all beings. It was that same heart-stopping void that appears in your chest when you're speeding along the highway and see the lights of a state trooper appear in your rearview mirror. It is that internal organ-kicking, inescapable admission that we have not behaved with righteousness, that we were in fact going 85 in a 65, and that we will be called to account for our wrongdoing. Without further consideration of the origin of the noise, however, and allowing that the feeling was the same no matter what caused it, I ducked down and covered my head.

One of the cigarette boats had arrived and was blasting its warning siren as it loomed over us with the crew shouting down with a megaphone.

"Ahoy, there, mateys," barked one of the crew members through a megaphone. "Do ye have ye old Salty Dog Discount Code?"

Watson and I both ignored the question as we leapt back onto the XR.

"The West Wing!" Stanton laughed, staring down at the webbing in his hand.

"Stanton! Not now!" Watson yelled. *"Get your chestnut-tanned ass*

over here!"

"With commentary by Martin Sheen for all twenty-one seasons!" Stanton cackled.

"Arrgh!!!" The pirate voice on the megaphone was pretty fake, but there was an underlying quality of real threat. *"Show me thy coupon, Scurvy Dog!"*

A second crewmember typing in commands on what looked like a control screen.

"Plus there's the *Hoosiers* boxed set with all 26 episodes of the PBS Indiana high school basketball documentary series!" Stanton remained fixated, his hands holding out a section of webbing laden with videos before him.

A swell formed on the surface of the ocean. I couldn't tell if it was caused by a subtle motion of the larger vessel that towered over us, or if it was a massive form moving deeper beneath several layers of videos. Without taking his eyes off the boxes in front of him, Stanton had begun sinking into the center of a slow-moving whirlpool that was forming.

"Time to move," said Dalton with a drill sergeant bellow.

The engine started and Klean hit the throttle hard. The engine whined as it strained against the resistance of the webbing still wrapped around the undersurface of the XR.

"You can't find these anywhere!" Stanton yelled up from the enclosing sinkhole with a garbled voice. His entire body up to his neck was buried in video boxes. "I've been trying for yerz to find *Deep Cover Two: In Deep-rg* with Lawrenz Fzzhhhbn."

A purple rope ladder had dropped over the side of the in-store coast guard vessel and a party of AllMart security guards in purple pirate costumes with purple swords and flashlights were descending toward us. The XR started to tilt into the sinkhole as a busted-off ski followed Stanton into the depths.

"With the letterbov centeniumm edishumm uv *To Kll A Mmmnbirm*." The top of Stanton's head remained visible, with his ecstatic arms raised above the surface of the boxes that were sucking him down.

All of us onboard the shopper had shifted to the other side to keep us from teetering over into the whirlpool as an unseen piece of webbing stuck to our hull dragged us down. The bow of the larger vessel pitched forward into the sinkhole along with Stanton, at the mercy of the electromagnetic tractor beam that the enthusiastic first mate had focused on us. The commander holding the megaphone tried to get his hands on the vehicle impoundment controller as they both tumbled down the slanting deck. The rope ladder swung out over the sinkhole as the vessel started following us down, tossing the pirate police like toys out over the sea.

Then—choreographed from some higher power—one of the pirates fell in slow motion with his sword extended and a look of absolute surprise on his bearded face. In that same instant, the sudden lurch of our vessel revealed the strip of plastic webbing that constrained our vehicle and was dragging us down, which the pirate's saber sliced through as he swung past.

With the webbing severed, the XR was free. In a violent forward thrust the vessel righted and continued at high speed toward the far shore. Behind us, the purple coast guard vessel, all its inhabitants and Stanton disappeared into the vortex on the surface of the sea.

The two remaining pursuit vessels arrived at the site seconds later to find no trace of the vortex and its occupants. Figuring that they could not match whatever force propelled the XR, they did not give chase.

"As far as Reggie knows, he's at the Counterintelligence Expo in Orlando," said Dalton, tremulous. His face was covered with sweat as he again reprogrammed the navigation system.

Watson was fighting back tears. It's hard to say what that was about. Stanton had been a 6-foot bronze statue thorn in her side the whole trip. He had disobeyed her orders and nearly gotten all of us sucked into oblivion by doing so.

Yet, he had also been a valuable member of the team and she hated to lose him.

Casual shoppers scattered like crabs as Klean blasted the horn on the XR and we waddled up onto the beach with one ski missing. Without slowing down, he flipped a toggle on his control panel that jettisoned the remaining skis out from the sides of our vehicle so that they tumbled a few feet and flopped over as we sped across the sand. A few purple dinghys close to shore were racing toward us, but they didn't appear to pose a real threat. Klean would never in a million years admit it, but even he looked rattled. Even if he and Stanton didn't see the world and its machinations in any way that could be interpreted in even a vague sense as similar, that didn't mean he wanted him dead.

Submission

Hey All You Purple People!!!
Help us welcome the new members of the Purple Power TEAM for the third week of October!!! Remember, there's no "I" in P-U-R-P-L-E!
Janice Haupenfeister, Washington Courthouse, Ohio
Cyndie Machulski, Marysville, Ohio
Marco Morettini, Steubenville, Ohio
Jeff Watkinson, Chillicothe, Ohio
Lawrence Edward "Larry" Klean, Bethesda, Maryland
Join us for a MEET AND GREET at the new Taco Deo in the Food Farm, 1-3 PM, Wednesday!!! Coupons will be available for a Toasted Meatshell Taco. If you're not on the schedule, join us for Chipito Races from 3-5 PM!!!

From **The Purpletrator,** the All Mart employee weekly newsletter, October 22

Once we cleared the beach, Klean didn't even ask Watson's permission to take us on a detour to the Temple of Hypnos, which was one of 5 small-scale versions of Pharmadelphia that were placed around the store for the convenience of shoppers. This one covered no more than a few acres and was identified by a central acropolis with a broad colonnade that was topped by a huge purple plastic beam. A banner hung from the beam with the message: YEAR SUPPLY ALLZAC (omeprazole/sildenafil 20/100) NOW $3.99!

Klean brought the XR to a stop at the base of a wide stairway painted to look as though it were chiseled limestone. Everyone piled out and headed toward the energy drink aisle or the rest rooms at the back of the acropolis. Overhead the cloud of metallic dust was growing thicker and sirens wailed behind us. We didn't know who or what were after us at that point. We wanted to get to the Mezzanine and then get the hell out of there.

No one said a word about Stanton. We knew he wasn't dead. He was lost. The more critical thing on our mind was how to complete the mission without 29% of our staff.

With the possibility of increased responsibility piled upon me in their absence, I stood and considered my own potential fate. I was drained of all energy for at least the third time that day. The adrenaline pipeline that had been kicking me in the head when Stanton tunneled himself into the depths was gone, and I found myself drowsy, feeling as though it were the middle of the night again. Rubbing my hand across my cheeks, I verified the thick stubble that identified me as a direct descendent of Paleolithic Eastern Europeans who remained well-insulated despite the presence of the occasional kilometer-thick glacier on the continent.

Watson didn't need to actually tell me to get a shave as she glanced up from the Terminate spreadsheet she was working on. Her look seemed to reinforce my notion that all the diversions of our mission had not exempted me from using my supposed special skills at some preordained time in the future. The telegraphed movement of her eyes toward the Boy Hair Removal aisle further emphasized her meaning. I needed to clean myself up a little for the moment when I would be called upon to reveal those skills.

I was certain that Watson was watching me, even though her eyes remained focused on the screen in front of her. Exaggerating my motion a little so she would know that I had gotten her message, I pulled one of my credit cards out of my wallet, grabbed an entry-level personal grooming system off a nearby shelf and headed to the lone checkout in that section of the acropolis.

The man behind the counter looked familiar, but I couldn't place him with his face half turned away from me.

"Lawson?" I whispered.

The man at the register resembled Lawson in height, and his facial features conformed to similar lines. But his clothing looked nothing like what the Lawson I remembered would have worn. Khaki slacks and a brand new purple-flowered Hawaiian shirt with a purple All Mart name tag. These were the indelible marks of the All Mart Supervisory Associate, which was one giant step above the ranks of the Purple Poncho. He did not turn when I whispered his name, but I could see a pause in his flow of thought. As if the name I had spoken excited remnants of memories that were already departed. The fever in the eyes further allowed me to conclude that even if his body came from the man we knew as Lawson, the thoughts and feelings that had constituted the original Lawson were gone.

"K," he said with bemusement, no longer diluted by the constraints of a professional working relationship. "You really had me fooled."

The ironic smile of the man in front of me was different from the one I had last seen in the Gorge. Before, I was an unknown adversary. Now, I was an object of respect.

"What the hell are you talking about?" I asked.

"The whole zero threat personality thing," Lawson chuckled.

"What the hell are you doing here?"

"I flowed out of the Gorge and was rescued, you might say. And then found out more or less immediately that McAlsteinetti and his senior people have been following your movements for years."

"Why would they do that?" I had no idea what he was talking about.

"You tell me," said Lawson. "You're the guy who's so deep in this thing that I bet the guys who think they placed you in the agency where Watson found you don't even know who you're really working for. Some people think you're in with organized crime in Africa. Nobody knows anything about you for sure."

"Did they say anything about what happens –"

"Look at me," said Lawson. "Right now, I'm a goddam store clerk slinging personal care products."

He swiped my shaving system across the code reader. Grabbing the credit card from my hand, he reached over and swiped it through the keypad while I stood there motionless. "I'm not connected enough to really know anything yet. All I know is that people at the highest level in this store are aware of your presence and your anticipated arrival at the Mezzanine. But I'm moving up fast. I'll find out who you're working for, and why, and then we'll have another conversation about it then, just you and me."

"What am I supposed to do?"

Lawson seethed. "Kill it, K. Please dispense with the total ignorance of your destiny and all that total immersion Daniel Day Lewis role preparation crap. This is real. Your card's denied."

"What?" I asked.

""Your credit card," said Lawson. He glared at me as if had scraped a rusty garden rake along the side of his favorite new car. "It just blew up the software. I'll have to find a senior manager to restart the system. Look, just take the freakin' shaver. I already earned a hundred of 'em with my Ecstatic Shopper

Purple People Points."

"I really am just a temp," I begged.

"If that's true, and I doubt it, then that's great. There's amazing opportunity in here. It's like the wide-open west. There's gold lying around everywhere. You get to decide. And don't tell anyone I'm here. Now, get the hell out of my store."

"And go where, exactly?" I asked. Can we just leave? What about that metallic cloud?"

"The Intentional Particulate Matter?" said Lawson. "Another one of the great product ideas from Dominational Dynamics."

"What *is* that stuff?"

"Dust. They take truckloads of plain dust and park them outside maximum security prisons, on the streets of gang-infested inner-city neighborhoods, next to meth labs in the rural Midwest. They have some long-term dust contracts with drug lords all over Asia and South America. Then they mix the dust with metallic filings from ground up vintage tanks, artillery, small arms, et cetera. And then they launch this stuff into the atmosphere. DomDye sells tons of this stuff to leaders of unstable developing countries. Super cheap to buy and easy to use."

"I can't even im-" I stuttered.

"Works like a champ."

"How?"

"*How should I know?* Psychic energy or some shit. It works. Now, I reiterate. Please get your specially-skilled ass out of my store."

"And go where? The Mezzanine?"

"I wouldn't even bother going there. It's all unraveling. Therein lies the opportunity for regular guys like me. McAlsteinetti, he's dead." Then he thrust the shaver into a little plastic bag, flung it at my chest and stormed off in search of the manager.

I didn't say anything when I got back to the parking zone. Though I wanted to tell Hardin that Lawson was alive, I justified my silence with the thought that this might not be true. There was also the fact that I had no idea what he was talking about. But everyone else was silent, too. For all I knew, they had also seen him. Or maybe they had seen others who had disappeared from their lives in the years since the undertaking of Store Number 1.

There was no way to process any of these things until much later, much of it with the help of the Agency therapist. Seconds later, with my stubble controlled, my sideburns and eyebrows beat back, we were moving again. All that remained was a little pick-me-up. This last detail addressed with a few quick slurps of DewAll, the Mart's signature caffeine distillate gel. Klean had chunked a case of it down onto the deck behind the driver's seat for all of us to share. Already speeding along a large central aisle, we all grabbed a handful of the convenient esophageal injection devices for the last push to the Mezzanine.

"DewAll! Gets it all together!" The sound of McAlsteinetti's enthusiastic voice made me think that some of the packets were loaded with promotional audio sound chips. Then I noticed that the little video screen on my laptop had opened which made me wonder if the DewAll packet had launched a transdimensional pop-up ad. I thought I heard the little voice say 'That Lawson's going far' but that didn't make any sense so I decided it was saying 'That launch is going far'—which sort of made sense as a promotional tag-line for DewAll. That is, caffeine can launch you. Or help you launch something else. Whatever it was, I didn't try to replay the clip and the little screen dropped off my desktop.

It didn't feel like a good time to be doing anything but putting all my energy into trying to figure out those special skills that were still hanging around out there in the void. Stanton and Lawson were the two guys who I figured would jump out and improvise for themselves whatever it was I supposed to do at the appropriate time and place. Watson's face was even more lined than before. Being out of control wasn't working for her. Dalton had checked out and hadn't said anything since his final commands shouted out to the sinking Stanton. Hardin had freed herself of the communications collar but looked even less comfortable than before. The network icons on her com screen all had red X's through them, which indicated that we had no active communications with anything either outside or inside the store. Klean drove on.

By then, no question remained that the time spent freeing ourselves in the Videocean had blown our cover as a secret operation. Security guards on carts, scooters and low-flying battery powered purple ultralight aircraft were everywhere. I found it beyond miraculous that they hadn't spotted us yet as we were exposed at this regional Temple of Hypnos. Our only hope of arriving at McAlsteinetti's office without stopping was to make for the White Aisle and use that as a superhighway to cruise at top speed to our destination.

The White Aisle is your year-round home for Christmas decorations, wrapping paper, lights, candies, cookies and stocking stuffers that cuts like a twinkling shaft into the heart of Store Number 1. Even though I had never even been inside the store, I knew this to be true. The single recent photo of McAlsteinetti showed him standing on the stairs leading up to his offices and apartment at the apex of the White Aisle. Blurred, no more than a few dozen pixels in size and smuggled out of the store by a management escapee, the photo showed his pained face surrounded by the perennial displays of inflatable snowmen and dirigible Santa sleighs.

The White Aisle itself posed no danger to us. It was the traffic that was deadly. The continuous emphasis on holiday merchandise created the highest known density of bargain-hunters on earth. Even more treacherous than the numbers, however, was the uncertainty in the motives of these shoppers. Was the man next to you picking up some holiday greeting cards because he needed to get last year's greeting out late? Or was he so meticulous about his affairs that he planned on getting his greetings for the upcoming holiday out by October 15th? No one, perhaps not even them, could be certain about what motivated such a person.

Then there were the new promotions that McAlsteinetti ran along the

White Aisle. It was his little test strip for the world. His barometer of how the greater mass of humanity might take to a marketing plan of his design. They were never advertised on the outside and would be rumored inside the store. Even after they occurred, details of the sales were withheld from the media, with eyewitnesses often unable to agree upon the degree of price reduction they had seen. Adding even more mystery to the place, those present might not even be able to recall the manner in which such prices had been offered. Nevertheless, all parties could agree that they had never seen *anything* like a McAlsteinetti White Aisle in-store special.

Taken as a whole, the White Aisle represented the ultimate black box of market forces.

Yet, we no longer had a choice about our path, and Klean and Watson both knew that we would have to risk it.

As we made our final turn onto the Aisle, I saw an All Mart employee standing at the edge of traffic hunched over and wearing what appeared to be a purple buffalo costume, complete with a fluffy purple mane and a hollow plastic snout with hollow plastic horns. I was guessing that the huge mat of hair around a buffalo's neck is called a mane. The avid historian of the American Frontier such as McAlsteinetti could have named all the external features of a buffalo and been able to interpret what it might mean to have a character disguised as a buffalo standing beside the aisle. I suppose if you had read the roadside displays along the highways of Wyoming and Montana, or studied the nomadic tribes of pre-railroad North America in a postgraduate history class, you might have been able to cobble together in your mind the details of the upcoming promotion. Both these provisions excluded me. The few times that I had driven out west, I was on a mission of pleasure and my road trip companions and I took turns driving while the others slept through the pristine emptiness. The wilderness was no more than space that separated us from the comforts and delights of southern California, and we had no time for understanding the logistics of Native American hunting practices.

Apart from the issue of my inability to decipher these signs, the man in the buffalo suit was one more of the encyclopedic details of McAlsteinetti's ongoing experiments that he cherished for his own sake. He didn't care if anyone else *got it.* He loved the adherence to a structured order that was his alone, even if the marketing department managed to desecrate his vision in the fine details of the final product. I know this because, in the end, I am the keeper of his final words.

"Hm," mused Watson as we passed the buffalo man stamping his feet at the side of the aisle. Was the unveiling of this new promotion intended for our benefit? Since he knew we were coming. Even after watching his final monologue over and over again in my apartment, that detail remained unclear.

"What the –?" Even Klean, whom I later learned had survived more deep ops than all the others combined, could not grasp what lay ahead.

Hardin recoiled as her pod cruised past the buffalo man. I watched as her face tightened and her eyes narrowed at this first sniff of unknown territory. She was rechecking all the com channels to see if we could get any kind of signal.

'Nice work, Hardin,' I thought, *'try to get a call in to HQ and let them know that some new shit storm is going down.'*

For Dalton, something else was afoot. He still hadn't spoken since the vortex took down Stanton, and where I once saw a solid measure of icy confidence in his eyes, I now saw nothing. There was no way to gauge whether he even saw the buffalo man as his face stayed fixed on the ever-changing green navigation display of the store's entire floor plan and inventory that was being projected in front of him.

A cold prickle rose on my spine as I spotted a few more buffaloes a few yards ahead, on both sides of the aisle. Klean, sensing our collected edginess, or responding to some personal sense of danger, sped up. Other shoppers around us were doing the same. Those on foot began trotting rather than walking. The whine of nearby electric carts kicked up an octave as drivers increased their speed. All this defied the serenity of the powdery faux-snow that was spray-tacked onto the surrounding displays of holiday merchandise, reflecting the yellow twinkle of the LED fake gas flames in the street lights.

The sight of a few more of the purple buffalo costumes further ahead sent the crowd moving even faster, although the aisle itself seemed narrower.

I could hear the wheezing of nearby foot shoppers as they strained to increase their pace. Klean had us weaving around them to get us out of there faster, but their closing ranks prevented us from advancing very far. Headlight eyes strained to find some sign ahead of what this all might mean. The now familiar smell of nervous sweat arose as a communal cloud from the running mass of humans.

Above the main aisle, timed to reflect the progressive changes in our mass movement, a series of lighted signs flicked on with the message:

'All Mart Welcomes You'

The people around us began moving at a fast jog—but with fresh smiles of anticipation. Perhaps they were here today because this promotion had been rumored at the Food Farm. Or, like us, they happened to be on the White Aisle at that moment by pure coincidence. How we all got there didn't matter. Each of us knew inside that this was how McAlsteinetti introduced new purchasing sensations to the international business community.

The signs changed: *'To An Entirely New Concept in Discount Shopping'*

Those on foot were running, attempting to pass each other with their push carts, although also to avoid being run over by the electric carts such as ours. A young, athletic woman in jeans and a sweatshirt squealed, snatched her child from the front of her cart and tucked him under one arm. Using her free hand to crash her cart into a lighted Host of Shepherds lawn display, she squirted through a hole in the crowd ahead like a pro running back. A huge, middle-aged man—who had the mass to suggest he might have *been* a former NFL player—raced off behind her. Those in electric carts leaned forward in their seats and strained their hands against their already wide-open throttles, as if these actions might further increase their speed.

Huge neon purple letters flashed overhead: *'WELCOME TO:'*

Wild shouts, cheers, laughter, gasping and wheezing filled the air as shoppers sprinted along. More employees in buffalo costumes with drums banged out a rising tempo. Klean fixated on the power readouts as the engine whined. Tinsel, a thousand racks of greeting cards, radio-controlled celestiotronic angels and reindeer flashed past.

In unison, the signs flashed the purple words: *'BISON PRICIN!'*

Then, the people in front of us dropped off out of sight—down, we saw an instant later, a 45-degree ramp that channeled all traffic into what appeared to be a sub-level to the store that was opened up for the express purpose of accommodating this new sales phenomenon.

Turning down onto the ramp was like the first rush of a roller coaster. You felt the whole-body pull of gravity as your cart accelerated downward. The natural response of flesh to this unexpected reality was terror. Hence the screams. But then laughter when you realized the next floor level wasn't that far below, more like fifty feet, fifteen of which you traversed in the very first second. It was analogous to a theme park ride with the terror of the velocity real in one second, replaced with the absolute delight of escape in the next. I had no doubt that McAlsteinetti had worked with engineers and aerospace medicine doctors alike to determine the optimal angle at which instantaneous fear would be induced, followed by an intense feeling of exhilaration as the mind realizes that you survived.

Once you were laughing out loud about your survival, more than halfway down by that point, you could discern that the ramp ended and the sub-aisle was funneling all traffic toward a finish line, where carts were further getting funneled into little chutes. There, employees wearing purple fake-leather fringe buckskins and purple headbands with purple feathers waited for shoppers to pass through.

A huge banner overhead read: *'Bison Pricin'—All Merchandise Free For ONE YEAR!'* In a line of smaller type below that: *'For Selected Customers'*

Ahead of us, those who had hung onto their push carts lifted their feet off the ground so they could coast even faster down the remainder of the incline. I could see the woman who had run ahead with the child. She was in one of the chutes embracing one of the employees, with her child seated in a shopping cart decorated to look like a ceremonial war canoe—except that all the markings were shades of purple and the totem-like carvings were molded from still more shades of purple plastic. The NFL guy was on his knees at the base of the ramp and weeping. The screaming of the crowd was in stereo. There was a baseline of primary screams as the shoppers behind us descended the ramp, but the secondary screams were getting louder as people were finding out if they were among the select shoppers.

Klean was wrestling with the steering so that we wouldn't go through any of the chutes, but the shopper seemed to be taking us toward a chute off to the left.

"Some sort of remote guidance system," Klean said, ready to explode. After pounding on the control yoke a few more times, he gave up trying to control the machine.

"Any ideas?" Watson had stepped back into role of commander as we slowed down and were propelled toward the entrance of the chute. Ahead of us, two elderly companions were leaping and hugging each other.

"The FATASS XR can be operated remotely for shopping in toxic environments." Klean leaned back with his hands off the controls and his lips pursed with disgust. "And someone's doing it now."

"I'll do the talking," said Watson. "I'm sure this place is loaded up with security guards."

Under its own power, and the control of someone or something else, the XR edged into one of the finish line chutes where a petite female employee dressed like a Native American of the Great Plains waited with a purple plastic tomahawk. Her costume suggested Sacajawea, but I had seen her face before.

"Welcome to Bison Pricin,'" she squeaked, giving a few spiritless strokes of the tomahawk through the air. "Today only, select customers will be eligible for FREE MERCHANDISE." You could *hear* the capital letters in her rehearsed promotional pitch. "With no dollar amount limit for ONE YEAR from today."

Hardin had burst into tears, leapt out of the cart, hurdled over the edge of the chute and stood beside the woman. *"Angela!"* she cried, moving to embrace the other woman.

Sacajawea glanced at Hardin and dodged the hug by stepping aside and giving a few warning strokes with her tomahawk. She seemed to be enjoying herself despite the intrusion of Hardin. I suppose it must have been exciting to be at the spear tip of any great new discovery that was much bigger than oneself. "Do we have any select customers in your party today?"

"I don't think so," Watson said, looking around the chute for a way out. "Hardin, I don't think it's your sister. Just look at her. Get back in here and let's move."

"Let's consult our Bison Pricin' Medicine Man." The happy little Fauxcahontas didn't let her smile slip a single millimeter as she leaned her head to speak into the end of one of her plastic braids that I suspected doubled as an intercom. Making me wonder if Hardin and she shared an interest in designer concealed communication systems. Her eyes lost focus on us for the tiniest instant as she listened to the reply that was reaching her ears through the purple tresses that covered her head. "Our Medicine Man says that the select shoppers in your party will be any of you—or all of you!—if your birth-date contains a nine!"

Then, though it strained my understanding of the limits of human determination, her smile got bigger. "Do any of you have a birthday that contains a nine?"

"Not me," Watson snapped. "Anybody else? No? Good. Thanks for letting us play," she said, forcing a saccharine smile. "Now, can we get out of here? Hardin, it's definitely not her."

Klean moved the control stick and the wheels moved in response. The engine revved up. He was ready.

"It is her. Of course it is," said Hardin. "Even if she doesn't remember me, my sister is in there somewhere."

"May I see some sort of picture identification to verify your status as a Bison Pricin' select shopper today?"

"Hardin!" Watson hissed, *"don't do it!"*

Klean edged the XR forward a few feet in an attempt to get out of the narrow chute sooner than later, but the traffic ahead wasn't going anywhere. In fact, we couldn't see anything ahead except a leaden cloud that had settled around all the carts and people in front of us.

Hardin reached into the pocket of her Bengals jacket.

"Hardin, don't do it." Watson looked desperate. "We can send a party back here later to bring her out."

Tears trembled in the catch of Hardin's lower lashes, and then streaked down her cheeks as she pulled a small coin purse from her pocket.

Klean's voice resonated above the drone of all the other shoppers around us. "You don't need to do this. I'll come back myself to get her."

Her tiny movements were those of a little girl, uncertain of everything about herself. "I think she'll remember me. It just might take a while."

"Hardin," Klean growled. *"Put—down—the—driver's license."*

"No, please, not you, too." It was my own voice, hoarse from the lack of sleep.

"...and," said Hardin. "I was really wanting an extended leave from work...after..."

Watson was up out of her command center and stood at the side of the cart, tugging at Hardin's sleeves, pleading with her as Angela, a journalist who had disappeared the previous summer and now a proud Bison Pricin' Associate, was standing by.

Crowded in by a small tribe of employees that had gathered at the prospect of welcoming a new Bison Pricin' Select Shopper, Hardin struggled to turn her head against the crush of the purple buckskins to speak one last time.

"What's the point of continuing to the Mezzanine, anyway?" Hardin asked as she disappeared amid the throng of well-wishers.

Religion in my family was little more than elaborate wallpaper that was present in our house but had no influence on our daily lives. Still, armed with little hope and with some hidden blackness about to consume yet another member of our team, I allowed my eyes to drift toward the ceiling.

I confess that I had no idea how to interact with whatever all-powerful being might be available to intervene on Hardin's behalf, but I forgot that issue as my eyes were drawn to a thin gray line that ran along the bottom of the overhead banner announcing the promotion in which we were embroiled. It appeared to be a line of fine print, which was little surprise in the context of the enormity of the discount being offered.

With Watson and Klean both pleading with Hardin, as well as attempting to stand down the purple war party that was trying to drag her away, I pointed my ShopScope skyward and had a closer look at the banner. Even with the Hubble-like optics of the scope, I had to use the zoom feature to bring the sub-atomic font into focus. Scanning the scope across the bottom of the banner, I read. *'Offer valid for permanent residents of All Mart Store Number 1 ONLY. Verbal commitment to permanent residency acceptable. Void where prohibited.'*

Bending over my turret toward Hardin's pod, I screamed with every cubic millimeter of volume my lungs could muster, *"Noooooooooooooooooooo!"*

Hardin was already being herded toward a purple teepee with 'Medicine Man' printed on the side in Old Century Saloon Extra Bold. The teepee, I then realized, was the field office for the promotion and the source of the trivial and random criteria that separated the select shoppers from the masses. Some midlevel manager was inside there deciding that a birthday containing a 9 would establish the criterion for the disruption of entire families. My immediate disillusionment with the whole affair did not stop there. Whatever attention to detail McAlsteinetti had prescribed in planning Bison Pricin' seemed hollow. I could not imagine that real shamans of any Native American tribe would have considered any of the aspect of Bison Pricin' as medicinal. Yet, no one in the vicinity of this debacle seemed the least bit bothered by this glaring historical aberration.

Smiles beaming everywhere, employees in purple buckskins draped purple buffalo costumes over the shoulders of the select shoppers and seated them at purple plastic picnic tables molded to appear as though they were built from rough-hewn logs. There, the winners signed stacks of forms that I supposed would offer them residency inside the Mart, and, if they further desired, employment within the long lineage of the Purple Poncho.

"I tried to help them both," Watson sobbed. She started to get up out of her pod, but looked too weak and sat back down again. She poked at the controls in front of her. Her entire body shook. "I brought Hardin so she *could* find Angela. But I didn't know how bad it was."

Her whole body quaking, she drew her legs toward her chest and rested her head on her knees. "I'm not a monster," she murmured through a steady flow of tears.

Klean looked torn up with Hardin's loss, but was banging on the display screens in an attempt to re-establish control of the XR and maybe get us to the Mezzanine. I wondered if Hardin were right—what the hell were any of us going to do when we got there? Turn ourselves over to security forces that would be all around the perimeter of the executive offices of a major world corporation? Or wave up to the drones who were being flown by who the hell knows and for what purpose?

Dalton continued burrowing into some darker place that was far beneath our current situation. His sunken eyes remained fixed on the detailed laser rendering of the Bison Pricin' ramp and its associated traffic. His powerful, trembling hands moved through the display with a purpose that I could not begin to fathom.

Klean had crawled the XR out of the winners' chute, but we could not go any further. A thick cloud had gathered and the legion of carts and celebrating shoppers within it were too chaotic to move forward. The nearest I could figure, we were guests at a post Bison Pricin' barbecue. Among the dark shapes around us, I could see smoke roiling out from long rows of gas-fired grills and rotisseries. A greasy steam rose from a battery of deep fryers and mingled with the smoke to create an oppressive smog. Long tables, festooned with foam-core cutouts of Kokopelli, were heaped with ears of roasted corn, trays of scorched burgers and chicken, vats of potato salad and coleslaw, and decorated with edible rosettes of beer battered and deep-fried yellow squash. Native American-themed New Age music with what I considered to be excessive use of tom-toms and chanted phrases of uncertain meaning boomed from speakers wired into the thatched roofs of wigwams that housed the soda fountains and coolers. It was way more than hokey, and the presence of Kokopelli made me ill. His flute-playing likeness wouldn't have been found within a thousand miles of a Plains Indian buffalo jump.

Watson looked exhausted. The aromatic cloud of steam and fryer grease had wilted her professional veneer.

Klean was attempting to contact the aerial observation plane in hopes of getting an updated floor plan that would account for the sub-level aisle in which we found ourselves. I was hoping we could get our hands on an architectural schematic of the wigwams and food troughs on his screen, which could also help us get out of there.

Dalton—the poor guy, so easy to ignore by then in his twitchy withdrawn state, slipped beneath the grasp of reason—had fixated on the latitude and longitude data that was displayed along with the animated 3-D representation of the barbecue. I could see his lips moving, as if seeking the strength to speak something of importance.

"It was here," he whispered. I had to lean over the edge of my turret to hear him.

"What was here, Dalton?"

"The whole thing was right here."

"What whole thing was right here Dalton?" I asked, a lot louder, after recognizing that none of the revelers in the smoke even noticed us.

"BlubberMade," he said, with his usual moxie returning with each syllable, despite his haggard appearance and the apparent failure of our mission. Without a response from me—probably neither expected nor wanted—he continued.

"BlubberMade was founded in 1632 by Angus MacHaggis, a Scottish immigrant to southwestern Ohio—though it hardly bears noting that he was Scottish with a name like that. But his nationality really isn't relevant. What is significant is that through a combination of a strong work ethic and a little luck, he figured out a way to vulcanize whale blubber into a soft, pliable and extremely durable biological polymer that he was then able to mold into farm implements. The first BlubberMade Plow is on display in Smithsonian's Dirt and Soil Museum in Washington."

Klean, who had turned to listen, offered him a bottle of mineral water from the cooler behind the satellite dish. Dalton took a tiny sip, cleared his throat and charged ahead.

"He expanded his product line to include household utensils and containers. The business was passed down through successive generations and survived the ill-timed foray of the company into apparel before the Civil War. The culture of the day was not yet ready to absorb form-fitting and entirely waterproof bodysuits, though this market was successfully tapped later by the company's main competitor, SupperWear. Another blow came when the invention of the tractor completely wiped out BlubberMade's original, and, up until then, highly profitable line of hand tools. But the company survived into the 20th century. A chicken in every pot required a BlubberMade slotted spoon in every kitchen. During the Depression, BlubberMade provided modular housing, office space and even slot machines for WPO workers at Hoover Dam. When the war came, BlubberMade refitted its production lines to make lightweight fold-up mess kits that also served as portable flotation devices for troops jumping off landing craft during the invasion of the Philippines. In the 50's, BlubberMade introduced BlubberLife, the revolutionary family of products that allowed people to eat, work, bathe and worship—freely I might add—in front of their televisions. Well before the 60's, the Company quietly answered the call of environmentalists by re-formulating its primary product so that it would include neither blubber nor petroleum, which took some doing and probably violated some of the fundamental laws of physical chemistry, but today stands as one of the cornerstones of green consciousness. Even though, as you see, it isn't here anymore."

"Dalton, we all love BlubberMade, that's a great story, but *what* isn't here anymore?" I hoped I wasn't sounding testy. I had no idea what he was talking about and wanted to go home.

"The factory was right here on this spot." By then he was out of the cushioned seat of his pod with his arms spread wide, his goatee looking dusty and windblown and his eyes scary like that guy on the cover of the *Kansas* album, "and over there were the corporate offices, and –"

He paused to turn around, "– and over there was the post office, and there was the hardware store that did really good business thanks to BlubberMade, and a few doors down was the Blubber Inn, which housed the Blubber Box Café on its ground floor, and all around here –"

He whooshed his arms in great sweeping movements, "– were the houses of people who lived here."

"Lived at the factory, Dalton?" I still didn't understand. "What people?"

"The people of the *town*," and by then Dalton was rolling. "The town of West Aberdeen, named by the Scottish settlers who came here along with MacHaggis. There was a town before there was the company. Both grew together. There was a real love and loyalty among the city government and BlubberMade. They worked together. Then, well, you see, or should I say, *you don't see it*, do you? The town is gone. There may be the remnants of foundations far below this barbecue. Archaeological scraps that might remain for the very distant future to discover. But for now it's gone. Made waste by the advance of *this store* across the country. The one-nation exclusive license on manifest destiny now expired. The transcontinental shared delusional disorder now complete in its affliction. The Law of Conservation of Chosen Peoples was violated, but now will be restored. But even before the presence of this particular store and this particular barbecue on the landscape, BlubberMade had fallen victim to McAlsteinetti's methods. The MacHaggis descendents had done their best to compete. They briefly had a BlubberMade Outlet Pond where they allowed customers to fish for spatulas, salad tongs and the like. Which was actually quite popular during the ice fishing season and flew in the face of the Mart's own promotions and temporarily pushed back its encroaching shadow. But then All Mart forged a deal with SupperWear to sell similar spatulas and salad tongs for pennies. Homemakers could scrounge some lost change and purchase an entirely new set of utensils. You know the drill with McAlsteinetti's commercials. It's all hype and fantasy. Like the one during last year's Colossal Bowl. Jerry Jensen, owner of the Dayton Dragons does a cheer with the Dragonettes to tell the Dayton City Council that he doesn't need their tax money and then builds his team a new stadium with his own money that he saved by shopping at All Mart. The ones where All Mart introduced their partnership with SupperWear were a little different. Deadly different for BlubberMade. If you recall, they show a little boy accidentally melting a spatula while attempting to bake his mother some cookies. But then he finds a few coins in the couch and rides his bike to All Mart so he can buy another one. All in 30 seconds. The logic was so simple. The potential savings at AllMart too great. BlubberMade was doomed."

"But nobody died," I said. "The company went under but a lot of their employees moved away and found other jobs after a while. Some stayed on and struggled through. It's sad that people probably lost their pensions, but they're still kicking."

Dalton's gaze softened. To him, my comment was that of an innocent toddler who had spilled milk on the dining room table. "You just nailed it," he said. "Before the town of West Aberdeen, indigenous peoples passed through this very spot for thousands of years. Multiple cultures built mounds and villages, traded with each other and for the most part got along fine until Europeans came. Residents of the newly independent United States wanted more land so they came and settled West Aberdeen and the surrounding area. They didn't ask permission or attempt to do it legally. They just did it. The Indian families who lived here lost more than just a cushy factory job and their pensions when the settlers came. If you can find any of them, you can ask them how they feel about illegal immigration. But it didn't start or stop at West Aberdeen. Most towns between New York and LA grew in similar fashion. The logic of settlers in America was also simple. The desire for wealth and personal freedom so vast."

Dalton then climbed back into his pod, curled up, closed his eyes and fell asleep, as though he hadn't slept for years. No one around us had heard his words nor even seen the semaphoric display of his willowy arms. The barbecue was well underway by then and several Conestoga wagons loaded with kegs of KürtBrau had rolled in.

The Bison Pricin' early adopters knew how to party. They had no time to bother with the whereabouts of West Aberdeen, or even to ask the remaining three of us why we weren't joining them. But I believe they may have thought that Dalton had gone mad—for not admitting that his birthday was May 29th, and therefore a Select Shopper in his own right. His face was being blasted onto overhead monitors that used biometric reconnaissance scanners to catalogue everyone who came into the store and cross-referenced their features through the Human Face Registry that allowed the Mart to identify select shoppers in the crowd. Although I thought McAlsteinetti and his management team would have used more state-of-the-art technology for the new promotion, the fact that the surveillance was ongoing made it clear that they knew we were right there at the Bison Pricin' Opening Gala. Why didn't they come out and arrest us?

Klean and I watched the fog for signs of lifting. But it was no use. We might as well be buried a few miles deep in tar sand. It felt like it, too—choking, warm, stifling. The remarkable thing, though he had rambled on a bit, was that what Dalton said was absolutely true and that what we later described as a barbecue was yet another attempt at seduction. But the fare and its presentation were far from being desirable in any way that the darkness of our higher minds might harbor—rather, it was aimed toward the most primitive parts of our animal brain. More critically, it seemed as though it was undertaken with a sense of urgency, and its essence was designed to hasten some inexorable purpose.

The mission fell apart, I should say, floundered, after another few minutes in the fog. It sucked because we had no meaningful navigation tools and were about a mile from the Mezzanine where McAlsteinetti waited. None of the video map systems worked, the monitors were all flickering noisy images that had become uninterpretable, so Klean was driving by his own sight and instinct. Dalton's local radar was still working, but he had fallen into a deep sleep and there was no one to monitor it except me. Watson was still curled up into a ball in her pod, staring off into space, murmuring words under her breath.

When something big showed up in the radar, I yelled basic directions down to Klean and in this manner we picked our way forward and through the cheesecake dessert forest that was installed at the western edge of the barbecue. As we cleared the last of the fake trees hanging low with tiny plastic sealed boxes containing individual slices of cheesecake swirled with assorted fruit flavors, I saw a patch of real grass, a mere hummock of green, in the middle of the aisle. With Klean moving ahead, I saw that this bit of grass was the tapering end of what appeared to be a long indoor park, or rather a chain of consecutive beads of green containing some unkempt flower beds and dying bushes that rose back up to the original level of the White Aisle. This green belt then continued all the way to the Mezzanine—which had become visible as a gray slit far ahead of us in the haze. The grassy knolls were somewhat discolored, and looked unwatered and uncared for, as a lawn might look in the tail end of summer when the heat of August coupled with the malaise of homeowners results in the synergistic transformation of lush and green into brown and dusty. As far as I could tell, we could either have gone to the right or to the left of this dying grass. I didn't know which might be better, of course. The continuation of the White Aisle merchandise on either side—synthetic pines bearing tinsel and ornaments which continued the tree theme—looked pretty well alike.

As we entered the aisle, I became aware it was much narrower than I had supposed. To the left of us there was the long strip of neglected grass, and to the right, a high steep bank that was populated with a wide selection of metallic Christmas trees. Above the fake trees, a line of macroscopic snowflakes in an array of colors, materials and price point hung in a line that lead westward along the aisle. The snowflakes hung thick over the aisle, suggestive of a typical Midwestern storm, and from time to time a limb of one of the metallic pines fell off and projected into the aisle.

It was then late in the afternoon. We couldn't tell exactly what time because all the onboard clocks had fried out from the greasy mist at the barbecue. Klean and Watson looked gloomy, despite the steady, intense glare of the solar-grade fluorescent lights. In the mist, which brightened somewhat as we came out from the partial shadow of the cheesecake forest, Klean crept the shopper forward, while Dalton snored from his pod beneath my turret.

Without Klean we would not have gotten this far. His lean, unbrandished athleticism suggested a higher order of fitness, and his grasp of both the shopper's systems and the passions that drove the internal economy of the Mart spoke of fruitful years of higher education. With the secretive nature of our mission blown, he had ditched the V-neck sweater and put his jump boots back on. There seemed little skill, or point, in prolonging a ruse that had fooled no one from its outset. As a rule, Klean was the most stable member of upper management I had ever seen, and if he lost sight of you, he would without fail call upon his highest self to find your back and keep you safe and would not for an instant allow the shopper to fall into danger nor be overtaken by unfriendly hands. Although he drove in silence, I could see that his mind was going about a thousand miles per second. The departure of Hardin weighed on him, and Watson and Dalton were out of commission, which left him to complete the official requirements of the mission. What those might look like, of course, was cause for serious introspection.

I was looking up at the snowflakes, which were obscured by what looked like an overcast layer of clouds high up near the ceiling and feeling much annoyed to see that at each yard ahead there appeared to be even more of them, when I saw Dalton roll himself flat on the deck without waking. He kept on snoring and trailed his feet off the side of the shopper, which, by that time, was beaten up by the miles of our campaign. At the same time, Watson, whom I could also see below me with her eyes still wide open, ducked her head to avoid some unseen projectile. Then I saw that in that same instant that Dalton's feet had caught up in some of the damnable overhanging tree branches. And then—toothpicks, holiday party toothpicks with the tiny green and red plastic cellophane feathering on the ends were flying all around us. Thick as gnats, they were whizzing in front of my face so I saw tiny chunks of holiday smoked sausage and cheese that were pierced upon the sharpened toothpick ends, dropping all around me and piling up on deck. All this time the aisle and the tree displays still echoed with the drumming and chanting of the barf-inducing New Age music that emanated from the ongoing celebration behind us. With the music abating somewhat at that moment, I could make out the tinkling sound of the toothpicks landing on the deck—which, if I focused on that sound alone, perpetuated the illusion of holiday cheer. Just beneath that sound, however, at a lower frequency, there was the deep pneumatic hissing of All Mart's patented Snack Dispersal System that I guessed was installed behind the trees. Klean toggled the control stick and moved the XR to the left so that we cleared Dalton's feet of the branch and could continue forward.

Toothpicks with sausage and cheese. We were being fired upon by a programmable party host. I leaned over to lift one of the shields that would cover the driver in the event that he or she attempted any shopping in heavy weather. But then I saw that Klean had clicked on the autopilot and was already getting up out of the cockpit, clutching at his chest, his face contorted in reaction to yet another improbable circumstance that had arisen. A second later, Dalton's foot got caught again on one of the fallen trees and the XR spun around and rammed into the side of the bank. Attempting to correct the situation, I had to lean down from my turret to move the branch. In doing so, I saw a peaceful face amongst the aluminum boughs and cones on a level with my own looking at me. And then, as though a blinder had been removed from my eyes, I made out, deep in the shadows of the holiday display, little shacks thrown together from scraps of dry-wall and cedar paneling from Hardware Heaven. Looking deeper into the forest, I saw more shacks slapped together using wide-screen television shipping crates from Electropia and insulated 4x8-foot cartons used for the delivery and storage of Sequoia Brand Frozen Garlic Toast. The brush was swarming with delicate limbs of all colors, adorned with Purple Ponchos and engaged in the simple movements of daily life. The low-priced nickel-alloy Christmas tree limbs shook, swayed and rustled as another volley of snacks flew from the SDS hidden deep in the forest.

This was where the Converts laid their heads. Speculation abounded, but no researcher or reporter had identified their amassed permanent dwellings.

"Can you get us straightened out, clear of these branches?" I asked Klean, who was slouched over on the deck. He lifted his head and I could see that something had gone wrong with him. His eyes were wide open but they were focusing on something behind me, far away.

He mumbled something I couldn't hear and held out his hand, which bore a tiny balled-up scrap of paper. The faces in the bushes stared at us but showed no malice—nor any range of emotion outside of serenity and simple curiosity. Some of the children scurried into the shacks when they saw me. Through windows fabricated from food wrap—there was no real weather here and no need for thermal or wind protection —I could see appliances and entertainment centers. Miniature lawns of nylon pine-needle carpet were arranged in front of the shacks. Fleets of bicycles, tricycles, and electric motorcycles were lying along the edges of miniature driveways. Most of the small driveways had late model electric shopping carts parked in them. I didn't have time to study this microcosm within the Mart. Out on the deck, Klean had fallen into some new well of madness and Watson had uncurled herself and taken the lead in a shouting match with one of the helicopter dispatchers at Departmental HQ—whom she had reached on the single satellite line that she was able to resurrect on Hardin's com screen. The words *"get us out of here"* were salted with Marine Corps drill sergeant suggestions of what Watson threatened to do if the dispatcher refused.

Figuring we weren't going anywhere with Dalton's zonked-out legs getting caught in the trees every few feet, and with Klean out of the driver's seat and plunged into some well of self-pity, I climbed down onto the deck. First I had to step over Dalton without waking him. This became non-trivial when a sudden jerk in the control of the auto-pilot almost threw me off the deck.

Stumbling, trying to catch my balance, my right foot jammed into Dalton's ribs—which stabilized my fall but also imparted enough force into his chest wall to elicit a solid thud. When no reaction uttered forth from Dalton, I knelt down beside Klean.

A greasy hand print was smeared across the front of his shirt where he had grasped a tiny hunk of sausage and crushed it. In the center of his chest I could see the protruding end of one of the party toothpicks that was still stuck in the fine weave of his dress shirt. He held up the scrap of paper that had been stuck onto the toothpick along with the sausage. I had seen a number of these lying on the deck but had made the fatal assumption that they were recipes.

"I have to do this," Klean mumbled as I took the paper from him.

It took a few seconds to smooth it out so I could read it, since it had been soaked through with pork fat, but when I did, something happened in the center of my chest. It wasn't that my heart froze in response to some penetrating shock. I had read books in which characters say *'my heart froze'* when they see or hear something unexpected. It wasn't like that at all. Instead, it was more like if you could imagine that some company had figured out a way to put despair into liquid form and were marketing it as Despare!—the industrial strength vanquishing agent of the human spirit. In order to meet the growing demand for their product, they had hired a freight train of railroad tank cars and loaded up every single car with their liquid Despare!. And then, while I was home alone on a Saturday night, they crashed the train into my apartment at the precise moment that I shut down my computer after yet another night's work on my screenplay and had surrendered myself to the shadowy master of my own advancing age, with no companion to discuss the unpublished works of Kafka. Or, if I were to choose the topic of conversation with this hypothetical mate at the proscribed moment of the tank car impaction, I would be discussing the potential fate of a character in my screenplay named Rocco, who had flown to Nairobi to find his old boss, but then finds himself sitting alone at a sidewalk café, sipping a gin and tonic, then approached by a young Masai boy named Chitundu, who has arrived in the city from the plains to find a doctor to help his sister, Adila, who is suffering from a rare skin disease, which has no known cause and no known cure. My own inner despair of these questions was thus heaped on with the ruptured tank car load of the liquified and more potent form of despair.

This was how I felt upon reading the scrap of paper that Klean had handed me.

There, printed in plain English, Spanish, French, German and Mandarin, were the words that had reduced this noble professional to a heaving, tearful mass of uncertainty. 'Now hiring EXECUTIVE-level positions. Minorities encouraged to apply.'

"Lawson's up to something and I have to check it out," he said. "I saw him back there, like I know you did, and the only way to know is to get inside."

"What?" I grabbed him by the shoulders and squared him to face me. "Are you crazy? This is not a good fit. They'll eat you alive up there."

"What?" I grabbed him by the shoulders and squared him to face me. "Are you *crazy?* This is not a good fit. They'll eat you alive up there."

Klean pushed himself away from me. Even though he was slumped over, I found his own immense strength was still sustaining him.

"K, my new-found friend, you're probably right," he said. "But it's way more complicated than me just me going in there to stop Lawson. The Media Ordinance Division is a dead end for me. 'Coupla' magazine execs get together and decide Whitney Shears has lost her teen glow, Morpheus can find a replacement and people have a new superstar to adore. McAlsteinetti driving down ad revenue by producing his own quality family entertainment and giving away bandwidth on his own network? Who do you think they're gonna' call to guide the narrative? Do these missions of nudging the paradigms of our popular beliefs amount to a life? A purpose? I'm no different than anyone else. We all want something bigger than this. And who's to say that maybe I won't have some part in whatever good might come out of this place? There's people of good will everywhere. And wherever they are inside here, they could probably use my help."

"I have no idea what to say." I didn't. I couldn't think of anything inspirational, funny or even lame to say, and I didn't feel like I had any sense at all what his existence in this world was really like.

Klean saw the desperate blankness in my face and smiled. "Of course, you don't," he confirmed. "But I know you're at least trying."

He straightened a little and gave me a look that frightened me and I didn't understand right away. But I knew that he was going.

I grabbed onto his shoulders and shook him, *"Morpheus! Stop. In the name of –"*

But it was too late.

Watson looked over from her emergency evac efforts and held up her hand to me, as if to indicate that I should let him go.

Klean stood up on the deck. Something new convulsed him as the old life fought its final stand for control of his body. I almost expected some bellowing last words as he took a huge deep breath, as if preparing for a fight.

But then his breathing stilled, and he appeared to focus his gaze on the Mezzanine that was ahead. "Watson, please see to it that my 401K gets rolled over to All Mart."

"You can do it yourself on the Department Intranet. You'll have access for 30 days from the time your resignation goes through. And *don't* forget to make sure that all your receipts from this trip and your advanced vehicular training in Dallas are *taped* onto individual sheets of 8 1/2x11 paper," Watson warned. "You know they won't take 'em if you staple 'em. Or, you can scan them and e-mail them."

Klean wasn't listening anymore.

"The Department wants you to be happy," Watson said as she pulled some performance evaluation sheets from a file drawer that opened into her pod. "Do you have some time for an exit interview?"

But Klean had leapt off the XR, freed himself from some of the hanging snowflakes that entangled him in mid-air, and then ran off ahead of us toward the Mezzanine.

Acceptance
Dude, thirty-seven more days!

Jed Fritzman, first in line, camping outside the KumQuaTech Computer store on Michigan Avenue in Chicago. On January 4th. In anticipation of the company's release of their new quantum paradox encoded panmedia player—the eQuaZen

The extended wood flute solo in the New Age music soundtrack had stopped, and the Converts in the trees had either gone back into their shacks or headed eastward for the Black Light Blowout that would be starting again soon. The smoke lingered. Dalton snoozed. Watson had given up on getting us a helicopter and decided in her somewhat revitalized state to attempt a meeting with McAlsteinetti. Or at least fulfill the motions of preparing for the meeting. To this end, like Klean had done, she changed back into her slacks, blouse and paratrooper heels and was practicing her MetaPoint presentation. But her voice carried a hint of exhaustion, as if some physical limit that was not believed to exist had in fact been reached. And in between the animated bullet points she was reviewing, her silence spoke of a burden that was unshakable by all usual and customary means.

On the other side of the White Aisle, on the open lane across the little strip of dead grass, a line of armored vehicles flying the flags of multiple nations was moving away from the Mezzanine. They weren't regular army and they were picking up any customers or Converts who had hadn't scattered into the forest. Loudspeakers on the vehicles were shouting out warnings in multiple languages as they rumbled past. Their presence made sense when I remembered that there was a huge airfield on the roof of the store for use by corporate jets who had meetings with McAlsteinetti and his executives. A few charter services also used it for day trips to the Gorge. The airfield itself was surrounded by vast rooftop fields that were planted over the last few years as an awakened effort to offset the mammoth carbon footprint of the store, trucks and factories needed to supply it.

The All Mart security forces had given up on us and were also rounding up people in what had all the overt signs of an evacuation. People were running and screaming, lamenting and jumping onto the sides of the passing military vehicles with a few sacks of possessions slung over their shoulders. I couldn't see the metallic dust particles anymore—they must have infiltrated through cracks in every window and door in the central part of the store. Instead, through the skylights I saw hundreds of jet trails crossing the sky high above the store. I didn't understand it right way, but the sky itself seemed distorted, as if the window glass was warped. Dalton's navigation and radar monitors— which were cycling through images of air traffic over Ohio, the Midwest and all of North America—depicted the electronic version of the air traffic situation above the store, so that the reason for the apparent distortion became even more confusing. Hundreds of aircraft, the size of tiny seeds on the radar screen, were moving at the periphery of a flickering, pixelated area over the store.

I settled down into the driver's seat and figured out how to get the XR to move straight ahead. After mowing down a few score of lawn elves, I felt bad and stopped so I could go back and stand them up again, but Watson wouldn't have it. The single stern glance I received said that she was grateful that I was showing some initiative and that she appreciated that I was accepting the responsibility for my mishaps, but there was no time to offer extended courtesy to LED-studded cut-outs of imaginary creatures.

On my left, the thin strip of dying grass continued all the way to the base of the stairs that lead up to the Mezzanine, which I could make out in the haze, about half a mile straight ahead. The holiday displays of the White Aisle had given way to rows of vending machines and dining tables. These were surrounded by bulletin boards bearing minimum-wage postings and multicolored scraps of paper announcing the sale of used cars, babysitting and other goods and services that employees traded. The size of the store demanded that this was one of many employee break areas. So, there was nothing special about this one. Except, of course, the employees who worked near this one filled higher-level clerical trenches for the company—human resources, finance, marketing. My first thought was that these people would have regular contact with McAlsteinetti. Would some of them suspect that he had become overly obsessed with the nature of the subatomic universe? Would he have in passing let slip his prediction that the great technological age of humans was ending? Would they know who his real friends were?

The lack of details about his private life was not the result of any absence from the favored watering holes of the world's richest people. Nor, early on, was there any obvious effort on his part to avoid the media or shelter his eccentricities from the outside world. To the contrary, he was a regular at yacht clubs, Grand Slam tennis tournaments and Aspen chalets. He had dated multiple lingerie models along the way, most notably more than half the women in the yearly calendar for Annabel's Knickers, the British supplier of intimate apparel. The dramatic overlapping of these affections had in fact made him a regular feature in the tabloids. During these years, he seemed to enjoy interacting with journalists and talk-show hosts of any stripe. With a wink and laugh, he doled out titillating but harmless naughties about his girlfriends and billionaire buddies, dished innocent anecdotes on the politicos who ingratiated themselves to him or waxed economic on the trends that he foresaw. All this media attention was met with an understanding that questions about his early childhood were off limits. After he started construction of Store Number 1 and became a permanent resident of the Mezzanine, however, the clever anecdotes and quotable business advice ceased to flow. Numerous reporters from most major metropolitan papers and international news magazines had scheduled interviews with McAlsteinetti and then never made it to see him. Not in the capacity as a member of the media, anyway. Like the aid workers and sociologists who entered the store intending to help and study the culture of Converts and then never left, many reporters never even arrived at their scheduled appointments. Hence the rarity of photos and reliable word of his more recent activities. Even vendors, many of whom ventured inside to establish new outlets for their products, never reached the Mezzanine. No foul play was ever considered. Instead, signed letters of resignation got out to their former employers. Extended families received heartfelt letters of invitation to rejoin their lost loved ones inside the store, and all personal assets were transferred to the All Mart Credit Union. Months earlier, Terri Grand of IPR's *Clear Sky* had scheduled a taping of her show with McAlsteinetti at the Mezzanine. Three weeks later she reappeared, smiling, natural gray hair flowing and looking healthier than ever as a Babel Babe.

At the other extreme of media interaction with Store Number 1 and McAlsteinetti were those scant few who did walk out of the store but found themselves with no market for their work. Which was surprising, given his personal worth and the absolute dominance of All Mart over all other discount and retail outlets. Most famously, German documentary filmmaker Hermann Schmerzhogg spent three years inside the store attempting to tell the tale of a band of his native countrymen who had Converted and were said to have established a small village somewhere in the Wholesale Highlands. Schmerzhogg's first round of financing vaporized after he crashed a shopping cart loaded with camera equipment while hauling it over one of the 12 peaks of the AlmoZone—the successful region of the Highlands stacked with Kurt's Klub Assorted Nut Shipping Containers. Schmerzhogg had scraped together a smaller budget from a few European cultural NGO's but then had to postpone production for a month when an epidemic of Selection Fever blistered through the Highlands. Broke, pale and with a total cholesterol of 327, he stumbled out of the store with an estimated 2000 hours of footage that no one wanted to see.

The 5 hour and 47-minute finished film, that he edited in his own basement, premiered and closed on the same day at an early morning session of the Trondheim Arts Festival. The Board of Directors for the well-regarded though Kroner-strapped Norwegian festival felt the content of the film was too disturbing, even for the liberal-minded local audiences, and without sufficient entertainment value to justify a wider showing. Bootleg copies of the film, some bearing the original title, *Das Abbott,* were available for download. Even those were said to be missing the haunting scenes of German families dragging sledges loaded with liquid laundry detergent and breakfast cereal back to their camp in the Highlands. These unauthorized versions also lacked a controversial 2-hour long interview with McAlsteinetti himself. No one except Schmerzhogg and the 5 festival-goers and 7 critics who saw the whole film that morning in Trondheim knew what McAlsteinetti had said in those hours. The story that Interpol showed up at the festival and confiscated the film circulated for a few days, as rumors do at film festivals. The premier of Sqwintin Tarantella's new film, *Slash Until You Laugh, Volume VII*, soon eclipsed the already-fading protest against the censoring of Schmerzhogg's work.

That documentary came to mind again as we approached the Mezzanine and an outsized man in flowing lavender robes with a shaved head picked his way down the stairs with his hands extended in greeting. Families and children ran past him down the steps and headed off down the White Aisle, away from the Mezzanine. Watson motioned for me to slow down as we got closer.

"*Velkommen, velkommen,*" said the man with a Midwesternized sing-songy Scandinavian lilt that, on top of sounding a little shaky, also sounded familiar. He *looked* a little shaky, too, and he had a goofy half smile and far-off focused eyes that made me think his college recreational drug experimentation had persisted beyond his senior year. "Vee haf—a—bin waiting, for yeeew?"

His monkish robes swished back and forth as he pointed toward a parking spot at the edge of a nearby strip of purple carpet. As I was shutting down, he ambled over to the shopper but seemed indifferent as to whether we got out or not.

"We had an appointment for ten o'clock this morning," Watson apologized, climbing out of the XR.

"*Ja*, I knooow," he said, waving off our concern at being late with perfected disinterest. His robes were decorated with multicolored splotches that documented in texture and color a long and varied dietary history. The wettest and darkest of these stains, and the one that capped the dome of his generous abdomen, looked like a pool of teriyaki sauce. The few grains of rice stuck around the edges of the stain supported this hypothesis. His grubby feet were displayed through the split seams of a scuffed pair of Allverse high-tops. He might have been thirty, or maybe even sixty. I couldn't tell from the indeterminate blondish color of the thin stubble that covered his face, neck and, to a lesser extent, his head. In between waving at the departing hoards and chuckling at jokes that seemed to be coming from somewhere over his left shoulder, he watched us get out of the shopper.

"We were detained," said Watson, stepping onto the carpet with her laptop case over her shoulder, "on multiple occasions."

"*Ja*, dot's fine," said the monk.

As I moved within a few feet of him, I found that I was beginning to understand his odd speech, as long as I ignored the *'ja's'* he kept slipping in. More compelling, however, I caught the first whiff of his personal bouquet. There was the anticipated strong undercurrent of fermented sweat, with tones of pickled herring and, as I guessed earlier, teriyaki. I didn't think for a second that he was a slob, or that his abstinence from scheduled bathing was wanton. Quite to the contrary, the impregnation of this man's wardrobe with organic matter was purposeful. Every square inch of residual food or beverage on his purple robes had a story all its own. Every stray bit of broccoli tempura that remained in his teeth and on his sleeves had a meaning that I could not yet grasp. The pattern of overlap of these stains and crumbs could be used to interpret the exact sequence of *motivated* spills and slurps that had occurred during months leading up to our meeting. He was an artist. A tortured one at that.

"We'd still like to speak with Mister McAlsteinetti, if he can manage to work us into his schedule. We–"

"You don't talk to McAlsteinetti," said the man. "Well, you listen to him."

"I'm Ted Kojwaclczsziziek," I said, "and this is Roberta Watson."

The man in the purple robes grinned as though he were listening, but since his eyes had drifted off toward the ceiling it seemed he was continuing to take delight in some unseen humor that surrounded us. "The man has an enlarged mind. He is a poet industrialist in a classic sense. Sometimes, he'll— well—you say *hallo* to him, *ja?* And, well, he'll just walk right by you in the cafeteria and won't even notice you. And then suddenly, he'll grab you and he'll push you in a corner and he'll say, *'Do you know that Ur is the middle word in 'purchase?'* Yet, he can be terrible. He can be generous. He can be right. He is saving us all, you know. He is a great man. I mean, I wish I had the words. I could tell you something like, the other day, he wanted to rescind my employee discount."

"What?" Watson said, narrowing her eyes.

"*Ja, ja,*" the guy in the robes insisted. "Because I took his picture. I was helping the kids with a print ad for one of their *skolen prosjkets*. He said, *'If you take my picture again, I'm going to cancel your employee discount.'* And, he meant it."

"I understand completely," said Watson. "But, I assure you, we are not here from the media, but on a business-to-business matter of the utmost urgency. Now, who are you and can you take us to Mister McAlsteinetti?"

"My name is Gunnar, but everyone here calls me Barney."

That's when I remembered why this guy looked familiar. He was

Gunnar Bjärniæløågson, the unpronounceable Norwegian cinematographer who disappeared a few weeks into Schmerzhogg's first shoot. As a known social existentialist and Norwegian national, he was the reason the film was allowed to be shown at the Trondheim festival. As a memorial tribute to the local artist's supposed death, of course. In terms of his popularity, he was no ABBA, but he had his following among serious aficionados of Scandinavian documentary film-making. I felt honored to meet him after all these years.

I wanted to ask him about the existence of the Schmerzhogg interview with McAlsteinetti but decided against it when Watson brushed past him and started up the steps to the Mezzanine.

After only a few steps, her pace slowed as her gaze fixated on something beyond the top of the stairs. Something not quite human. Something beyond morbid. Something that pushed her to the limit of her tolerance.

Barney tottered up ahead of her, looking obliged to reassert his role of host. A few feet behind, Watson stopped in mid-step and appeared ready to scream as she approached a framed color photograph on the wall.

It was Klean. Blank eyes, smiling at the camera, his skin lighter than I remembered, wearing a knotted purple silk tie. It was hideous. I took the last three stairs in a single move to get to Watson, whose fist moved to her mouth in an attempt to stifle her own scream. I didn't fare much better. As I got up close to the photo, I could see the true grisly nature of this chilling display of corporate hierarchy. On Klean's lapel, he wore a tiny purple tomahawk. And the pattern on his tie was tiny purple envelopes alternating with the All Mart logo—the words overlaying a purple infinity symbol. I had to turn away. My head ached and a wave of stomach acid burned the back of my throat. A small metal plate with his name and new title was screwed into a wooden plaque that was bolted onto the wall below picture. The tiny curlicues of sawdust around the screws spoke to the rawness of the installation minutes earlier: *L.F. Klean, Associate Vice President of Research and Development, Direct Marketing Division.*

That explained the little envelopes on his tie. He was in Direct Marketing. Even though I worked as a freelancer in the industry, I knew how deadly it could get near the top of a direct marketing agency and my heart feared for him. A drop in response rate from 0.01% to 0.0098% might mean heads will roll.

I gagged and staggered across the hall, arriving face to face with a photo of another young executive. Then I felt the horrific truth of that place—along the wall ahead were rows upon rows of similar photos lining the mauve-painted hallway leading to McAlsteinetti's glass office at the end.

There was Rodney Dokehammer, former CEO of Oakey Dokey furniture, the 27-generation family-run hand-made oak furniture company. Furniture that was now press-formed outside Mexico City from sawdust and glue imported from Borneo. Darlene Workman, founder of Kumquatech, who built a French-speaking teddy-bear in her garage at the age of 12—which, after acquisition of her company, spawned All-Mart's popular Kuddlee Killaz family of urban felony robo-pets. To what insane end all these cadaverous faces, more garish than a band of gypsies attacking a Mardi Gras parade? And the corporate art displays between the photos—a bilious collection of color-coordinated, decorative, floral still-life watercolors without a single thread of connection to the great sadness of the human race. The juxtaposition of the vile with the banal was too much for both Watson and me.

"Peter Wistman," Watson moaned, staggering, pointing to one of the portraits. "He was my supervisor when I interned at Dispersed Intelligence."

I tried to help but she reeled away from me, finding more portraits. It got worse. There were also photos of the executives accepting awards, out on big game hunts, or shaking hands with senators and foreign dignitaries. Watson pointed to a picture of a young woman wearing a starched white skirt on a red clay tennis. "And this, this is Tracy Lawdin. I played field hockey with her at Waspen Hall Academy."

Watson made a deep guttural sound, or was it me? Barney turned from his hurried pace.

"You noticed the portraits," Barney said. He looked as though even speaking about them troubled him. Beneath that was some hidden pain, welling up from a source that even he could not nail down.

"It's just, so..." Watson's voice sounded weak.

"I know," Barney said, forlorn. "The color is terrible. I usually don't do *portraitvorken*, but McAlsteinetti insists we have this gallery of our executives. I've been using some outdoor patio lights that I borrowed from Lawn Land. But I'm not getting the contrast I want."

Watson braced herself against the wall and averted her eyes from the nearest of the photographs. I handed her a water bottle I had in my computer bag. The few long gulps she took seemed to steady her a little and returned some focus to her eyes.

Barney studied us with a look of tired, torn detachment, as if he had seen a similar reaction from others. It was not the supposed imperfections of the lighting in the pictures that seemed to bother him so much. There was something conflicted in how he felt about the figures displayed in the images. He pointed to a photograph of an executive kneeling next to a bighorn ram that one had to assume was dead because the executive had one of his hands gripping onto one of the long, curved horns and was wrenching the entire head of the animal toward the camera. With his other hand, the executive was holding a high-caliber rifle with a mainframe-guided TheoMatic sight. The mountain range in the background looked like the Tetons, but it might have been anyplace in the highest Rockies out west.

Barney motioned toward the picture. "In this one, I was trying to contrast the gaping wilderness with the ferocity of the human spirit."

Watson didn't even look down.

"What?" I said. I knew even less about art than I did about marketing or mathematics. But I did know a thing or two about African safari gear which I had researched while working on my screenplay. "He's wearing a $20,000 Rhi-NO safari survival jacket. Where's the ferocity in that? And where's the sporting aspect of that scope? He could have shot that goat from the surface of the moon."

Barney either didn't hear my comment or pretended he didn't. "The human spirit. Indomitable. You might notice the forms. The sense of struggle. Evolution unbound. The potential for individual achievement in the face of massive tectonic upheaval. Uncertain sensuality. Animistic uncertainty. The curling of the antlers as allegory. Chaos. Decay. The struggle for potentiation of achievement. Uncertain massiveness. Individualistic animism. Sensual tectonism. Struggling allegorical upheaval, potentiated. The mountains as oppressor. Primal. Ritualistic."

I had never stood that close to an artist explaining his work before, so at first I didn't know what any of that had to do with the question everyone was asking: *what the heck are we doing here?* In an earlier time in my life, when I was starting to explore my own creative urges, I might have been intimidated by his words. But on that day, after watching the doors fall off the life and work of people much smarter than myself, I knew that Barney didn't know. And Watson didn't know. Even genius McAlsteinetti didn't know. All Barney could do, and he did his best doing it with whatever he had left in him, was point his chubby finger toward a grainy bleached-out color image of a rock shelter with a few smudgy figures huddled around a charcoal fire and talk around what might be in there.

I sure as hell had no idea what was in there. Given our circumstances in that moment, it didn't matter. We were so close to completing something, whatever our mission had become, and the thing we had to do right then was keep moving.

Lucky for me, Watson was getting herself back together. She looked stronger, as if she were restocking her will as we teetered at the fulcrum of our mission. I was feeling stronger, too. Maybe it was as simple as recognizing that even Barney was shaky on the details of what we were doing there. Perhaps suspecting for the first time that my part in all this was not yet complete. As long as everyone else didn't know what the hell was going on, I was no worse or better prepared to throw some special skills onto the canvas of human history than anyone else.

"When can we see him?" Watson croaked.

"Oh, *ja*," Barney turned his pained attention from the photograph and sighed.

With his head hanging down, he led us the last few yards down the hallway and into a waiting room jammed with vendors pushing samples, demos and prototypes of their multinational products. He pointed in the general direction of a few unoccupied leather chairs arranged around a square glass table. I would have thought an evacuation of the building might have deterred these mid-levels from being there that day, but I guess the possibility of delivering their goods into the All Mart revenue stream was too attractive a proposition.

"If you don't mind waiting for a few moments. He's been engaged in, um, *a very important meeting* all afternoon. The office is half-deserted now that we're getting close to the holidays. He's been drowning with all the upcoming promotions. October is the busiest month."

Watson and I sat down while Barney slumped off behind two tall glass doors that I presumed led to the innermost reaches of the All Mart Empire. Watson grabbed her cell phone and was speed-dialing Department of Commerce Special Forces Headquarters. Feeling that familiar creepy underarm sweat that demanded I also look busy, I took out my laptop. It occurred to me that I might be able to proclaim that my special skills had become inaccessible as a result of the Upraiders.

"Good," said Watson, noticing as I opened the laptop. She gave me a weak smile and her eyes bore the faintest reflection of hope. "You've made it this far. Let's see what else you've got."

Then I saw her listening to another voice. Her eyes focused on something else and her smile was gone. "Inside the Rabbit Hole," she said to someone at HQ. "Request mission completion protocol."

I could hear a Brazilian ensemble version of the *Marines' Hymn* in the background as they put her on hold.

"How much RAM do you have on there?" she asked. "This could get memory-intensive."

"It should be fine. It looks like they added a bunch." Right then the little video icon returned to my desktop. I didn't see McAlsteinetti's face, but rather a rapid sequence of people on a basketball court. It was a view from a head-cam and the person wearing the camera had in that instant tossed up an air ball.

I heard the hold music stop and the murmured voice of someone giving Watson a new set of instructions.

"You wouldn't?" Watson was horrified at whatever it was that they said they would do. "You have my recommendations based on years of study. Which were confirmed by Klean and Hardin's internal report on the restructuring. And you're talking about using the Langsford Bioeconomic Stain Removal System?"

Watson turned so I couldn't see her face. I shivered.

"You know," she said. "It's kind of hard to get promoted or even commended for completely eliminating a building, people and ideas from the fabric of space and time. How do you propose to get a medal for destroying something that no one will be able to prove ever existed in the first place? How do you justify the spending the agency's entire yearly budget to say that you destroyed something that there is no longer any trace of? And I don't find it very comforting to be told we'll be picked up along the perimeter of the event horizon."

Watson shook her head in denial as whoever she was talking to further explained their position on the matter. "Yeah, I know, we failed by conventional means," she said. "But we can salvage this thing. We have to at least give this guy a chance. He's made it this far so I think he's for real. The fact that you don't have any records on him is what gives me the most confidence—well, he does exist. He's sitting here with me right now."

The hold music came on again. Watson's face revealed nothing that I could interpret. She had locked me out.

After a few seconds, the music stopped and a different voice on the other end gave Watson what sounded like a series of instructions from a printed protocol.

Watson held the phone away from her ear and spoke to me. "I've received specific instructions on how to proceed with the skills that got you selected for this mission."

"I'm as ready as I'll ever be," I said. I felt calm. In my mind, there was little I could do to hamper the mission by that point. We had reached the Mezzanine and were within a few feet of McAlsteinetti.

"You're to open a new document in SniperShop on your computer and import the McAlsteinetti parameters that are being e-mailed to you right now. Once those parameters are loaded into the program, you are to open an Arsenal Palette. You are then to create a Legal Obfuscation Layer with an assortment of Financial Justification filters, the details of which I'll leave up to if you want to do something creative. If you look on the Department's website, there's a library of Plausible Deniability preset brushes that you can load. You might have some of your own from previous jobs, and those would probably be fine. As long they have sufficient resolution to meet international standards. And then, you are to proceed, as you would normally proceed, in FreeHunt mode. After you're finished, just mark the task as completed in your e-mail and I'll spread the word."

I didn't even pretend to hide my surprise at this request. "SniperShop?"

"Yes," said Watson. "You were the only person that we could get on such short notice who knew how to run SniperShop."

I had never heard of SniperShop. I did have SnipperShop on my computer. It was one of the several thousand cheapo video editing programs that were included in the box when you bought a new video camera. In this case, SnipperShop came free with the Sanyiba Z45...one of the next generation of cloud-based cameras that my brother had purchased for his son last Christmas.

A peace that surpassed my own understanding passed through me as I fessed up. "I don't have SniperShop on my computer."

I had no idea how long the gap between my last words and those of Watson might have lasted. It might have been a few seconds. For all I knew it could have been hours. She also seemed calm. Maybe it was me setting the tone, bringing her into the sphere of resignation. She looked so serene, sitting in that huge stuffed chair a few feet from me. The occasional turning of a magazine page by someone waiting there with us allowed me a tiny window into the ongoing passage of time.

When Watson spoke, her voice was softer than I ever could have imagined. "I'm sorry. Can you say that again, please?"

"I don't have SniperShop on my computer."

"You're saying you don't have SniperShop on your computer?"

"Yes, that's correct."

"You *don't have SniperShop* on your computer."

"No. I mean, *yes,* I don't have it."

"You don't have *SniperShop* on *your* computer."

"No. I don't have it on my computer."

"*You* don't have SniperShop *on your computer.*"

"Yes, that's correct," I said. "I do not have it. I don't have it. I mean, it's not here. That I'm aware of. I can't exclude the possibility that I might have had it at one time. Or that it's there and I can't find it. Although I think that's highly, highly unlikely. So unlikely as to actually not be possible is what I should say. I mean, I download a lot of stuff and a lot of stuff gets downloaded without us knowing it, of course. Who knows what's in all those e-mails you get from those, well, you know? So, it might have been there briefly. But I try to keep this machine running pretty smoothly and I have pretty good spyware detection software. And who knows what the Upraiders took on and put on here. Plus, I delete a lot of stuff on a regular basis. So it might have been there. But, for now, no, it's not."

"The program that you're supposed to be skilled at, SniperShop, is not anywhere on your hard drive."

"Yes."

"SniperShop. The program that is now required for completion of this mission as we have understood it. That you were hired specifically to operate. Is not on your computer."

"Yes."

"The program that when we called your Agency and said, *'Hello, hi, yes, you can help us today, we need someone to operate SniperShop,'* and then they called back about 5 hours later because they were scouring the entire Midwest to find somebody and they said, *'Yeah, hey, no problem, we found this guy, one of our regular guys, he's great at SniperShop, clients just love him. He's a little older than most of our freelancers but more mature, you'll like him. He's available, he hasn't worked for weeks but that's because he finished a new campaign that went on for a month and he needed some time off to work on his screenplay—oh, yeah, yeah, sure: Mob boss gets a heart and goes to Africa; thinks he has a good shot at getting it read. Oh, yes, one of our best, yes, and did we mention his extensive work with SniperShop? And it will cost you THIS obscene amount because, well, you know, SniperShop is becoming the industry standard now.'* That program, of which they were speaking, and of which I am now speaking, the program toward which many hard-earned tax dollars are now being sucked in order to pay your ridiculous hourly wage plus the Federal Reserve-crippling markup that your Agency skims off the top, *that program* does not occupy any of the several trillion tracks on your hard drive?"

"Yes, that's pretty correct."

"I see," said Watson. She *still* seemed so calm. Perhaps Barney's discussion of his photograph had also touched her in some way. "Well, what *do* you have on your computer?"

"I do have SnipperShop," I said. I had loaded the software on my computer at my brother's house that same snowy Christmas afternoon.

"Ah, SnipperShop. That *sounds* like the program I'm interested in. Perhaps it may be helpful. What does SnipperShop do?"

"You can make movies with it."

"I see. Making movies is a teentsy-weentsy-eentsy-meentsy little bit like what we need to do here today. So maybe it'll be fine. And you're proficient with SnipperShop, are you?"

"Well, I'm basically familiar with the interface."

"Familiar with the interface."

"Yes, I can open video files with it."

"You can *open* other video files with it."

"Yes." In order to provide confirmation of the apparent mix-up in the software titles, I had launched SnipperShop and opened a VPEG clip of my nephew jumping around in his pajamas.

"So basically, you just opened it up one day and played around with it for five minutes."

"Well," I said, slowing the clip down with one of the slider controls that I had clicked on. "I did spend some time with some of the advanced motion control features."

"And then you put it on your résumé."

"Yes," I said, flipping the video clip upside down with another of the random buttons I clicked, then turned my laptop so she could see it. I felt like I was getting a handle on SnipperShop while we were waiting. "I knew a lot of these video editing programs shared similar features. I felt like having at least one of them on my résumé was a strong point."

"And you spelled it wrong."

"Spell checkers can't keep up with all the new technical lingo."

"No, no, I couldn't agree more," Watson said smiling. Her face spoke libraries of emotion: a solid base of anger, a dash of humor, expansive awe at the magnitude of her misfortune and my unsuitability for her mission.

"I'm sorry," is all I could think of to say. I was. I didn't want to do what she thought she had hired me to do, but I did feel bad that my typographic error had caused her so much pain.

"No apology is necessary," Watson said. She was back to business and did not even look at me after that. She glanced at her watch, pulled out her phone, booted up her wrist pad, and began dialing and typing. "We're on to Plan D. Ideally without going back to either B or C. That is, *sans* the Crater or the Langsford."

I was hoping to get a little better understanding of option C but didn't get a chance to ask. Barney had slipped back into the waiting area and seemed poised to make a very sad announcement. His undertakerish enthusiasm, however, was contrasted by rivulets of sweat on his head and face, and even more wet stains on his purple robe, as if he had been out running around. It seemed to contradict the ditzy angst with which he faced the world, but it could have been the eternal nervousness that no doubt came along with his status as personal assistant to one of the world's most powerful business icons.

"Mister McAlsteinetti has been somewhat delayed, but his senior staff will be happy to meet with *you*, Miz Watson. And, uh..." Barney's voice trailed off as he looked over at me.

And that was it. I felt a wave of both relief and disappointment as I was excluded from whatever official Department of Commerce activity might be surrounding Watson's meeting.

"Mr. Kojwaclczsziziek, you have been invited to wait in our..." he looked a little panicked as he struggled to make up a word. "...Adjunct entertainment suite."

Watson packed up and was ready to move. I was off the radar, out of the loop, down for the count, face-down, belly-up and the object of whatever other euphemisms existed for sudden failure in business. Barney trudged down the hall ahead of us and opened a glass door, through which Watson entered without even looking back at me. Barney closed the door behind her and motioned for me to follow him.

As I passed the wall of glass, I could see an oval ring of people in business suits surrounding a 50-foot long wooden conference table, connected with other executives worldwide by TelePortMini Booths that were mounted along the central axis of the table. Multicolored bar charts, line plots, Wage-O-Static™ indicators, DemandoMetricSM maps and DictatorDodger® brand governmental stabilographic maps were projected on the walls of the conference room in a dynamic electronic display of global market data. On the main DemandoMetric simulation I could see huge color coded-bands radiating out from LA, sweeping westward across the Pacific like some climatopathic El Niño to engulf Tokyo. Whatever the current trend was represented, it was hot and spreading fast. They also had radar screens showing the accumulation of large aircraft over Columbus. It was interesting, there were also radar signatures moving in a line up the Scioto River that looked like submarines, with a picket line of radar signatures along the south shore of Lake Erie. And, although I didn't think it was possible in terms of orbital dynamics, satellites were also forming a cluster over the midwest.

"Please, Mister Kojwaclczsziziek," Barney said, touching my arm. "Follow me."

I wouldn't have minded slipping into the back of whatever meeting was going on. There was something inviting about the proceedings inside that room. It was akin to seeing a flash of sunlight reflecting from a gleaming object in the tiny creek behind my family's trailer and the instantaneous activation of whatever neurons connected me to the gold nuggets of the Sierra Nevada, through stories involving grizzled 49ers or the wanderings of Conquistadors, or perhaps through some deeper wiring in the species. Either way, I dreamed of wealth beyond imagine—which was *a lot*, because I confess that I have pondered impossible wealth in the deepest thicket of my mind. The people in that room controlled entire industries, took home salaries that could be mistaken for population figures in Asia, and held stock options that could, and sometimes did, fund their own individual interplanetary space programs. It was all right there, so close, and I'm not above saying that I wanted a piece of it.

"Mister Kojwaclczsziziek, *please.*" Barney said, grabbing my arm and leading me to a much smaller room at the end of the hall. With a smile, he shoved me through the door and lumbered off like a jilted pallbearer to attend to some other pressing concern. Neither entertaining, nor suite-like came to mind as I let myself drop onto one of two battered leather couches that had been stuffed into the tiny room. A room, I deduced, that had been a janitorial closet and been retro-fitted to fill in as an office for the security staff. A dented gray metal desk sat in the corner, strewn with papers, back issues of magazines and what looked like academic journals covering a range of subjects including economics, physics, cosmology and agriculture. These should have been my first clue about the true nature of the room, but I was too exhausted to put anything together. Above the desk, rows and rows of tiny color monitors scanned the nearby conference rooms and assorted other corners, doors, aisles, displays and stairways throughout the entire store, including the dying-grass strip that ran down the center of the White Aisle. In one tiny screen, I could see the FATASS XR still parked by the front stairs to the Mezzanine with Dalton's tiny sleeping figure curled up on the deck. This bank of monitors reinforced my initial suspicion that this was the occupational domain of a security guard.

On another monitor, I could see the All Mart senior staff eyeing Watson as she was being seated at the conference table. Since it wasn't my job to monitor *anything*, however, I became giddy with the realization that the room was the perfect place to grab a nap. Watching Dalton crash like a raver on the plane home from Reykjavik had reminded me how tired I was, so I allowed myself to sink back onto the couch, with no further thoughts about what Watson might be doing in there, and how I might still be required to play some part in the mission as it was unfolding.

Revelation

Our acquisition of the former Chinese province of Hunan will give us a solid foundation for our anticipated Asian expansion. Also, I'd like to say that we're all deeply saddened by the sudden and unexpected passing of my predecessor, Kurtis McAlsteinetti.

Stephen P Lawson, Acting Vice President of New Market Expansion, All Mart, in a press release announcing the proposed construction of Store Number 2.

Maybe it was my imagination, but as soon as I closed my eyes, the door flew open and Barney's sweaty back fumbled into the room. His plump, sticky hands gripped the ends of a stretcher that had been slapped together from a sales banner and a few aluminum Christmas tree branches. On the stretcher, protruding into the office, I could see two pale, skinny legs, covered with flowery tattoos, with the feet wearing high-top basketball shoes and one of the ankles piled on with ice packs.

"Well?" Barney blustered, as he struggled to back himself further into the room. Whatever internal deconstruction had occupied him was interrupted by the mission of getting through the doorway.

Jumping up and holding the door open, I saw the man lying there on the stretcher. He looked younger and leaned more toward geek than I had imagined. His hair had smooshed down on one side from sleeping on one of the couches, and his beard and Nazca-line sideburns had an adolescent, first-attempt at facial hair scruffiness to them. His cheeks were on their way to being hollowed and he was a lot thinner than any pictures I had ever seen of him. In the early photos of him during his ascent, he seemed more robust. But that might have been a Soviet-inspired campaign by the PR Department to convey health and prosperity to the outside by adding pounds to his photos. This was not the sunkeness I had witnessed in Dalton's corkscrew into unreality, nor the sinewy asceticism of a contemplative lifestyle. This was more the spidery appearance of someone who *forgot* to eat as often as not, and without the muscular windfall of any organized or consistent exercise program. As I studied him, I understood that this was the face I'd seen on the tiny video screen that had appeared on my laptop. On his purple t-shirt were the iron-on words *Hardware Heaven Heavies*, which contrasted with the t-shirt worn by the employee who carried the head of the stretcher: *Pharmadelphia Phantoms.*

"K! Glad you could make it!" McAlsteinetti laughed as his eyes met mine. "Sorry you missed my dominating performance in the first round of the Intramural Tournament."

"Ja, your mother," said Barney, over-the-top rolling his eyes as he and the other employee dumped their world-famous boss onto the other couch

along the wall.

"C'mon," McAlsteinetti said as he thumped onto the frayed and splitting cushions. "How 'bout a little respect here?"

"I believe you had a double single this afternoon, sir," said Barney. He sighed as he collapsed the make-shift stretcher and wiped his face with the folds of his robe. "One point and one assist, if I recall correctly."

I thought for a second about informing Barney that he had transferred a few grains of rice from his robe to his eyebrows, but I thought it might be an installation of some sort and let him and the other employee athlete from Pharmadelphia depart in peace.

"Barney's a good man," McAlsteinetti bellowed, lifting his ice-packed ankle onto the arm of the couch, "One of the few people around here who listens to me anymore."

I'm sure it was my turn to say something, but in his presence I blanked like a first grader on a thermodynamics exam. There, inside the corporate offices of the profit dynamo he had built in the same number of years that it had taken me to get to page 57 of my screenplay and build a preposterous amount of consumer debt, I'm not sure what he expected. Then there was the whole issue of my squeamish encounter in the Gorge, followed by the sight of the executive portraits. I had no clear idea how to process what might become of Hardin, Stanton, Lawson or Klean in the next year of their lives.

To his credit, McAlsteinetti must have seen the conflict in my eyes.

"Your friends are safe," he said and then laughed. "It was actually Barney who gave me the update on the status of their transition on the way over here. He's the best source for real-time information I have. As a very small token of my appreciation, I let him run around here in that skanky bathrobe. Among other quirks of hygiene, as you may have noticed. Not exactly up to Purple Poncho dress code."

The dress code comment surprised me, but then I remembered that there were plenty of people in the world who wanted their customer service associates to look a certain way. For his own part, McAlsteinetti looked like another new millennium iconic geek, not caring what anyone thought while threading his own way across the global business minefield, displaying the tendril tattoos that entwined his arms and legs and the petroglyph-pattern facial hair. Another feature that separated him from his employees was that his eyes didn't burn with the fervent stare of the Converts. Instead, and this was the part I didn't yet understand, he was looking at me as if I was an old friend. Long-expected, missed, and returned in time to catch whatever televised sporting even might be on that night.

So even though I didn't know what to make of the whole situation, I found myself relaxed in his presence. I had to admit that not having any freelance production artist responsibilities made it a lot easier to be there. Despite the humiliation of not being invited into the senior staff meeting, being banished from Watson's list of contacts made it impossible for me to have any agenda with McAlsteinetti. As it stood at that moment, my prospects for future freelance work with a Discount Outlets Unit didn't exist. With my lack of special skills now official, I realized that I could hang out with him for a while. Watson neither knew nor cared what I was doing by then. There was no pressure to achieve anything, no guilt-driven feeling that I should attempt to find a downloadable trial version of SniperShop and try to figure it out. As a result, my sense of well-being expanded and I found myself relaxed in his presence.

McAlsteinetti repositioned the ice packs and grabbed a remote control that had fallen behind one of the cushions. "Any requests?"

It was a little confusing when he pointed the remote up at the rows of monitors and started flicking through channels. I couldn't even tell which of the monitors he was changing. There were too many of them and I couldn't sort out all the movement. As I looked closer, I saw that many of the monitors were tuned to various cable and satellite channels. He wasn't only monitoring the store, but also the entire broadcast world.

What most caught my eyes, however, was that on one of the monitors—

the one where I had seen Watson being seated—one of the suits in the conference room was waving his hands over a detailed relief map of North America. With his hands, he traced a narrow purple belt that stretched from Philly, through southern Ohio and straight west to Denver, then warped a southward bend around the Rockies, headed north again to encircle the Grand Canyon, slithered down through the Virgin River Gorge in Utah, rolled through Las Vegas and charged toward the ocean through Bakersfield, San Bernadino, the Inland Empire and all of LA County. The executive was pointing out the various north and south jogs of the path while Watson looked on, nodding. They intended to build a store that sliced across the entire lower 48 states.

"No," I said in delayed response to McAlsteinetti's question about a request. "Nothing in particular."

At that, he stopped channel-surfing on one of the mid-week college football games between schools from athletic conferences that sounded more like cattle ranches than perennial powerhouses of gridiron talent. Maybe he saw the presence of a football game as a requirement to facilitate our conversation in some way.

"Drink?" he offered, reaching into a squat brown refrigerator jammed between the end of the couch and the wall.

I couldn't tell if he was stalling out of some discomfort of his own or attempting to put me further at ease with the situation.

"Sure," I said, a little nervous that he might want to do flaming *KränkenMeister* shots or something. Although I felt safe and relaxed for the first time since entering the store days earlier, I didn't have the stomach for any celebration. It was possible there were other parties afoot who might have the required skills to close the deal that Watson had undertaken. Lawson and Stanton were now free agents, and who knows who else might have dropped in at the rooftop airfield. I was relieved when he pulled two Kurt's Kolas from the fridge and tossed one in my direction.

"You got my messages. I'm sure of that. My buddy Ken in IT at the

Department assured me he installed the player during your upgrade. But you still don't remember me," he said.

Later, I had to admit that it was kind of him to consider giving me a little preparation time before bringing up our previous meeting. The reality was that the events of the previous days had more than prepared me for things that I neither expected nor understood. I hadn't felt so free of the future in years. Plus, I was rolling with the whole truth thing after revealing to Watson my lack of special skills.

"I'm sorry," I said. With that admission, my mind was freed to jog down the mile-long corridor of memory searching for when I might have met him before, feeling certain that I would have remembered an encounter with the man behind the world's largest discount store chain. But failing, I added, "I sure don't."

"That's okay." McAlsteinetti grinned and spread out his arms. "The Corky Porky. In Springdale."

As soon as he said this, the connections fired and the lines of his face became familiar. Seeing him in commercials earlier in his career, he was only a tiny figure on a TV screen, and it was an adult voice that you heard all over the media as the company expanded worldwide. If his voice sounded at all familiar it was because I and everyone else within radio and TV range of earth had heard it so many thousands of times before. "Kurtis? You're the *bag boy* Kurtis from Corky Porky? The *Jefferson and Grant* Corky Porky in Springdale?"

McAlsteinetti smiled with his own resurfaced memory from our earlier acquaintance.

I was a senior in high school and working part time as a stocker at the Corky Porky Grocery Omnistore on Jefferson Pike in Springdale, Ohio, half way between Zanesville and Columbus. Kurtis was a freshman and came to work at the store after winter break, which meant that our time there overlapped by a few months before my graduation. For our own juvenile entertainment, my fellow stockers and I would send him out to pick up carts in the parking lot on days when even the airport was closed due to high winds and icy conditions. There were other insults propagated using all manner of discarded foodstuffs from the stock room, but these were enacted with such frequency and on so many other younger workers that I had no specific memory of him as the target for our fun. It was easy to see why I didn't recognize him. Back then, he wasn't far enough along in puberty to even have zits yet, and the extended bowl cut was in one of its rhythmic cycles of popularity at the time, so that I never even saw his eyes during the time that he worked there. His voice was that of a boy. These factors must also be considered in the context that, as seniors, my friends and I were focused on getting the hell out of Springdale and failed to consider the feelings of everyone around us, including the stock boys.

Whenever it comes up with Dr. Sandra, the Agency therapist, she reminds me that I was 17 and didn't know any better. That's true, but it doesn't change the fact that some of the things we did to him were cruel. My freedom from the future meant that there was a little more of me available to feel things. Also, sleep deprivation had no doubt helped weaken my usual emotional defenses. A stream of sadness welled-up through a deep crack inside me. I felt horrible. Even if he hadn't become world famous, I think I would have still felt awful about those days. The memories of how we treated him and all the other younger bag boys and some of the older cashiers were ugly. There was no way I could reframe them as anything other than what they were. I stammered and didn't look him in the eyes. "I'm, uh–"

"Call me Kurt," he said, continuing to smile at me like we had run with the bulls in Pamplona, as opposed to bagging and stocking soup in Springdale. There was none of the menace that Barney had described, so it appeared as though he had either forgotten his mistreatment as a Corky Porky bag boy or he had used these years of adolescent suffering to arrive at some transcendent palace of forgiveness. He took a long slurp of the cola can that had his name on it—literally—and turned his attention to the monitors.

Either way, we chatted about what each of us had been doing for a bit. Then we pondered the potential whereabouts of the other stockers and bag boys. After that, he pretty much talked the rest of the night.

I'm sure he thought we had a conversation. But after we caught up on the Cork, I couldn't squeeze in a syllable with a hydraulic crowbar. In addition to the voluminous details that will follow, his message had a certain urgency, which at the time made me wonder why he couldn't pick up a phone and tell somebody else. Or with all his power, why not call a publisher and fire off a few hundred thousand words of non-fiction relating the very same end-of-the-world message that he was imparting to *me*? At the very least, he could have sent a Fritter message proclaiming that the end was near.

As the night went on I started thinking that, in addition to having a whole lot to say, he might have been lonely and wanted another human near him as he unfurled his flight of ideas in regard to the impending collapse of the global economy.

Whether that message might have been offered to anyone else who showed up in his office that night remained unclear. Was I chosen to hear his rant? The progressive downsizing of Watson's team, plus my forgotten childhood connection to McAlsteinetti made the case defensible. Or was I simply someone who stumbled in out of the rain? Who, against lottery-like odds, had known him years before?

I'll never know. Despite its inherent meaninglessness in regard to the national championship, I got hooked on the football game that was on television and didn't hear a lot what he was saying, even though the sound on the television remained off. It was near the end of the fourth quarter and I was trying to follow a last-ditch drive by Acorn State Mechanical Bible College, who were down by 6 to Southeastern Kearney Correctional. I'm not a huge football fan, but it was a good game and I was eager to not think about anything after riding in the XR for almost two full days. I tuned in to McAlsteinetti during commercial breaks but that wasn't enough to keep me following the points he was making about the wholesale dismantling of civilization.

Then a late-night talk show came on and I started missing the connections between his thoughts on the abrupt end to the Age of Information. In part because I was so annoyed with him for not letting me watch the stupid game—but also because those connections seemed a little loose to begin with.

Whatever frayed grasp I had on his words was even further compounded by the fact that I hadn't slept for 36 hours. But even without the all-day-all-night red-eye drive through the store that had resulted in the decimation of our team, I usually couldn't get through the first few minutes of any late-night monologue before starting to nod off.

Thus, all of what followed in the next 9 or 10 hours that I was with McAlsteinetti, I don't remember. The only reason I am able to relate any of it is because Lawson implanted a DeusX Kamera into the fabric of my band jacket when he whacked me on the shoulder, right before we entered the crowd of people heading into the store on Monday morning.

Dalton called me immediately after he got discharged from Walter Reed and helped me wirelessly download the video onto my laptop and disable the device so that Lawson couldn't access it remotely. Watson later explained through a form e-mail that it was standard operating procedure to monitor the activities of freelancers such as myself in this way for billing purposes, although in my case I think they were interested in documentation of a different sort.

Whatever might have been the true motivation for planting the gnat-sized camera onto my shoulder, the sleep onset video termination feature was implemented so that the camera would record when the freelancer—me—was alert and working. The idea behind the termination feature was that if I were snoozing, I would be doing so in a quiet place where no one was around and I wasn't doing anything, anyway. Thus, turning the camera off at these times saved valuable battery life and memory space, without threat of missing anything important that might be happening. From an administrative perspective, however, if I did fall asleep, the broad gaps in the recording could be used to make appropriate deductions from my paycheck.

On one of my visits to see Dalton at The Meadows, before he started working on his poems, he explained to me some of the basics of brain waves and how they related to the multibillion dollar a year remote personal omniscience market. I think I already knew what an electroencephalogram was—a recording of electrical activity in the brain using a number of external electrodes placed on the skull. I had seen those in medical shows on television. But Dalton told me how the DeusX Kamera monitored brain waves through a single electrode that had to be implanted into a small nerve on the back of my shoulder, which Lawson had nailed with a dead-on first stab of my trapezius muscle. This tiny nerve branch connected the camera to the Accessory Nerve, also known as Cranial Nerve XI, which connects to the brainstem. Through this pathway, Dalton explained, the activity in the auditory and visual centers in my brain could be monitored.

The reason for assessing brain activity was simple. When the subject of remote monitoring was awake, the camera stayed on. The most common type of brain activity observed during the waking state in the modern world was so-called beta waves. Alpha waves, the next level of brain waves down the ladder toward sleep correspond to a more relaxed state. Next down the list is theta waves. The problem with theta waves is that the boundary between waking and sleeping is not as clear as we imagine. That is, these waves can occur when someone is awake and relaxed, or in a drowsy half-sleep state that often afflicts people sitting in conferences, meetings, lectures, or, of course, behind the steering wheels of large pieces of machinery and motor vehicles. Recognizing that people experiencing theta brain activity might be either awake or doing head-bobs in a staff meeting, or even in a meditative state, the architects of the DeusX software decided to keep the camera running during these periods.

Dalton further explained that once something called sleep spindles and K-complexes showed up on the brain wave tracing, the person was in deep sleep. These brainwave patterns were so distinctive and so strongly associated with true sleep that they provided the developers with a useful marker to shut down the camera. In addition to power saving, this spared the end-users of DeusX Kamera data the agony of fast-forwarding through hours of footage that depicted a close up of a pillow, or a desk top.

The biggest problem with these parameters was that the mission planners could never have imagined that someone as important as McAlsteinetti would continue to recite his apocalyptic message even as I slept.

With all that said, there should be no doubt in anyone's mind that my video record of that night is incomplete and ripe for misinterpretation. The activities of Ren and her parents, and Hardin and her sister Angela are also fragmentary. Without the aid of the video, and before McAlsteinetti even got to his executive summary of the apocalypse, I do remember the first few minutes of our supposed conversation. After that, things got blurry fast. As far as I can figure, I kept dozing off into light sleep with the camera still running. After the football game ended my level of vigilance further declined. At other times I was awake and kind of remember him talking about some gloomy aspect of the near future of our species. At still other times, the camera turned off as I went into deep sleep. During those times, he might have said a lot more, clarified our way forward a little, as it were, but I have no record of it. Either in my memory or on the DeusX chip that was in the camera.

But with McAlsteinetti the unwitting victim of my hellish high school years, and my immature behavior at the Cork a factor in *his*, I have decided that I cannot let his genius be lost. Thus, spurred on by an ounce of camaraderie mingled with a truckload of remorse, and with Schmerzhogg's film that carries the same message ignored, followed by widespread disinterest of the media, I have attempted to reconstruct the words and images of that night and present them for the world to hear. For the sake of attempting completion, I include the heroic efforts of Klean, however flawed this record might be.

"I was born in Circleville, not far from here," McAlsteinetti begins. "Of Judaeo-Celtic parents who thought my own last name should reflect their individual origins. How the Italian part of it got thrown in there remains a mystery. I was too young to wonder, and no explanation was ever offered by the relevant parties. Anyway, that's a detail that's unlikely to be revealed anytime soon. The more important piece of my origins is that Circleville is the home of the Pumpkin Show."

In the background, there is a sound of rustling of leather, as if something is moving on one of the cushions, and then he continues. "The Pumpkin Show is ranked among the largest agricultural celebrations in the United States and yet is no mean festival. Billed as The Greatest Free Show on Earth, it plays a major role in driving the local economy around Circleville. It should therefore not be surprising to learn that my plant geneticist father was employed by a local seed firm that stood at the vanguard of pumpkin development technologies.

Throughout my earliest years there, he was attempting to create a series of plasmids that would insert themselves into the pumpkin genome and cause the resultant fruit to be seedless, and, of course, sweeter. As I'm sure you're aware, plasmids are pieces of DNA that are usually found swimming around in the cytoplasm of bacteria. The nice thing about plasmids for genetic engineers is that they can force their way into any larger strand of DNA that they want to. They've been around for billions of years and aren't that big of a deal. With plasmids, the sweetness and seedless part of his job was easy. He just found some sweet pumpkins and some seedless pumpkins, found the DNA that codes for sweet and seedless, and stuck those genes into the plasmid—which he then inserted into the DNA of the designer pumpkin."

At this point, I should state that during McAlsteinetti's discussion of the Pumpkin Show, the DeusX Kamera was also capturing whatever was occurring on the multiple monitors in his office. Although the images are small, I have been able to zoom the video on my laptop at home using SnipperShop in order make out faces and create a partial record of events happening concurrent to McAlsteinetti's historical and subquantum rampage. On a grouping of screens in the top right corner of the video field of view, which appeared to monitor the winter holiday section of the store surrounding the White Aisle, I saw Ren, Quinoa, Pesto, Hardin and Angela, plus a few braves wearing purple buckskins, moving in the direction of the Mezzanine. Their faces were intermittently illuminated by the multicolored displays as they moved. Angela, who looked fully focused and aware and was no longer wearing the fake plastic braids, led the group through the maze of trees and lighted wire-frame animals and mythical figures. Hardin, keeping her promise, had brought her back.

"More challenging, however," McAlsteinetti continued speaking to me while I was in a half-sleep. "Was the company's goal of causing the pumpkin to puree itself after it had grown to an optimum size. The idea of having a pumpkin that would convert itself into pie filling was extremely attractive not only to local farmers, but also to those who stood to profit handsomely during the Pumpkin Show, even if they weren't officially part of the festival. But there wasn't just local interest. The international pumpkin community was also quite interested in this project. My father quickly solved the part about making the inside of the pumpkin moosh itself. This was simply a matter of creating a DNA-based pumpkin mass index calculator plasmid that he inserted into pumpkin chromosomes that would cause individual pumpkins to monitor their own height, weight and circumference relative to their age. Of course, there was no *conscious* monitoring of the pumpkin's size—it wasn't as if he gave the pumpkin a nervous system that was able to sense anything, let alone *monitor* its own height, weight and circumference. There were no pumpkins looking in mirrors and thinking *'Oh, look, I'm fat, I think I'll just go smash myself.'* Instead, and I'm still proud of my old pop for thinking of this, the plasmid he created that coded for sweet and seedless also coded for a series of proteins that changed *shape* in response to changes in the hydrostatic pressure within the pumpkin cells. As the pumpkins got bigger and heavier, the proteins continually changed shape as the pressure inside the pumpkin cells increased. Once a critical size corresponding to maximum suitability for being liquefied and poured into a pie crust was reached, the proteins would be pressed into a conformation that allowed them to bind to the Fas death-domain within the cell which would initiate a novel Caspase-8-independent Fas death-domain mediated apoptotic pathway."

On the screen monitoring the senior staff conference room, Lawson arrived in the room wearing a sports coat over his Hawaiian shirt, surrounded by assistants—or bodyguards?—in suits.

McAlsteinetti doesn't even flinch and continues his discussion about auto-destructive pumpkins as Lawson sat down at the conference table across from Watson on the monitor.

"Okay, that's a mouthful," says McAlsteinetti. "But mind you, this was long before recombinant squash and gourd workers had even mapped out all the interactions that begin with binding of a protein, *any protein*, to the death domain of the Fas protein, which is then followed by the irreversible cascade of protein interactions that culminates with the death of a cell at its own hand. Okay, not at its own hand, of course, since individual cells don't have hands any more than pumpkins can look in mirrors. It's more like death at its own cytoplasm. What I mean to say is that the successive binding of proteins along this pathway leads to the cell killing itself, and this is called apoptosis. It's a naturally occurring pathway within all eukaryotic cells, including our own. In the case of my father's work, without really understanding the big picture, he had arrived at the way of initiating this progression of protein binding that eventually caused every cell inside the pumpkin to essentially shoot holes into its cell membrane and then just die. My father called it the PieWay, which we all agreed was a silly name, but this is the kind of thing that geneticists get away with all the time. Sonic Hedgehog, for example, is the given formal scientific name for a gene that codes for a protein that helps direct traffic during the embryologic development of vertebrates. Including humans, of all things. Anyway, the PieWay worked. Too well in fact."

"Test farmers would come out to their patches in the morning and find puddles of liquid where there were noble pumpkins the night before. He was working on a mechanism to preserve the rind and skin of the pumpkins so that they would serve as a sort of collecting vessel for the insides that became liquid when a black tractor with no markings showed up at his lab one night. Witnesses said it was one of those monster tractors like they have at tractor pulls. Have you ever seen a tractor pull, K? These tractors have like 20-foot-wide tires and flames come shooting out their exhaust. They're basically monster trucks with bigger wheels on the back and little wheels on the front. Of course, there was no license plate on it. It was probably registered with the Agricultural Intelligence Agency. Typical."

The faces of Ren, Hardin and Angela appear on a video screen monitoring a hidden corridor in the Mezzanine. I believe that Angela's role as one of the planners of Bison Pricin' must have given her detailed knowledge of these passageways. Quinoa, Pesto and the costumed braves enter an abandoned employee break room in the sub floor beneath the Mezzanine with a security guard. Pesto presents a handmade beaded belt to the security guard in exchange for dusty boxes of unused equipment which the two lads and the braves then haul away.

McAlsteinetti appears to glance sideways and smile at the sight of the young men taking away the boxes, which he sees from the edge of his vision. Still, he continues: "Even less surprising than the black, fire-shooting tractor that took my father away in the middle of the night, however, was when the entire watermelon crop of central Asia turned to mush the following summer. The CIA said 'oh well' and blamed it on a weather pattern they called the Trans-

Zagros Tropospheric Inversion. But none of my climatologist buddies had ever heard of such a weather pattern. The fate of the watermelons sounded similar to that of my father's experimental pumpkins, and I was thus able to embrace the belief that he was still alive out there. Enslaved as a watermelon killer maybe, or worse, but alive.

"After that, my mom didn't feel safe anymore and we moved to a trailer park in Springdale. By then she was paranoid they would find us if she went back to work for any of the colleges or universities around there, so she took a job waiting tables at a diner. It didn't pay much, as you can imagine, but tuition was free for me at the SuperCollider school, which she had re-enrolled me in under a fake name. All she really needed was to earn enough to pay the modest rent on our trailer.

"Things went pretty well like that for a long time. We got to know our neighbors and found they were just like us. My mom ended up getting together with some of the ladies once a week to drink wine coolers and watch reruns of *MacGyver*, which, of course, have been continuously on TV since the turn of the century. Sweetly, charmingly in fact, she claimed that she enjoyed the technical aspects of the show, the gadgets and stuff. But I have no doubt that she, like many of the other ladies, was more captivated by the eternal hotness of Richard Dean Anderson. She was quite lonely by then.

"Our life at the trailer park was simple. I studied aerospace engineering and cosmology during the day. She served omelets, burgers and late-night coffee to regulars from around town. When we were together, she made me read huge stacks of literature and history that I wasn't getting in school. Ancient cultures were her field at Antioch, and she was particularly fascinated by the Indus Civilization. Which, as you know, falls into the 'where are they now?' bin of civilizations. Along with the Etruscans and the people of Kush. One millennium you have these great brick-paved streets with a carefully-planned sewage run-off system, maybe some pyramids to let the surrounding barbarians know you're ruling things, and the next thing you know you're a mound. With peasants who can't even read the inscriptions on the bits of rubble that are scattered on the surface of your mound. And sheep grazing on top of you. Textbooks a few thousand years later will devote a small portion of a single chapter to the ruins of your sophisticated waste-disposal techniques and depict a few of your household goods with captions describing their supposed ceremonial functions."

On the video screen Hardin and Angela both embrace Ren, who is crying. The two older women appear to be encouraging her. Wiping her tears, Ren appears to be strengthened by the words and leaps up the stairway and out of the field of view. Hardin and Angela watch her for a few seconds and then exit the range of the surveillance camera via an unarmed service entrance to the darkness of the store outside the Mezzanine.

On the DeusX video, McAlsteinetti is watching this scene and is moved. He is unable to hide his admiration for the courage of these women, though it is impossible to tell which part of it touches him most: Ren advancing into the unknown ahead, or Hardin and Angela heading back to face the darkness inside the store.

He continues: "At the fringes of serious archaeology in that same future, an army of wackos will be convinced that your civilization both arrived and departed earth in a huge mother ship that traveled from the neighborhood of Proxima Centauri using a technology that, despite its ability to safely traverse between stars, will ironically not be able to survive being buried under a mound of dirt for a thousand years...and will be mysteriously lost forever. The argument will be given that this technology does not involve metal and electronic components which constitute our machines. These same nut jobs will meet regularly in the low-budget convention facilities of airport hotels, or whatever the futuristic equivalent of such hotels will be. Meeting yearly, they'll all get together and sip Mai Tais to discuss the new findings in your mound that support their hypothesis that your civilization blasted off into space in the aforementioned mother ship after the rainfall patterns changed catastrophically, or some river changed course, or after you hunted the local giant ground sloths into extinction. If you haven't noticed, the fall of entire civilizations is often blamed on the loss of water, or some animal that went extinct about the same time that the civilization is believed to have checked out. I use the ground sloth metaphorically, of course.

"These fruitcakes will also attempt to decipher your inscriptions—believing that the spray-painted scrawls on the crumbling walls of your former cities contain detailed instructions on how those who attend enough of their conventions might escape to a world of higher understanding without the trouble of stepping onto the mother ship. This is your fate as a mound. The best parts of you are lost. The rest misunderstood forever. Co-opted by earnest kooks at yearly conventions for eternity.

"But, I digress.

"Life went on quite pleasantly for my mother and I in Springdale up until the time that our landlord, his name was Russell and that's all I remember about him, decided to almost double our rent at the trailer park. I know my mom would have preferred if I could have focused on school alone, but the tips she was getting at the Dine-O-Mighty in Springdale weren't huge. Which led me, of course, to pursue employment at the Corky Porky."

Ren appears on another of the video screens, creeping along a concourse of offices and kiosks on the professional services level of the Mezzanine. Probably one level down from where McAlsteinetti and I were at that moment. Passing by the 24-hour DentAll Clinic, Ren hides her face from the receptionist.

"I have only the vaguest recollection of some prank involving ricotta cheese," McAlsteinetti chuckles. "And—"

His monologue cuts off there, which I believe coincides with the first time that my sleep spindles fired and the DeusX Kamera turned itself off. The time stamp on the video feed indicates that I was out for 21 minutes after that point, during which time I have no idea what McAlsteinetti said, if anything. I must have remained a little groggy after I woke up, because even though the video clicks on as soon as I was conscious again, I have no specific recollection of these next few minutes of his monologue. My first real memories from waking up, at least what I believe to be real memories, begin about the time he started talking about the final resting place of all human knowledge.

"— but mom had no intention of ending her association with the women she'd met at the trailer park," McAlsteinetti was saying.

I believe this is one of the key points he was making about the well-documented fact that his mother handed him an envelope containing $11,000 on the day she left Ohio in the company of a group of women who have never been identified, a few weeks after his 18th birthday. Witnesses at the trailer park describe them as early middle-aged, though with youthful and radiant demeanor. They were driving a bright-purple painted school bus loaded up with thousands of old books and manuscripts. Biographers have speculated that this school bus was the inspiration behind McAlsteinetti choosing purple as the All Mart corporate color. A bus bearing that description was sighted in northwestern Montana a few days later, but McAlsteinetti's mother was never seen again. All stories about his success begin the chronicle of the All Mart with this day and the envelope, with each new book including new supposed sightings of the school bus.

My head was clouded from sleep, but I thought there might have been a little moisture around his own eyes as he got to this moment of his childhood. But the video was a little smudged and I couldn't tell for sure. All I can figure is that I had slumped my shoulder onto the couch while sleeping and smeared some greasy potato chip dust onto the lens.

Soon after that, I remember rolling over and sitting up to glare at him for waking me up. Since the following segment of the video is clear again, I have hypothesized that my rolling motion allowed the lens to somewhat clear itself as I rubbed my shoulder across the couch cushion. After that, I attempted to go back to sleep by laying straight back on the couch and covering my face with a small pillow—which allowed the camera on my shoulder to remain pointed in McAlsteinetti's direction.

"Are you familiar with superstrings?" he began again. The video shows him locking his gaze onto one of the monitor screens overhead, which by great fortune was in the field of view of my shoulder camera.

On the screen Ren rushes forward to embrace a man who is standing behind the counter of the 24-hour AllDent Oral Care Center kiosk. The man—

who has the same eyes and smile as Ren and is clearly her father—passes off a new set of dentures to a customer and then closes up the kiosk.

In the background I giggle and mumble something from my half-sleep.

McAlsteinetti didn't acknowledge whatever it was I said and continued watching the screen. "For a long time, physicists have been trying to peacefully reconcile the elegance of Einstein's general theory of relativity and the world of quantum mechanics. I'm not sure how much physics you've had along the way, but there are two theories of relativity. The *special* theory is the one that quantifies how time slows down as you approach the speed of light. The *general* theory of relativity is the one that describes how massive objects distort space around them and thus impart gravity to objects that are nearby or happen to travel past them in space. Actually, it's not just massive objects that warp space, but, on the contrary, any object that has any mass at all is able to warp space. The upside is that we humans are individually of such relatively small mass that we don't distort the space around us very much. Which is good, because otherwise we'd be flying into each other every time we got near another human being. The earth and the sun, by contrast, are of sufficient mass to really get a good grip on space, warp it with feeling, as it were, and thus keep things in orbit around them. The moon, for example, according to the general theory of relativity, is continually falling into the warped space that surrounds the earth. Our moon's orbit is the curved path of this continuous falling. Simultaneously, the whole earth-moon system is falling into the even more dramatically warped space that surrounds the sun. Due to the earth's velocity, however, this falling is defined by a curved path, our orbit. Which, like the moon's orbit, is fairly stable over the short term, speaking in terms of cosmic time on the order of billions of year. This relative stability of our orbit is a really good thing because otherwise, earth would be zinging off into space right now, which would quickly though temporarily surpass global warming as another thing for countries to argue about."

On the screen monitoring the conference room, Klean is standing at the head of the table pointing out inflection points on a series of graphs. Looking at the zoomed video images over multiple viewings, I have determined that one of the panning cameras in the room captured what was being projected onto the main presentation screen in the conference room at that moment. The text on the single MetaPoint slide was simple black type on a shaded purple background, laid out by Klean himself after arrival in his new position. The words read: "Don't worry!"

McAlsteinetti continues his monologue. "Be that as it may, at the other extreme of scale from the solar system, down at the level of individual protons and electrons, we find that things are not as elegant and orderly as Einstein preferred. On the contrary, things start to get a little paradoxical, which always spooks the old timers in any field of inquiry—Einstein included. To wit, it turns out that photons, the fundamental particle of light, behave both as particles and as waves. Not so kooky with all the craziness of the modern world, huh? Well, turns out that such a duality could be established for all the fundamental particles you learned about in 8th grade. So, it *should* be a little unsettling for you.

"The electron is not the tiny blue beach ball flying around the center of an atom that you were taught, but a weirdo-hybrid wave function—an equation—whose very existence in a particular area of space can only be predicted by a particular *probability* that it might be there at any given instant in time. In the quantum world, you can't pin anything down. The energy and location of all fundamental particles are expressed as a *probability* of being such and such an energy at location X. Or Y. How would you like to be told that you're an equation and only *likely* to be here now? The electron might or might not be in a particular place around the atom today. Now it's here. And now it's over there. There's a chance it won't show up at all. Or that it will tunnel right through the concrete wall of your electron examination chamber. Scandalous! This led to Einstein's admonition against divine dice rolling. Thou Shalt Not Conduct the Universe from Vegas, Baby. You can imagine the indigestion in the academic physics meetings of the day. I hate to break the bad news to the puritans of reason, but *somebody's* rolling some dice with the universe. The wave functions describing particles have been repeatedly verified experimentally throughout much of the twentieth century. As a result of this agreement of math with reality, quantum mechanics is now almost universally accepted in the world of theoretical physics."

On the monitor screen, Klean had finished his presentation and Lawson was now striding back and forth in front of the conference table. I didn't need the zoom on SnipperShop to read the details of Lawson's single slide. There was a graph with an arrow directed upward to the top right corner of the screen. The type reads: *Expand to infinity. And then expand some more!*

Glancing at the screen, McAlsteinetti grins, shakes his head and continues: "Fortunately, for Einstein and the rest of us, these effects of uncertainty overall cancel each other out as you move up to the scale of macroscopic objects such as humans and airplanes. So that anytime we're flying we're never suddenly without a pilot, or without an airplane for that matter. The particles making up the pilot and the airplane are so numerous and the scale of the space they occupy is so large relative to the wave functions of protons and electrons that, overall, the pilot and the airplane remain tangible, and with reliable locations in the space that they happen to be occupying. Which, I stress, is a great source of comfort for all those who dare to travel in airplanes.

"None of this is immediately relevant to why I'm building a store that will envelop a huge piece of North America. But it's part of the bigger picture, which we shall see.

"Continuing our journey into smaller and smaller distances, if you go *further down* beneath the microscopic level, ridiculously smaller than the level where electrons might or might not exist, the quantum uncertainty about the location and energy of particles increases. Actually it doesn't simply increase, it skyrockets by multiple orders of magnitude, which leads to chaos. Not the cute chaos caused by kids in a daycare center, nor the more nightmarish chaos of failed coup attempts, but chaos so extreme that any vestige of reality becomes completely obscured. The result is that what we think of as tiny little plots of quiet, peaceful space in the universe are actually a rip-roaring foam of particles that form spontaneously from nothing. From nothing. Just like that. These particles take a few well-deserved billionths of a second to find an antiparticle partner, at which time they collide and annihilate each other in a flash that returns the energy that created them back into the void. Space is not empty. Anyone who tells you it is, is a liar. There is no interstellar nothingness. It's all something. Electromagnetic fields gyrate wildly. Familiar notions of space and time break down. Our trusted friend Euclid, whose points and grids keep us geometrically snuggled in our personal realities, is unavailable for comment. In the last few centuries, Reason has been the obedient pool boy of science, whistled into service to skim the leaves off our clear view of the physical world. Along the way, the matter that makes up the clear water in the pool was thought to be indestructible. But *these* are now the sentiments that get self-satisfied chortles from the junior physics faculty in the back of the room. Reason, despite his elegant strokes with the skimmer, can't get the pool much cleaner than downright muddy in the quantum world. And matter, even though we're immersed in it, is both created and destroyed all around us at every second of the day in the most violent possible way.

"Yet violent and elegant rarely have lunch together publicly, and to compound the situation even more for the physics damage control team, each time someone tried to unify quantum mechanics and general relativity mathematically, bring gravity and the easy-listening music-of-the-spheres into the headbanger brothel of the quantum world, as it were, they kept coming up with results that contained infinity.

"Which, of course, is an absurd result. What does it mean that something has an infinite probability of happening? It either happens or it doesn't, right? Or, there is a percent chance that it will actually happen. A probability of one implies a one hundred percent chance of something happening. A probability of one that it will rain means that there's a one hundred percent chance that it will rain. If there's a 50% chance that it will rain, that's a probability of 0.5. Flip a coin. With a probability of 0.5, half the time it will rain and half the time it won't. If it rains *harder,* the probability of it raining doesn't increase to more than one. It's already raining. Your probability of one point zero corresponded to whether or not it would rain at all. *Harder* rain has a probability of its own that's between zero and one. It will either rain hard or it won't, or with some *chance* of it raining harder somewhere in between. If something has a probability greater than one, and infinity is quite a bit greater than one, that thing doesn't *more* happen if it does happen, or superhappen, if you will. It happens or it doesn't happen. It either is or it isn't. Or is it? Should we even bother to ponder what a probability of infinity means?

"Then along came superstring theory, or, more formally M-Theory, which provides a means of unifying quantum theory and general relativity and completely absolving us all of those boorish infinities. The basic premise is that instead of thinking of fundamental particles as points in space with a particular mass that might or might not be moving at a particular velocity, individual particles can, and should, be thought of as extremely short, one-dimensional strings. Like any string you keep around the house, you can loop it, wiggle it, dangle it in front of your cat. Whatever. The point is that these strings can be either closed into a loop or open-ended, and they can *vibrate*. And here's the money thought inherent in string theory: it is the vibrational *patterns* of these strings, and whether or not they are closed or open or extended into membranes, combined with the frequency and intensity of their oscillations, that determines the mass and charge of *all* fundamental particles of matter. Including, conveniently, those thought to transmit the force of *gravity* throughout our universe, which are called gravitons. *'Gravity has its own particle?'* you say. Well, sort of. If you believe in particles as particles. It's really easier to think of them as mathematical entities that add up to make stuff. And stuff can be either matter or energy.

"But it gets even better. And here's where my motivation behind the Black Light Blowouts might at last take on a hint of sanity.

"In order to completely account for all the fundamental particles of our known world—including the whimsically named muons, neutrinos and quarks—string theory requires that additional dimensions of space exist so that strings can vibrate *into them*. In order to vibrate at whatever frequency and amplitude are required to make them either a photon or an electron, or a whatever particle, strings need extra room, extra dimensions, in which to vibrate around in. It's a little bit like having some hidden closets around your house in which to store things that you don't interact with in your everyday life. You still own them and they're part of your household, you just don't see them.

"The reason we don't see these extra 6 or 7 dimensions, depending on which equations you subscribe to, is because they're tightly curled up at the same scale as the strings themselves. In our known world, we can only see length, height and width—the familiar 3-dimensions of spatial relationships, which are soberly accounted for by Euclid, as I have already mentioned, who was no fun whatsoever at cocktail parties. And we can indirectly observe the fourth dimension, *time*, through changes in objects and persons. The graying of my hair, for example. And yours, of course. The gradual decay of collagen in my skin. The progressive erosion of the Rocky Mountains into a few piles of gravel lying out on the prairie. The rolled-up dimensions of superstring theory contain space alright, and possibly some time dimensions, but that space and time is inverted beneath, or involuted within, or curled up like a roly-poly bug far below the smallest things in our 4-dimensional frame of reference.

"Which is, I stress, very small. Small enough to not be noticed and not interfere with the work of our familiar world.

"Still, just because they're not noticeable doesn't mean they're not useful. The smart dollar in the world of business looks for two things: space and oscillation. Trust me, oscillation is the next big thing. In my earlier years, I might have cared about understanding the nature of these little strings. I might have even ended up working at the Salzporck Particle Accelerator if not for the unexpected success of my first All Mart store. In fact, whenever I drive over the Hyperconducting Hypercollider that underlies major parts of Ohio, Indiana, Illinois, Wisconsin and that one tiny corner of South Dakota, I occasionally get a little wistful about my days smashing atoms at the Super Collider Charter School. More often, however, I merely look for opportunities to use my enormous blessings to assist my fellow humans.

"Which leads me nearer to the peak of my current discourse, since I know you're still wondering why I basically give away so much stuff.

"The Quantum Paradox Encoding of Information piggybacks an oscillatory signal onto photons that vibrate in the curled-up dimensions of time and space. By carefully modulating and monitoring this signal, we can both store information in these curled-up dimensions and transmit information *through* the quantum void. Well, big deal, you say. Isn't that what radio and TV do? Modulate a signal on a carrier wave? Wireless internet and other applications of electromagnetic radiation have allowed us to send information through space for decades. Aren't quantum computers already operating at top secret labs in Silicon Valley? What would be the big advantage of using superstring vibrations to transmit information using the quantum void?

"Well, I told you why it would be a big advantage but you didn't catch it because it looks like you're sound asleep. But here it is, anyway. We can also *store* information in these curled-up dimensions in the quantum void. Current information systems require a digital or analog encoding of information that is accessed from servers, where it is stored, and then transmitted to the end user. In the Quantum Paradox Encoding, or QPE as its known on the street, all the information you want or need is around us at all times. By adjusting the probabilities of the desired information being near the end user by the touch of a pressure-sensor on your lifestyle device, the information doesn't have to travel anywhere. It's already there when you need it. Every note of music, every second of every film and television show, and each digital picture ever taken by anyone at any time and under any circumstances will be available instantaneously to the user. That's the obvious thing. You won't have to wait to download anything. Whatever you're watching or listening to will begin playing immediately without any dependence on the speed of wires or hard drives.

"There are additional advantages of using such a system of information technology. First, as I have already hinted at, these billions of hours of music videos, movies, television shows, plus trillions of full-color web pages will occupy the rolled-up hidden dimensions that are predicted by superstring theory. In this capacity, media content providers are no longer limited by the curvature of the earth, the thickness of wires and cables, and the maintenance costs of satellites. Nor are they limited by what can be stored in the vicinity of earth. The quantum foam in which strings exist extends to the very edge of the universe, at which point no one really knows what happens. There might be black holes in between, of course, but up until the time that we have to deal with storing information around black holes, we can use every possible cubic light year in the universe to store media that people will want. Actually, come to think of it, with the extra dimensions, they won't even be speaking in terms of cubic light years anymore. They'll become octantic, decantic light years? Whatever Greek or Latin name is ponied up by the engineers to account for volume in greater than three dimensions.

"Of course, the implications are staggering. You could access a complete library of movies at a remote mountain campsite—with no added weight to your backpack. You could record every second of your child's first eighteen years and have access to it through a tiny QPE player locket, or keychain that you carried with you at all times. You could program a sequence of songs onto your OmegaPod that would play continuously for the rest of your life. The possibilities for modes and volumes of delivery are literally unimaginable once we abandon our current reference of three spatial dimensions and one time dimension.

"Like every new advancement, however, there's bound to be a drawback or two—which I believe is why so far you can only buy QPE players in Taiwan. One of the main problems with Quantum Paradox Encoding is that media lawyers can't figure out a way to copyright protect or restrict access to the information that gets into the extra dimensions in the quantum void. Unlike the internet, which relies upon carefully guarded servers with multiple layers of security to protect information that can only be accessed by authorized users, once somebody uploads a piece of Quantum Paradox Encoded information, it's in there forever, and anyone can get to it.

"Why then would media companies choose to offer their content in QPE format at all? Because there will always be *more new content* that someone will want to access! In the quantum void, just as on the electromagnetic spectrum, content is king. And there's an added bonus: upload a 30-second ad to the string void and it's also in there forever. Running continuously. Reaching ears and eyeballs for eternity.

"But this situation becomes even more problematic. As I see it, it would only be a matter of years before *all* humanly generated information will end up encoded into these hidden dimensions. Including stuff that isn't even close to being entertaining. The electronic archives for parking tickets in the City of Chicago currently requires every cubic mile of an abandoned iron mine in the Upper Peninsula of Michigan—and that's in cubic closest packed silicon-tetrahedron encoded flash memory modules. Chicago will clearly need more storage space for their parking ticket records. And so will everyone else.

"Before long, *everyone*, okay, so I really mean every human being who attempts to navigate in the world of modern technology, will by necessity start putting all their valued information into these hidden dimensions because storage space in our visible universe simply won't hold it all. Birthday party pictures, home videos, every movie ever made.

"So, everything will be in there, and everything will be shared. Once all this entertainment and information gets in there and becomes freely available to everyone, any kind of *competition* will become meaningless. With freely flowing knowledge of all things immediately accessible, anyone can make billions on the commodities market in a single day. Remember, information on *how to play the commodities market* will also be available. If you'd prefer to make your billions in real estate, all the market predictions, trends, angles, lessons learned and listings will also be available. Anyone who wants to be a billionaire, and that's almost everyone I know, and probably *most* that you know, will be able to do so with relative ease—so most everyone *would*. Here in the digital age, the flow of information is still restricted, despite claims of so-called democratization. Not everyone has a computer. But everyone will have a QPE player. My friend Ken in IT and your new friend Klean will see to that. I wish I could say I hired him, but that's not exactly the case."

On a video screen close to the one displaying the conference room, Ren and her father are jogging along a hallway. Ren's father looks nervous as he stops to show his purple ID badge to a security guard who stops them.

"Of course, there are also numerous drawbacks to this situation. The most basic downside is that, well, everyone would be billionaires. Very well-informed billionaires. And no one would want to, or have to, work at Tengo Taco anymore. Which would be a problem for me personally, because no one would want to work in my store. Entire industries will collapse because there will be no more factory workers to sit in front of the television and longingly watch the UltimoBall Jackpot each Wednesday night. They won't have to play the lottery; they will have made their own millions on wheat futures. There will be absolutely no incentive whatsoever that anyone can think of to go to work if you become wealthy through manipulation of information that you pluck from your QPE phone. Even the people who farm wheat will decide that trading wheat futures is more profitable. But you see where this is headed. From every available frame of reference, no one will be able to think of any reason whatsoever to go out into the stress-filled, knee-crunching, back-slapping, nose-grinding, humiliation-drenched endeavor that we have the audacity to call 'employment.'

"Many people, however, a very large number of people, in fact, *will* want to be actors and pop stars, and produce their own music, films and television series—which will continue to fuel both the demand and production of media content that I mentioned above."

"So, you wouldn't be bored, with all that media out there. But, obviously, financial institutions will collapse in the face of postwar Germany style inflation. With everyone holding billions, whoever has a store with any goods still in it, and there won't be many, will charge six figures for the proverbial loaf of bread. And you'll be lucky to even find any.

"Governments, principalities and seats of power will also subsequently crumble. With everyone knowing everything there is to know about Constitutional law and international trade, suddenly regular working folk like you and me will know what it means when the United States sells a whole bunch of machine tools to Bulgaria, or why those people on television are so skinny, or, critically, which of the 300 or so other countries in the world are not even considering launching an invasion on our borders. Which, I can tell you now, is basically all of them. So, with such knowledge in the hands of common citizens, politicians will simply no longer be able to rule using the timed-honored methods of fear and lies. *Finally*, in the long sad history of this membrane we call civilization, every politician on earth will be laughed out of existence. The military can be reduced to the size of local scout troop, with a budget to match. Homicidally convenient ideologies will lose their appeal. In the absence of organized armies, paid militias and elected sociopaths, wars as we know them will finally cease.

"Then things start to get really interesting. With bloated Swiss Bank accounts in every pot, and no place to spend them because no one works in stores or factories that makes anything anymore, and with no politicians to blame for the condition of the economy, most people will decide that they're better off growing tomatoes and raising some goats in the extra 12 bedrooms of the mansion they bought with their first ten million dollars. Technology will quickly lose its appeal. With everything equalized, there will be nothing to gain from any of the thousand devices that will allow you access to the sub-quantum field of information.

Some people will log off and start to make shoes because they *liked* working with leather. Others will bake bread and pastry because they *liked* the warm, comforting smell of yeast rising early in the morning. And then people will trade their goat milk or bread for shoes again and everyone will be content, and as long as people put in an honest day's work in their own gardens or workshops, they'll have enough to eat.

"Oh, there'd be a few marauding bands who insist on pillaging, but even these ne'er-do-wells will have Madinera's complete works available for their listening and viewing pleasure. Her complete discography, concert footage, films, books, sacramentals, children's fashion shows and consensual broadcasts will be available on their QPE players. Mostly they'll be glued to the dirt floor of their huts enjoying every possible camera angle of her career and won't come into the villages too terribly often to steal food.

"Trust me, this is the end. The entire planet will sink back into the Dark Ages. But it won't seem so bad, as Dark Ages go. You might say that I'm actually trying to facilitate this process at multiple levels. 'Bison Pricing' is one small part of my greater plan for the future of our species. Of course, you do understand that I use the term 'Dark Ages' as a purely descriptive term. Historically speaking, it's inaccurate. What I mean to say is that Dark Ages does not describe a discrete period in history but is used colloquially to describe a span of the Medieval Period in which ignorance, poverty and intractable disease occupied much of the world's people for most of their foreshortened lives. In Europe, anyway. Most of the world did fine during these supposed Dark Ages. The Chinese, for example. The Maya. The Mali. Anyway, please understand that I am using Dark Ages loosely, which doesn't make it any less appealing, nor does it soften my conviction that this will all occur quite soon, whether I'm involved or not.

"But this is precisely why I am here in this place in this particular time in history. I thought differently about it all until recently. I am creating this store as a refuge for the meek during these dark years. Which don't have to be dark if we choose otherwise."

On the central video screen, Lawson's bodyguards position themselves behind Klean's chair in the conference room. Lawson stands again, says something which is not heard on the video, but which causes the other executives to burst out laughing. Watson, barely visible at the corner of the tiny screen, looks ill.

McAlsteinetti stops talking for the first time and looks up at the conference room monitor as Klean stands up and shouts something at Lawson. McAlsteinetti's face tenses as Klean is hauled out of the room by Lawson's personal assistants.

On yet another screen close to the conference room, Ren and her father open a doorway in a dim, deserted hallway.

McAlsteinetti looks back down in the direction of where I am sleeping. "The messiest part of this whole thing, and something no one on either side of the debate seems to want to talk about, is that way down there underneath the floor boards of both the graviton and the Higgs boson, everything appears to be interconnected. Not with like a network of pipes or wires but completely inseparable. It's all one thing. The ultimate conclusion is pretty simple, and I do kind of have to hurry because I'm going to get my ass dragged out of here in a few short minutes—is that, if everything is interdependent, then nothing is completely random. The dice is always loaded. And always will be. Einstein can play his violin in peace, wherever whatever he was may be. The good news is that some, er, hm, *people*, have known about this forever and have taken steps to…*assist* is a good word. To assist humans in not completely destroying some of the nicer gains we've made since the technological boom of stone tools. Rose gardens, for example. Eggplant parmigiana. Single malt whiskeys. *Amazing Grace* played on bagpipes. All worth keeping, in my opinion. To that end, there has been an intervention, if you—"

The door behind McAlsteinetti opens and Ren and her father close in around where I am crashed on the couch.

"It's clear to the edge of the fields," Ren's father says. "Thanks to Ren here, all the roof workers are down at the Bison Pricin' after party."

"After party?" McAlsteinetti laughs.

Ren smiles and shrugs. "We followed the Watson team and watched the whole thing from the cliffs. All the barbecued meat bummed me out a little, but I still hated to see the leftovers get wasted. So I sorta' spread the word. Seemed like a win-win. It's nice to meet you."

"Your father's told me a lot about your project," McAlsteinetti says. "Which we've been following with interest. Hope you don't mind." Struggling to his feet, he gives Ren a brisk hug and turns to her father.

Ren's father grabs a loaded daypack from behind the couch and drapes McAlsteinetti's arm over his shoulder. "You two can bond later over some tofu scramble. Let's move."

McAlsteinetti looks down at me, as if speaking to the camera on my shoulder as he is being helped out the door by Ren and her father. "I'm a derivative, we're all derivative." McAlsteinetti flinches in pain and hobbles closer to the door. "Yet the derived equation solves the problem with limits."

On the conference room video screen, Watson is disturbed and pleads with Lawson.

"We cannot change our nature as derivatives. The derivative of ourselves identifies the rate of change of ourselves at any point in history. Using the derived equation, the limits of our function can be identified. But to solve the problem with limits you must abandon the original equation and use the derived equation. The solution of the derived equation is dependent on the exponential values within the original equation."

Ren's father looks outside in the hallway, visible from where I am sleeping. He nods to McAlsteinetti.

Ren and her father move the injured McAlsteinetti closer to the doorway. He is in pain but understands the need for haste. He continues speaking as they struggle to get him out through the door. "Did you ever see *The Formula?* Great movie."

"Please!" Ren's father wants to move right now while the hallway remains clear.

"It's Brando. He has this great line," McAlsteinetti says, and then does what I consider to be the worst Brando since Brando did Brando in *The Island of Dr. Moreau.* *"I'm an Arab. You're an Arab. We're all Arabs."*

Ren closes her arm around McAlsteinetti's waist and uses all her strength to get him through the door.

McAlsteinetti smiles back toward me, half waves his hand that is hung down over Ren's shoulder, and does his best early-electrifying-stud Brando as opposed to old trippy Brando. *""I coulda' been a contenda. I coulda' been som-body."*

He turns, uses his good leg to help propel himself and the three of them disappear down the hallway.

""K!" Watson's voice hissed through the open doorway. "Are you awake?"

"I am now," I groaned.

"Listen," she whispered, "my meeting's all done and I was thinking about heading down to the executive Focuzzi for a little dip. I was wondering if you wanted to join me?"

The door moved open a few inches wider and I could see the tan, smooth, contours of her torso.

I tried to sit up and not look too eager and was surprised by how calm and confident I felt. I'm not sure how it happened, I guess I must have changed after watching the game with McAlsteinetti, but I was wearing a gold lamé jockstrap and it all seemed so right. My quadriceps muscles rippled as I stood up, and my 12-pack abs undulated in the soft radiance from the row of monitors. My biceps flexed and glistened in the light as I moved to open the door for Watson. It seemed weird, but McAlsteinetti was still on his couch going on and on about gravity and medieval Europe, but I couldn't understand a word he was saying. The door swung open and I saw Watson standing there, her long dark hair lifted by the breeze flowing down the hall. A black pinstripe jogging bra strained against the taut, black diamond hardness and pointed presence of her breasts. A matching thong wrapped around the smooth, marble contours of her thighs.

"I was hoping you'd bring your special skills," she said. Without hesitation, her eyes met mine.

"Mais, oui," I said, draping a silk Happi coat over my shoulders. Continuing to meet her gaze, I stepped into a pair of red leather flip-flops studded with chrome rivets that were waiting at my feet on the floor and moved toward the door. I hadn't spoken that much French since high school, but I could see by the faint parting of her lips that she enjoyed it.

"And what about the graphs you promised for my *dees-sertation*?" It was Leila, the Tunisian Babel Babe who had smiled at me when I first came into the store, speaking in her lightly-accented English. I had forgotten that I had offered to create some graphics for her behavioral neuroscience research in exchange for a dinner of red hot *chakchouka*. It was strange. I usually didn't forget such arrangements.

The slit in Leila's long white lab coat flashed the entire span of her legs as she approached, and the thin straps of her spike-heeled shoes allowed me to study the porcelain smooth sides of her feet.

A polite conversation in Arabic began as Watson turned to confront the younger woman. The interchange escalated and reached the temperature required for nuclear fusion within seconds, their words spiced with staccato flights of French, English and Nafusi. That Leila could speak this shrinking Berber tribal language was exotic, yet not unexpected given that her homeland was North Africa. That Watson could speak it, and that I could recognize it as such, seemed odd. But I wasn't about to question it.

I stood and watched myself in the mirrors that surrounded the three of us, with McAlsteinetti chattering supine on his daybed in the corner. Overall, from the perspective of that moment, I felt that this was the best temp job I ever had. I allowed myself a few moments to remark on how healthy and happy I looked in the mirrors. I had made some new friends—most of whom had disappeared, of course—and I had reconnected with my old friend Kurtis. In that moment, I was no longer aware of my floundering life as a screenwriter, my inglorious fossilization as a bottom-feeder temporary graphic artist, nor my significant unmet financial obligations. Instead, I was grateful that I had found a spiritual partner with whom I could share my reflection—who was smiling back at me in multiple profiles as I gazed around. I'm not sure how my teeth had become so white. It made no sense. I drank way too much coffee to have teeth that looked like that.

"MeadMeister!" An elfin voice called me from the wilderness.

This was the voice of a 9-foot tall, blue-skinned woman wearing a reindeer skin bikini. I had met her on Valhalla Net, which was an online 3-D gaming world in which I spent many hours wandering across a virtual tundra looking for the counsel of Odin's Orbs and destroying the offspring of the half-bred wolf bane ThorKil. Somewhere in my online wanderings in the game I started chatting with the tall blue woman who was approaching me in full color 3-D. Her name was FreyaKin8877 and she was of the Viking Vixen Class. On our first meeting the conversation had gone well and she had given me some healing TaigaRoot in exchange for my 9-blade fire axe—which was promising, to say the least. In my mind, the next natural thing was for me to suggest that we head over to Loki's Lair, one of the several dozen virtual nightclubs on the tundra that were designed to look like Viking feasting halls. That invitation had brought her to me now. With a bundle of tundra wildflowers in her arms, she glided toward me down the long hallway of the Mezzanine.

Watson and Leila continued their white-hot discussion in the background as FreyaKin8877 pushed her way into the room. I fell back onto the couch as her glowing, 2-meter long blue legs straddled me. The caribou skin of her bikini pressed against my loins. Her skin looked so *real*. Running her fingers over the tops of my sculpted abs with one blue hand, she dropped wildflowers onto my chest with the other. Her gentle voice speaking my name caused me to tremble.

I shuddered.

It was then I noticed that the tundra wildflowers fell on my chest in slow motion, which sent a signal to my rational mind that what was happening wasn't real. FreyaKin's face moved closer to me and I knew that she wasn't real either. Even in the waking world, she existed only as coded lines that conformed to my desire.

With that realization, the blue limbs faded, and the sound of Arabic and Nafusi insults gave way to the mournful, unyielding hum of the monitors overhead.

Dalton laughed out loud when I told him about this segment of the video. REM Ripper was a 3rd-party plug in for DeusX Kameras that started up once inhibitory signals were detected in the brainstem—the same signals that stop our arms and legs from acting out our dreams while lying in bed. He explained to me that DeusX had developed a series of applications that sampled neural activity in the occipital cortex, the visual center of the brain, and extrapolated the signal into sequential video frames using statistical samples of images from the video of our waking state, which were weighted based on sex and age data that were entered into the camera before installation. The algorithm estimated how your brain would use visual images from your waking state to create videos of your dreams. As a mathematical extrapolation of what our actual dreams might look like in our minds, it was accurate to the point of embarrassment. The camera thus served the dual purpose of documenting the waking hours of the wearer, but also their hidden fantasies—with the lost time of one's deepest sleep edited out. With stiff revenue goals in place for the mission, Dalton wasn't surprised to learn that Watson had opted for the REM Ripper feature in my camera. Millions of hours of REM Ripper video dreams were delivered hourly to hungry paid-subscribers in advertising agencies, fashion magazines and cinematic studios at all levels of artistic aspiration.

At that moment of waking from that dream, however, long before I could laugh about the red leather flip flops, I was mortified that I was lying alone in that dark, cluttered office somewhere inside All Mart. I checked myself to make sure I hadn't done anything that might require extra attention at my next visit to the Laundromat—and I hadn't—but that didn't make me feel any better. McAlsteinetti was gone. Of course, this was before I had watched his departure with Ren and her father on the video in the DeusXKamera, so I had no idea when and how he might have disappeared. It wasn't only his absence that made me feel so lonely. I couldn't shake the feeling that not a single person in the world either knew or cared that I was there.

Since I didn't have the video yet to fill in the gaps of what all McAlsteinetti had said, those moments were disorienting. I tried to focus a little by trying to awaken some memories of him at the Corky Porky, imagining that we had stayed friends the whole time and that I hadn't been so mean to him after all. I understood that his childhood was nothing like mine, even though we had both worked at the same grocery store for a few intersecting months. He might have passed through the same automotive and glandular gauntlet as other teenagers, but I couldn't tell. I wished I had asked him if he knew whatever happened to Daphne Taggert, one of the cashiers at the Cork. Everyone knew he had this impossible crush on her that compelled him to hang out at the end of her check-out line, volunteering to bag groceries even when her customers had just one or two items. She was 10 years older than him, single, and had a kid. It was almost cliché. The teenage guy in love with the older single mom—both heading in opposite directions socially and economically. I heard him say one day that he wanted her to have 'a different set of circumstances.' I have no doubt that he meant it even back then. Nevertheless, she ignored his mooning affections and continued to cycle through a pantheon of patho-adolescent boyfriends, submitting again and again to the contents of the bulging, rusted worm can of poverty into which she was born. I thought the room had become darker as I thought about her, but realized it was a change in the lighting and activity on the monitors.

As I lay there studying the space before me, a few shadowed figures holding each other hobbled across the screen of one of the monitors, captured for a few steps in the silver radiance of a floodlight that illuminated one of the store's hundreds of loading docks. Since I hadn't seen the video from my shoulder camera yet, I didn't understand that the limping form was McAlsteinetti and the young woman and the man supporting him were Ren and her dad. Without that knowledge, it made no sense to me why the limping figure seemed tormented as a minivan pulled up to the loading dock. A woman with her hair in curlers and wearing a bathrobe jumped out of the driver's seat and embraced Ren and her father. As the family reformed their sequestered bond, McAlsteinetti leaned against the side of the van. His haggard face writhed as he yelled out toward the sky, proclaiming some anguish that I could not hear. I didn't understand it then and still might not, but it looked like he was directing his anger at the roof. Then, hurrying to escape some unseen pursuit, the four figures climbed into the minivan and sped off into the night, outside the view of the security cameras.

In the central portion of the bank of monitors, my eyes were drawn to the small screen that monitored the proceedings of the executive meeting that had carried on into the night. Several of the main suits were up moving around the table, directing their comments at Lawson and gesturing toward a series of graphs, lines and bar charts that all plummeted toward zero. This was followed by an animated slide showing a cartoon dead cat bouncing up and down, with a few blips of positive territory on the graphs before everything bottomed out. I have to admit that the series of still images that followed the dead cat were pretty impressive by any standards of photo retouching. Somebody in the marketing department had changed the National Mall into a pasture, with cows and goats grazing along and a few sleepy guys in tattered dress slacks standing around, shepherd-like.

On the screen, Lawson raised his hands to calm their fears and tapped a control at the edge of the conference table. The still images faded, the lights dimmed and the main video display in the conference room came to life. It was hard to see the screen because the wide-angle lens of the security camera that was capturing the action distorted the field of view, but I did manage to catch the title of the little movie that was starting: *All Mart: Accelerating the Inevitable!!!*

The stop-action animated short film began with model ships arriving at and leaving the shore of a plywood cut-out of North America. In the next scene the ships were stopped and bright orange zeros appeared in the center of the United States, over Asia and the remainder of the continents. Which I now take to mean the point McAlsteinetti described where mass production of goods on our planet ended. Then there was a little paper airplane made out of a $20 bill that did a tailspin and crashed into the fake ocean. It looked like they animated it further so that the little airplane collapsed on itself once it hit. After that, the film jumped to a generic big city scene in which clay models of regular people were walking along a sidewalk, riding little model buses and directing traffic of little model cars and motorcycles. There was even a little claymation homeless guy standing on a street corner panhandling. Then they faded the scene out. After a few seconds, the city scene came back on again. The second time, a lot of the people had a small glass box strapped to their foreheads. Then they faded out again but the city scene came back on a third time with even more people wearing the small glass box. The city came to life a fourth time but in this last version everyone—including the homeless guy—had the little box on their head. A text box appeared on the screen that read: *QPE Global Penetration.*

In this scene, they used some brighter colors for the sky and all the minuscule bits of claymation trash were gone from the streets. But then, a huge infinity sign flashed on and off the screen and the sky went dark. The next few scenes showed the small metal cars and trucks stop and crumble into rust. But it happened in the space of three frames so the animation didn't look very real. Then they jumped to another part of the city in which people tossed tiny cell phones and tablet devices into small but real fires that were burning in the street. I was impressed that they had considered the environmental dangers of burning electronic components and had a little claymation guy wearing a respirator salvaging the tiny bits of molten metals that flowed out from the base of the fire and into little ceramic vials. Other clay figures were running with their mouths wide open and waving their arms. They might have been screaming but, of course, I couldn't hear the sound track. A few of the claymation rioters threw tiny clay bricks through little shop windows. The next scene showed little clay model looters running out of shops with little fake televisions, fur coats and diamond watches.

Then the camera panned to the edge of the city where brilliant white light was beaming from a model All Mart store that stretched off across the horizon—store Number One.

I may have dozed for a few seconds after that, so that the next thing I remember is little claymation Converts in tiny Purple Ponchos teaching their children to read newspaper ads and shop inside a miniature mock-up of a giant All Mart store. Broad beams of studio lighting shot down through the miniature skylights so that everything was bathed in a warm, comforting glow. The next scene showed the Converts and their children singing songs around a tiny campfire in the middle of a Convert village. In another daylight scene, the claymation Converts climbed ladders that extended up through the skylights and went to work in green fields planted on the roof. At the end of the 5-second work day depicted in the film, shortened for cinematic convenience, teams of Converts lowered baskets loaded with claymation vegetables back down into the store. The last scenes showed purple-robed clay figurines, all of which looked like Barney, strolling along the little aisles, taking inventory and shining and oiling all the merchandise that required either gasoline or electricity. A line of Germanic Gothic text, like you'd see in a 4-foot tall Bible from an old monastery, came across the screen: *Useful items at the end of a Dark Age!*

Then there was a bad edit so it looked like the Barney scene got cut off before it was over. In the next scene, clay figures were up on the roof of the store driving tiny metallic models of some kind of harvesting machines. It was a little like those pictures from out west where you see a whole line of combines moving across a wheat field as a unit. Then, in what I thought was the most cheesiest part of the film, models of giant cargo planes swung down onto the rooftop runway. After landing, clay model farm workers drove little forklifts up to the planes and loaded little fake green bales into the cargo bays. Then the planes took off again and were shown to fly toward Asia, Africa and South America on a little spinning claymation globe. On the roof of the store, waving to the departing planes was a tiny, chiseled claymation figure wearing a Hawaiian shirt. Even from where I was lying on the couch I could see that the little figure was modeled to look like Lawson, though a few years younger and with more prominent cheekbones than he had in reality. The next scene showed a line graph with the title ENGINEERED TOTAL NUTRITION = RAPID CORNERING OF MARKET + SUSTAINED GROWTH DURING RECONSTRUCTION at the bottom, with the line soaring upward. The problem with this set of scenes was that the clay figures didn't have the same look as in the previous scenes, and the lighting was brighter, so the entire mood of the film looked and felt different. In my mind, this portion of the movie with the harvesters, the airplanes and little Lawson had been added after the original had been finished.

After the profit graphic, they showed a 2-inch paper calendar with the pages tearing off to indicate the passage of time, which was followed by the front doors of the store flying open and children and adults skipping out into the sunshine with stop-action smiles exploding on their faces. In this last scene, the clay figures looked like the ones in the first part of the movie, so it was easy to imagine that this segment was part of the original ending.

Whether it was or not didn't seem to diminish the effect of the film on Watson. As the credits rolled, she looked tormented—shaking her head that this was not the script that she and Klean had envisioned. Her sunken eyes that hadn't slept for days spoke the horror of what she was thinking. Her mission had been to stop McAlsteinetti from taking down the economy. That was now all but guaranteed and no one could stop it. The question that remained—who would we all be when the darkness lifted?

Lawson stood there, looming over the entire room. The rest of the senior execs stared at Watson. She said something to them and I saw by the movement of her hands that she was again begging Lawson to reconsider. He shrugged and again tapped the console at the edge of the table, which brought up a single image on the screen: a satellite photo of the Midwest showing vast stretches of checkered farmland—an additional tap of Lawson's finger on the console morphed the image into a crater that spanned from the Appalachian Mountains to the Mississippi River.

Watson nodded that she understood. Even before the lights came back on, she reached for the keypad of the TelePortMini and began typing in a long series of numbers from memory. I knew what she was doing because a TelePortola sales rep had done a demo at Wimsley, Van Der Küüken, Smith and Dreque, Direct Marketing Resources, Inc., which was one of my regular gigs on the temp circuit. Seconds after Watson finished plugging in the numbers, three action-figure sized humans began to materialize in the UltraGlas teleporter booths in the center of the conference table. The physical reconstruction of the three individuals she dialed-up looked nothing like the flashing, radiant-energy displays that had popularized teleportation devices on such shows as *KosmoKwest.* Instead, the figures appeared first as small, darkish clouds of dust that were collapsed with a graviton pulse until a faint ember formed near the center. The clouds were then bombarded with the psychon map that all subscribers to TelePortola had to upload to the company's central cloud storage. Once the psychon map data reached the ember clouds, the actual flesh of the individuals emerged from the chaotic field of virtual particles that seethed around us at all times.

To describe the machine as a 'teleporter' was not accurate, of course. No one traveled anywhere. The original person or object remained in their original location and what appeared in the booth was a bilocational twin—*not a copy*, but an actual second manifestation of the person in space. The hallucinogenic math of quantum physics had recognized decades ago that bilocation of matter was possible—in addition to the implications that McAlsteinetti had rambled on about. TelePortola was one of the first companies to capitalize on this principle. The miniaturization feature was added for the supposed comfort of the individuals being ported, but everyone knew it was so that the few companies who could afford the thing could tower over the people they dialed up. The cachet value of *getting* called up and appearing in the machine, however, far outweighed any psychological disadvantage the mini-portee might experience, so it was an arrangement that all parties could live with.

I immediately recognized the three mini-twins who appeared that night, primarily by their attire, which by virtue of the machine's localization software was identical to what the original was wearing, but also by their faces, which I had seen in media reports of their global acquisitions, personal scandals and outrageous displays of ego.

Standing in a bathrobe, with puffy eyes and sleep hair—although it was late morning by then in Europe—was Blut Stehngruber, CEO of Hellemacher, the boundless global supplier of everything every country needed to defend and assert itself, with diversified holdings in textiles, mining, pharmaceuticals, entertainment and food products. The company had won several international design awards for their new line of incendiary confections, but his biggest piece of news in the past year was his assertive takeover of the JetEX overnight shipping service.

Next down the line was Harvey Turnstone, the Tasmanian Media giant who owned enough networks, radio stations, newspapers and magazines to reach 99.9% of all the people on the planet. It was rumored that the remaining one tenth of one percent of humans would be within the reach of his news empire following his forced buyout of *Bhutan Today*, the biweekly magazine of the high Himalayas. Wearing flowered Bermuda shorts and an un-matched floral print shirt, his perennial sun-burnt nose was evident even in his miniaturized state, as was his perpetual disregard for the conventions of a coordinated wardrobe.

Last, recumbent on a daybed, with his legs crossed sheik-style, puffing on a sheesha, was none other than Achmed Bin Azraq, sole proprietor of Sharbai-based Global Engineering Unlimited. The presence of the complete water pipe, including the mouthpiece, which Bin Azraq kept in his mouth as he puffed, affirmed that he had paid major extra dhinars for the Proximity Field Upgrade to the basic TelePortola subscription. The PFU allowed for the added teleporting of objects or parts of individuals that were in close proximity to, or in contact with, the primary person being teleported. Not everyone who could afford this upgrade, however, did so, since it had resulted in the boardroom appearance of compromising and complicated bilocational entities more appropriately viewed in a bedroom. But the Sheik was wise enough to keep his alliances well outside the range of the port and attempted to create an image of himself as a bit of a homebody. Indeed, despite his company's pan-planetary reach, the Sheik retained his residence on his island nation of Sharbai in the Persian Gulf, which encompassed 400 square meters of sandy gravel. Although the island rested at the apex of a submarine domed salt structure containing an estimated 87- trillion barrels of sweet, light crude, Bin Azraq had earned his international reputation as a go-to-guy by virtue of his ahead-of-schedule construction of King Khalid Military City on the Arabian Peninsula, the President Dalton Schrump the 6th Military City in Florida and the Hector Noriega Playa Peligroso in territorial central America.

Taken together, these three men stood at the highest possible echelon of world financial power and were never more than a board member or two away from influencing every known human industry on the planet. The fact that Watson knew the Teleport numbers of any one of them was prodigious. Astounding, in fact, and no doubt why she had been placed in charge of the original mission. That she called all three of them *and they answered* at the same time implied no less that the earth would shake, or that something wonderful was about to happen. Indeed, they all smiled as Lawson and the executives explained their plan for the leveraged global meltdown, and each extended their tiny hands to touch the pinkies of Lawson as their ported minis made verbal agreements and then blinked back to singular localization of their consciousness.

I don't remember seeing or hearing anything after that. I'm sure it was because I had moved down into deep dreamless sleep. It reminded me of watching old movies on Friday night with my father. From the limited archive of that time, I recall watching *The Old Man and the Sea*, starring Spencer Tracy. One minute the old man would be heading out to sea while I began dozing, and then I'd wake up and they'd be showing the picked-over carcass of the huge fish or, just as often, the national anthem would be playing and the screen would then dissolve to fuzz. Of course, those were the days when programming ended in the middle of the night.

Realignment

We are pleased to announce the completion of negotiations in regard to our proposed strategic partnership as they relate to the various acquisitions and executive restructurings by means of inherent architectural changes in leadership and considerable relocation of paradigms that have been facilitated as a direct result vis a vis due process of a peri-legislative, pre-emptive undertaking that has resulted in our virtual merger with several international consortia, which will enhance our revenue stream in perpetuity.

Rex Troglett, Undersecretary, Department of Commerce, Office of Antitrust Operations, announcing the designation of All Mart Store Number 1 as a sovereign nation, during a press conference prior to the inauguration of President Stephen P. Lawson.

"C'mon," said Watson. "We have to move. Deals have been made."

The first thing that I saw when my eyes opened again was Watson's face moving into a small opening in the door to McAlsteinetti's office. I wouldn't see the video from the DeusX Kamera for another few days after that, so I had no idea why I was trying to stare through her blouse. It was almost embarrassing. What was I looking for? Pinstripes, I recalled from somewhere in the deepest corners of my mind. But, *why*? I closed my eyes and tried to retrieve the memory that would connect me with this longing, but it wasn't there. For the first time in our journey, I felt like crying.

The monitor that showed the proceedings in the conference room was black. On most of the other monitors, regular customers moved through the aisles in their normal shopping. But there were a few surprising additions to the daily routine in the store. On one screen, focused on a clearing in the artificial Christmas tree forest off the White Aisle, Quinoa was teaching a yoga class, wobbling in a tree pose in front of a group of Converts. I recognized some of them as people who had peered out through the trees at me the previous afternoon. On a screen next to this, Pesto was dumping whole carrots, beets and bunches of greens into a juicer, and handing out glasses of fresh juice to Converts on their way to work as they passed him in the aisle. A few screens away, deeper in the holiday tree forest, Angela was interviewing a group of less affluent shoppers who sat around a make-shift waiting room with a purple cross painted on a banner overhead. And there was Hardin, in that instant, wearing a white coat with a stethoscope draped over her neck, leading a patient through a doorway. A free clinic, for the many thousands of shoppers who lived inside the store but for whatever reason weren't working and weren't on the company health care plan. I took comfort in these scenes, seeing them as signs that all would be well inside the Mart and that I could go back to sleep. But then Watson pushed my feet off the couch and I figured I had better get up. I was, after all, still working for her. Although it was a only a technicality at that point.

"Things are going to happen fast," she said. "We have to catch our flight."

"He's gone," I mumbled. By then I had placed myself in the proper context of time and place and allowed the trace memory of a nonspecific piece of pinstriped athletic wear, that I imagined on her body, to dissipate from my mind. "It was him. He was here."

"Yeah, we know." Watson was shaking her head and exhaling a long overdue sigh. "Woulda' been nice if you could have kept him around a little longer. But I don't suppose it'll matter much in the end."

"Supernice guy," I said. "We worked together at—"

"Save it. I have a ten AM meeting in Arlington," said Watson. Whatever the meeting was about, it pissed her off to the core of her being. But there was nothing she could do to stop it, and it would serve me well to not piss her off any further.

I sat up and put on my band jacket, which I had pulled over myself as a blanket at some point during the night. Much later, I would have to consider the possibility that I manually truncated the video record of McAlsteinetti's prophecy, as opposed to my brain waves, believing that I dislodged the tiny electrode from the nerve in my shoulder when I took off the band jacket in the middle of the night. But that thought wouldn't come until I had gone over the video multiple times a few days later—hoping there were further clues to where McAlsteinetti might have gone. Right then, a question came to my mind, out of the blackness of my sleep. I was still pretty out of it and looked over at Watson. "What the heck is a derivative?"

"It depends on the context," Watson scowled. "A derivative is a financial contract. The value of the contract is dependent on performance. Using derivatives of equations is also a way of solving mathematical problems."

"A derivative? Huh." I knew even less about math than I did about finance. "I think of things that are, you know, derived from other things. Like a chicken is derived from–"

Watson shook her head to indicate she didn't want to hear any of it as she phoned in our egress. "On the roof. At the central pad. Three minutes."

I was struggling to get my shoes on while Watson was already at work on her next presentation on her wrist pad. Curling her nose, she pulled a ShowerQuick pre-moistened towelette out of her designer-camouflage BlitzBagg and flung it toward me from across the room. I made a few passes at key sweat gland locations with the towelette and was ready to move.

As we were about to walk out, Barney's face peeked around the door. I couldn't say how long he'd been listening or watching. "He's gone?" Barney asked.

"Yes, but I have no idea where," I said as I exited the room past Barney and was whisked back along the hall of photos in Watson's slipstream.

I was hoping to say goodbye to Barney but he had turned and slunk down into a seated position with his back against the wall, his hands rubbing the sides of his head in apparent torment.

But Barney didn't hear me. Watson let slip a dark chuckle and led me toward the long stairway that descended back down to where the FATASS waited. I was surprised at how nimble she looked, bounding down the stairs two or three at a time. With fluid strides, she sprinted toward the shopper that remained parked where we had left it the night before.

Watson didn't even look back as she hopped into the command pod and geared up for our final drive up to the roof. I reached the shopper a few seconds behind her and climbed into the driver's seat, careful not to kick Dalton who was still sprawled on the deck sleeping.

Watson was down in her control seat punching buttons on her cell phone. "Can you get her up and running?"

The engine was already howling. "No problem," I said.

The XR had few actual human controls. All you could do was basic steering, make it go faster, and stop it. Most of its lights and readings referred to information and events in the marketplace, outside its well-appointed confines. The remainder of the readouts were designed to take the burden of driving and operating the FATASS *away* from the humans on board and place it in the hands of computers or remote advisors. Even without all the shopvionics and the automation, however, Klean had made the machine do amazing things with the few simple controls. For my part, I could make the XR move, but that was about it. Not waiting for a specific command, I started off back down the White Aisle. The acceleration of my one-note driving caused Dalton to roll over a couple of times, but he still didn't wake up.

Watson looked up from her phone and turned to face me as I increased our speed. On her tired face, there were the first tiny facial muscle movements of a smile, which had pushed up through the raging details of our departure. Compared to what she had witnessed overnight, her opinion of me had changed, at least for that one moment. I had stuck around and shown up when she needed me most. I was powerless in almost every respect compared to her and those at the executive meeting, but I was still there and ready to help in whatever way I could. After the whole special skills misunderstanding, there weren't going to be any compliments. It was accidental that any part of her appreciation had slipped out. I knew not to expect more than the micro-smile she had given me.

I half nodded to indicate that I knew how grateful she was, that she didn't need to say or do anything else, and that she could go back to taking care of everything else and I would keep driving.

Convinced at that point that no amount of G-force I threw at the shopper would disturb Dalton's sleep, I made a squealing turn and backtracked along the failed landscaping project that ran down the center of the White Aisle.

As I veered toward displays and early morning shoppers at high speed, I was forced to admit that Klean had made driving the FATASS look easy. Like everything else he did. He was one of those people whose level of performance had moved beyond the arithmetic sum of his training and experience. His job with the Agency may have gotten tougher toward the end, but you couldn't tell from the outside. He seemed above it all the whole time and I wished he was with us.

Then, across time and space, across all imagined lines and boundaries of human existence, I understood the look that Klean had given me in the moments before he headed off to take the executive job, and why it had scared me so much. He, above all the others, believed in me and knew that I could get Watson and myself out of there. He also told me in that glance that lasted the smallest fraction of our time, the lifetime of a distant flash of lightning, that I needed to tell this story, all of it, whatever I had seen thus far, and whatever might come after we had escaped. I don't know how he knew it, but he did. It wasn't anything he said, it was how he lived. Confident in himself and all those around him to do the right thing at the right time. I imagined for a second that birds must feel like this when they fly for the first time. How the heck do I know what birds feel like? I don't, of course, but I couldn't categorize the sensation any other way. It is within them, even as what I needed to do is within me. There was nothing to think about. The necessary action flows between their bodies and the compliance of the atmosphere, waiting to be expressed.

In the same thread of our existence, Klean's decision to move on to senior management gave me hope that he would take those qualities with him. It would be several months before I would get a few nice voicemails from him after he left Allmart and started his own not-for-profit that shipped medical supplies to clinics in developing countries—keeping Hardin well-supplied on the side. He would ask about Dalton, whom I went and saw weekly, and about how my writing was going. Each time I heard his voice, I hoped that he was in Chicago for business, that we could meet for coffee and I could tell him that I had committed myself to telling our story and the final words of McAlsteinetti. But I guess he already knew that and trusted that these stories would be written.

Sirens wailed behind us. Whipping my head around, I saw about ten security carts racing up behind us with their purple and white emergency lights flashing.

"Don't worry about them," Watson yelled over the roar of the sirens.

She pointed toward a ramp that would take us to the roof, but I had already seen it and was steering in that direction. The power display showed that the beverage dispersal system batteries still had plenty of power, so I had no fear of jamming the voltage regulator past the red line and into the ultraviolet line—hoping to pick up enough speed to get up to the roof without stalling.

"Are we going to make it?" Watson barked without looking over to the steering pod.

The wailing sirens and flickering lights were getting closer.

"Yeah, I think I can get a little more," I yelled back to Watson. Hoping to free up some juice for the wheels, I shut down the refrigeration compartments and the master switches to the communication and marketing pods, which were empty.

"More is less than you think," Watson shrieked as we hit some bags of fertilizer that were stacked in the road.

Airborne for a second, I glanced sideways and saw that her face cracked yet another transient grin. Then, when the engine growled and we hit the base of the ramp around 75 mph, she seemed satisfied that she would make her meeting after all.

The sirens were right behind us. Then I saw that two security cruisers had pulled up right beside us, one on each side. In the passenger seat of the cruiser on our left, there was a hunkish graying gentleman, wearing the purple dress uniform of an AllTight Elite Security General who saluted us. Stanton drove the vehicle. His tan was faded, but his complexion looked more natural and alive than I'd ever seen him. He was also wearing the purple dress uniform of an AllTight senior officer. Each of those observations I found acceptable in the context of everything that had occurred inside the Mart. The bizarre part of it was that he was smiling at me. The older man lifted a military style salute and waved for us to continue on up the ramp, using his long purple flashlight as a directional beacon. Then they sped ahead of us, acting as our escort.

Out on the roof, the sunlight blinded me, forcing me to drop the speed of the XR lest I crash into the shapes that crowded the path leading to the helipad. When my eyes adjusted to the brightness, I saw irrigation pipes that rose up from inside the store and fed into the sides of industrial sized planter boxes that stood like high walls on both sides of us. The helicopter sat, rotors shuttering the sunlight, a few yards ahead with the security cruisers parked beside it. I didn't wait for Watson's signal but instead drove right into the spot where Stanton and the general waited for us beside the helicopter's side cargo door. Stanton gave both Watson and me huge warm hugs and whispered something in my ear which I couldn't hear above the roar of the helicopter. With the aid of some lower level security guards, Watson and I hefted Dalton's limp, sleeping carcass into the passenger cabin. The pilot looked back to make sure we were in while the technician winched the XR on board and secured it in the cargo compartment behind us. All this consumed no more than thirty seconds, with no celebration for the mission and no acknowledgement for our scattered comrades.

Watson was already working on her next presentation and didn't even look down when we lifted off.

As we ascended, I allowed my gaze to scan the roof below. Stanton, shoulder to shoulder with the general, waved as we flew over. Once clear of the airstrip, all I saw below was fields. A cultivated single crop that covered the entire span of the roof as far as I could see in all directions.

"Any idea what they're growing?" I asked.

"Looks like sweet corn," the pilot drawled back through the intercom. "But it's some kinda' hybrid. Those ain't corn flowers growing out the top there."

Hearing these words, Watson fought back tears and continued working as we passed over a Convert family resting from their morning labors on a blanket spread out in a clearing in the field. An infant frolicked on her mother's lap.

"What kind of flowers are they?" I asked.

"Poppies," said the pilot, turning his attention to the sky as we climbed.

Then, we were over the clearing, still climbing, and the scenery below became all green again.

Made in the USA
San Bernardino, CA
10 August 2020